BOBBY DAZZLER

Philip Collins is the director of the Social Market Foundation, a political think tank. He formerly worked in politics, academia, television and investment banking. He is married and lives in London. *Bobby Dazzler* is his second novel.

T0318004

By the same author

The Men from the Boys

PHILIP COLLINS

Bobby Dazzler

HarperCollins*Publishers*

HarperCollins*Publishers*
77–85 Fulham Palace Road,
Hammersmith, London W6 8JB

www.harpercollins.co.uk

This paperback edition 2004
3 5 7 9 8 6 4 2

This novel is entirely a work of fiction. The names, characters
and incidents portrayed in it are the work of the author's
imagination. Any resemblance to actual persons, living or
dead, events or localities is entirely coincidental.

A catalogue record for this book is
available from the British Library

'OKLAHOMA' Words by Oscar Hammerstein II and Music
by Richard Rodgers 1943, Williamson Music International,
USA. Reproduced by permission of EMI Music Publishing Ltd,
London WC2H 0QY

ISBN: 978-0-00-717856-8

To Min

Acknowledgements

My agent, Tif Loehnis, has been a source of invaluable support and critical intelligence. So too has my editor, Susan Watt at HarperCollins.

My thanks of course to my family, to Liz, David, Ben, Dominic, Jon, mum, dad, Ganga, Krishnan, Krishnan and Ravi. Most of all thanks to Geeta whose dogged refusal to allow me to be miserable jeopardised this book at every stage. It certainly could have been written without her, and a lot quicker too.

I should acknowledge some influences. Michael Ignatieff's elegant *The Needs Of Strangers*, the black comic voice of Thomas Lynch and the stoical wit of Philip Larkin lurk beneath the surface of my text and sometimes, I hope, on top of it.

This book is dedicated to my grandmother. She is its life force.

But still, the fates will leave me my voice
and by my voice I shall be known.

Ovid, *Metamorphoses*

1

The Highest Judge of All

The audience rose as one to acclaim Georgie Lees. *This* was the point. This was why she took the lead at the Heywood Amateur Operatic and Dramatic Society. It was that noise, that applause, these people, this moment. It had life within it. It seemed like over-kill but Georgie thought of Heywood Civic Hall as a kind of temple. The theatre ventilated her feelings. Blew them away sometimes. On stage she was herself: solid and sound, trying on a part (not the whole) and destined to live again, to be re-played. As Georgie Lees stepped forward, Heywood Civic Hall gave forth its verdict. She took a shy bow, vindicated, cherished, looked after, granted life by the women and children.

By her side, her husband, Preston, was taking his bow. He had played a good Billy Bigelow. Preston had a smooth voice. But Georgie Lees was the one with the gift. She raised her eyebrows in mock surprise as the audience refused to desist. In the front row, her mother Mary led the cheers. Georgie Burns (stage name, maiden name, daily name Lees) held out her hand and motioned to Mr Rogers the conductor for the planned spontaneity of an encore. The percussion started a teasing introduction. The oboes, clarinets, bassoons and horns joined in, the trumpets followed on behind, dragging along the tuba and trombone. Then the violins, viola, harp and cello began the melody, which brought a roar of recognition from the audience. Georgie led the cast through another reprise, the second, of 'You'll Never Walk Alone'. Her son, Bobby, came downstage, alone, from the back, where he was hidden in the

1

children's chorus, to join his mother at the front. He stared out into the dark, not singing, as the tune soared.

The principals took a second individual bow as Graham Collins changed the backdrops with his sophisticated system of pulleys behind them: from the clambakes and lighthouse of a Maine fishing village to the archangels and harps of heaven. Colin Smethurst as Mr Snow bowed to the applause. Then Preston Burns came forward. The carnival barker, Billy Bigelow, is panicked into becoming the accomplice to a robbery when he learns that his girl, Julie Jordan (Georgie Lees) is pregnant. Facing the shame of imprisonment, Billy takes his own life and spends the rest of the show 'up there' in heaven. Georgie refused to believe it was really heaven that Billy went to. Her mother had taught her that heaven was reserved for good people. Fifteen years later, Billy is permitted to return to earth for one day's recompense. He encounters the teenage daughter he never knew, at her high school graduation. She is a lonely, friendless child, her father's reputation as a thief and a bully having haunted her throughout her young life.

One by one the principals came forward a third time. And then in their pairs. And then, as one, as a cast, an ensemble, the Civic Hall community.

In the dressing room, Georgie stared into her mirror to wash away her thick stage makeup. Georgie put a strawberry cream into her mouth and it disappeared into her long, drooping cheek which, in the years of her forties, had started to billow and now formed a dome running from her pretty, narrow tawny eyes to her amply padded jaw bone. She smiled at herself. She looked younger, she could see the pretty girl she had been not so very long ago. Too many strawberry creams down the years, though. From behind her, Olive Platt, the producer of the show, shouted that there was somebody out in the foyer who wanted to speak to her. It was probably an agent, she added as an afterthought. Georgie ignored Preston's complaint and ran out half-dressed. The last of the audience were still leaving. It broke down the enchanted distance to see Julie Jordan in her underclothes skipping through the emptying auditorium.

2

Georgie was expecting a fat man with a cigar and a zoot suit. Wasn't that what all the agents wore on the Northern club circuit? But there was nobody there. Maybe this was Olive's idea of a joke. Not a very funny joke. Georgie had never known when she hadn't wanted to be a star. Once upon a time it was a less remote ambition than it was now. Georgie had been put through singing lessons from the age of five. She had been a child star, appearing on an ITV regional talent show when she had been fourteen singing Doris Day numbers. Her head-hugging, long-tailed fair hair and 1950s glamour model figure had meant that she had featured on the bill of the Manchester clubs as 'Heywood's Diana Dors'. Georgie had turned away the chance to sing professionally when she had been invited to join the chorus for *Hello, Dolly!* in a London revival. She had assumed that the chance would come again, when she was ready to leave her mother's home. In fact, it never had. Georgie had got as far as the chorus at the Palace Theatre's production of *Iolanthe* and a small attendant part in *The Gondoliers* at the Bolton Octagon. She had gone back to the clubs for five years until she had married Preston and had Bobby. From then on she had been content with being the biggest fish at the Heywood Amateur Operatic and Dramatic Society. Georgie had always received the best notices in the *Rochdale Observer* and the *Manchester Evening News* but she had never got close again to the professional theatre.

A tiny man, small enough to have been brought in with the fruit or shot out of a cannon a hundred years before, appeared from between two old ladies who towered over him. He was wearing spectacles with thick black frames, as if he had stepped out of a photograph of his own father's youth. He addressed Georgie in a high pitch: 'That was a great show. I thought you were super. How come you played Julie Jordan though?'

Georgie didn't know what to say.

The man went on before she had gathered her thoughts: 'I mean to say, it's a part for a young woman and I don't mean to be disrespectful but I'd say you're a lady of a certain age, do you know what I'm saying?'

Georgie did and she didn't like it very much in part because it was true. Georgie Lees had been an odd choice as Julie Jordan. Georgie had always been a large, curvaceous woman but her curves were lately threatening to dissolve into weary fat. A tube of cushion-skin insulated her shins and ankles, like felt around a cylinder. The flesh now crouched on the tongue of her dressing room slippers, like the head of a toadstool. She was forty-six years of age and was incredible as a woman half her age. There was too much of the world in the lines under her eyes for the naïve New England mill worker, Julie Jordan.

Archie went on, without waiting for any reply: 'Hey, look, let me introduce myself. I'm Archie Gregson, pleased to meet you.'

Archie held out his hand but withdrew it before Georgie could react. 'I'm putting together a show for the Bolton Octagon. They're putting on *Hello, Dolly!*. We're looking for a Dolly Gallagher Levi. Do you know the part?'

Did she know the part? It was only the best part in the canon. *The* triumphal part for a woman. *Hello, Dolly!* had never been put on in Heywood while Georgie had been the *grande dame*. She had taken turns as Nancy in *Oliver!*, Liza Doolittle in *My Fair Lady*, Magnolia in *Show Boat*, Anna Leonowens instructing the King of Siam in dance, Maria teaching scales to the von Trapp children and Annie Oakley getting her gun. Georgie Lees was the Carol Channing, the Ginger Rogers, the Martha Raye, the Betty Grable, the Mary Martin, the Eve Arden, the Dorothy Lamour, the Pearl Bailey, the Phyllis Diller and the Ethel Merman of the Heywood Amateur Operatic and Dramatic Society. But she had never played the role that all her heroines had in common: Dolly Gallagher Levi.

Archie continued, without pausing to breathe: 'I'd like you to audition. It's not guaranteed. There's lots of good actresses in the area and they all want to play Dolly. So it's not guaranteed. But I'll recommend you. And take it from me, if Archie recommends someone, they stay recommended, do you know what I'm saying?'

'Thank you. That's very nice of you.'

Archie had a habit of ascending the vocal register the more

4

breathlessly he spoke. By the end of a long sentence he was audible only to dogs.

'And let me tell you something else. I have a number of female vocalists in the area and none of them, not one of them I'd say, is anywhere up to scratch with you. Now you might think I say that to all the girls and you'd be right. I do. But this time, for once in my life I mean it. You've got a grand voice, truly you have. And there's something else too and this time it's guaranteed. I'm putting together a team. To go on tour. I've got a couple of young fellas, a bass and a tenor and a lovely old bird who's a contralto, she's on her last legs really but, oh what a voice, and I need a soprano. I've got some dates in Ireland and Scotland, a little tour, you'd have to leave home but that's show business, if that's the life you want to lead, that's the life you have to lead, do you know what I'm saying? But that's not for a while, a few months away but I want people to commit soon, it takes a lot of organizing does a tour, do you know what I'm saying? In the meantime anyway, I'd like to take you on and get you some bookings, I do lots of songs from the shows-type things around the place but you'll have to be available at the drop of a hat, do you know what I'm saying?'

By now Archie was shrieking so hard it sounded as if he were in pain. Before Georgie could assent he had produced a sheaf of papers from his briefcase and handed her a pen. When she asked for time to consider Archie told her *carpe diem* Georgie, *carpe diem*, if you seize the day now it stays seized. Georgie told Archie, politely, that if he was truly as keen as he seemed to be, then he could wait a day or two for her decision. She would certainly audition to play in *Hello, Dolly!* but she needed to discuss going on tour with her husband. And she had a young boy to consider too. He was in school although taking him out was not such a bad idea. Archie squeaked that Georgie should not take long and wandered off as abruptly as he had arrived. Georgie went back into the dressing room and decided to talk to Preston later, when Bobby was in bed.

Georgie told Preston she would see him at home. They had rowed before coming out, over Bobby, who was being bullied

5

at school. She left the Civic Hall by the staff entrance and turned towards home. Georgie, Preston and Bobby Burns lived in Nightingale Street, fifteen minutes' walk down the dip from Heywood town centre. In this short walk Georgie turned over four dimensions: her husband, her son, her mother and her work. Georgie and Preston had been married for ten years now, a decade of devotion, on his part, to his work. The Operatic and Dramatic Society was just about the only time Georgie and Preston spent together. Their marriage had become a dull ache in separate rooms; nothing too painful, but never quite free from discomfort. They ignored one another for the sake of Bobby, their only son.

Bobby went to the primary school at the end of their road, St Stephen's. Georgie admitted to herself that he wasn't the brightest boy in the class, but knew she was understating it. Bobby hated the tests he had to do at school. Bobby was also both bullied and bully – one of which went unchecked and the other put him in trouble with the head teacher. There was a threat that he might be expelled. Excluded, as they called it now, but expelled was what they meant. Bobby might be better off going to Ireland and Scotland. That was a daft dream though, wasn't it? She couldn't leave home because a funny little fellow had asked her. Georgie had her mother to look after. And the stall on Middleton market. The two came together. Tears formed in Georgie's eyes as she recalled her mother leaving Heywood in 1935 to attend the Royal School of Needlework in London. Mary's own mother (Georgie's grandma, Louise) had threatened to disavow her if she gave up her job as a weaver in Heywood Mill. But Mary had always been sure that she was an artist and that her talent required her to go to college. She had persuaded her mother that the School's royal charter meant that Princess Alice of Schleswig-Holstein personally handed out the places. Mary had come back two years later with a diploma and the belief that she was a pioneer in embroidery. It had seemed only a matter of time before she opened her first shop. Mary had had dreams of empire in those days. When she had married Jack Lees (Georgie's beloved dad), in the late third act of her life, those dreams had begun to gather dust. But Georgie had revived them. She had stood on the market stall now for thirty years, for more than a decade since her mother's retirement, alone. And still the idea of a shop. There was one in the precinct at Middleton, next to Preston's parlour. Maybe she should give up this dream? That was, after all, the only thing it had ever been. How close, in truth, had Mary ever been to realizing it? As a child, Georgie, of course, had never questioned her mother's capacity to do what she said she would do. If Mary said they would have a shop, then one day they would have a shop. But Mary and Georgie had now stood on the same pitch on Middleton market for more than sixty years between them and still there was no sign of the business going indoors.

Georgie turned off the main road into Nightingale Street. She had grown up in this street and had come back to buy a house when she had married Preston. She passed the entrance to the allotments where she had played as a young girl. Jack had taken a large plot, which Preston had inherited. Georgie opened the gate and sat on the park bench that she knew was just by the wire fence, out of sight in the dark from passers-by on the street. In the scrub down below, Georgie felt the sharp rebuke of the dead nettles, the celandines, the potentillas. The illuminated lamp-post opposite looked like a stooping concrete giraffe ready to graze on the plants of the allotment. A thin white film of wax on a bloom of perpetual carnations caught the light. Georgie knelt down to touch the soil. She took a clump of groundsel in her hand and uprooted it. Her father had taught her weeding technique years before. She ripped away a proper pest – the hairy bitter cress, one of the most fecund of weeds. Its pores popped open as Georgie fought to release the roots from the ground. Seeds scattered, ensuring the weed's victory. Undeterred, Georgie gripped the sticky hooked stem of the cleavers, the goosegrass, and wrenched it from the dirt. She lifted herself up from the bench and made her way home, feeling less and less of a pull towards this land.

2
When the Children are Asleep

Bobby had been listening for three months. His parents packed him off to bed (Up you go Bobby Dazzler, let's be having you before Fungus the bogeyman gets you, followed by a scary chase up the stairs by his dad – it was meant to be fun but it wasn't). They gave him half an hour, sometimes not even that. Then they started. He had heard the full story: his mother's allegations that his father was having an affair with Susan Platt, daughter of Olive from the show. Bobby hated Susan Platt now, even though he didn't know who she was. His father kept denying it, at least he had when Bobby had been listening. He may have missed something, he couldn't keep up all the time. This evening, after the awful show that Bobby never enjoyed, the dispute started over. It was always difficult for Bobby to pick up the thread of an argument. He usually missed the beginning of the row because it always took him ten minutes to decide that he wouldn't be able to sleep and that he had better sit on the stairs and find out what was going on. He knew he ought to get some sleep. He had to go to church with his mother and grandmother in the morning. Bobby didn't like church much. It was boring. Bobby's dad agreed with that. He thought it was boring too. Sometimes his mum and dad argued about church. That was when they weren't arguing about his dad's work or whether his dad was going out with that lady from the show. Bobby's dad spent a lot of time at work and his mum thought he wasn't really at work, he was with that woman instead. Bobby liked going to his dad's work. It was a bit spooky but it was better than going to school. That was boring too. They kept giving him tests at school and he kept getting all the answers wrong. It made him feel stupid. At least at his dad's work nobody made him feel stupid. It was a bit weird though, seeing all those dead people.

As Bobby's thoughts meandered, he settled into position on the third stair from the top. He knew the sound of the stairs now. There was a floorboard loose under the next step which gave him away. Three steps down was just far enough to hear what was going on. Bobby took a few minutes to attune himself to the conversation, to gain a foothold in the discussion. But then the dispute followed what had become a familiar pattern: his mum would moan at his dad and his dad would say something that infuriated her because he wouldn't answer the question properly and then his mum would try to say what she thought he really meant and then he would say that it wasn't that, that wasn't what he meant at all actually and then his mum would call his dad hopeless and his dad would say that his mum never really loved him and she'd only married him because granddad wanted her to. And then his mum would say that she wished he would give up his work because it was like living with a ghost. And his dad would say what would they do for money if he gave up work and his mum would say they could turn the shop into a wool shop and sell things that grandma made. That was the usual conversation, or something like that anyway.

As Bobby made himself comfortable on the third step down, this was where he tuned in: 'Why can't you sell the bloody place? I hate it. I don't know why you bothered getting married. You're never here.'

Preston nervously played with his hair. Preston Burns was a small, chubby man with a round head and thick hair that curled into tight circles. He could often be seen straightening his curls around his fingers, unaware he was doing it. Preston's jowls rested loosely into an expression that, even at its most animated, was haunted and lugubrious. He wore round glasses that sat too high up his head because they didn't fit properly behind the ears. This misplacement also drew the eye above the line of the frames, to his imprimatur. A conspicuous birth mark was painted on to Preston's temple. It was a raw gash in a pair of sergeant stripes or two red pencil moustaches. Preston had always felt dominated by his mark. It seemed to him to glow. Preston got up to pour himself a measure of whisky. He was not much more than five feet three inches tall and the Cuban heels on which he tottered like stilts fooled no one. Apart from Preston, of course, who could fool himself that black was white if he talked long enough without mentioning anything quite so tangible as either.

Preston explained there had been such a spate of business lately – he didn't know why, perhaps some dormant disease waking – that he had fallen behind on his paperwork. You wouldn't believe the regulations that now audited undertakers, the extensive inspectorate and ombudsmen that he had to answer to. And government instructions, local worthies and central command. It all needed watching and that meant that the boss had to be on guard, even at the weekend. And, in any case, as Georgie knew too tiresomely, too frequently, Preston was for ever on call. Like the other onlookers when we depart, the doctors. Preston overdid this comparison. He liked the feeling of professional confraternity it allowed him. He started another tedious paragraph on the attention his intricate trade had begun to attract from government.

Georgie knew her tone was far gone from peremptory but she no longer cared to be polite: 'Press, shut up will you? I'm sick to death of bloody dead folk. You never talk about anything else. You're at work all the time and then when you're not at work you're sat in the shed surrounded by your bloody vegetables. And our Bobby's being bullied at school and he needs special attention and you don't seem bothered . . .'

'Of course I'm bothered.'

'Do something then. You should have gone down and sorted out that bully. If you'd boxed his ears at the beginning Bobby wouldn't be in all this trouble.'

'I can't do that. I can't go and hit young lads. Bobby has to stick up for himself.'

This was a new subject. Bobby hadn't been the cause of the

argument before. He felt he was in some way the cause rather than the subject. The toughest boy in the school had set his acolytes on to Bobby. It wasn't fair. There were three of them. The second, third and fourth cocks of the school, all at once. Bobby dreaded the journey to school in the morning because they intercepted him when he came out of the wood on to the main road. He went a different way for a few days but then they worked it out and found him. They battered him when he got to school anyway even if they had missed him on the way in. He had mentioned it to his mum because he had come home with a black eye twice and she hadn't believed that they had both been from running into swinging doors by accident. His mum said he should tell the teachers but she didn't understand that they would get him even worse if he snitched. He needed a big brother to go and bash them up, although they had big brothers as well so it might not work. He was heartened by his mum's idea – which was the nuclear variant of the big brother plan – for Preston to go and bash them.

His mum and dad didn't seem to mind all that much though. They had moved on: 'Press, that man who came to see me after the show was an agent.'

'I know he was. Olive said.'

'He's asked me to audition for *Hello, Dolly!* at the Bolton Octagon.'

'I wouldn't, if I was you.'

'Why not?'

'I don't know about the Bolton Octagon.'

'What do you mean?'

'I just wouldn't.'

Discussing an issue with Preston Burns was like trying to carry a constant amount of water in your hands. His conversation, hinting, gesturing at content, was unsummarizable. This peculiarity was accounted for, by everyone who knew Preston, by death. Preston had been an ordinarily lonely young man until he had started work with Jack Lees at the Heywood Funeral Parlour. The sight of his first corpse, so they said, had stilled him into emptiness. It was the experience of certainty that had left him so unsure. Now, after more than thirty years of his undertaking, Preston Burns was making a good living from dying but he could speak clearly on only this single topic: the fact of death. The banal, bodily fact of death, not the imponderable, disagreeable question of a spiritual place beyond. Death had left Preston with an extensive technical vocabulary but nothing to say and so he talked and talked and talked the world ghoulishly into shape.

'And I've been asked to go on tour.'

'With the Bolton Octagon?'

Even Preston knew that the Bolton Octagon was in Bolton.

'No, with Archie Gregson. He's the agent. He's putting together a group to do songs from the shows around Scotland and Ireland some time next year, he didn't say exactly when. He wants me to go on it.'

'That sounds like a daft idea. You can't go on tour.'

'Why can't I?'

'How many reasons do you want? Your mother, for one. She's getting worse. I caught her trying to put the cat out yesterday in her nightie at eleven o'clock at night.'

'We used to have a cat.'

'I know you *used* to. Your mother needs to go into a home. She can't look after herself any more.'

'Press, it'd kill her. She'd be worse in a home than she is now. She's fine with a bit of looking after.'

'She's not fine.'

'She would be if you'd help a bit. If you weren't so bloody obsessed with your bloody job.'

'I'm not obsessed.'

'I wouldn't mind so much if it wasn't such a bloody awful thing to do for a living. I hated it when my dad did it. I can't believe I've gone and got myself hooked up with another fella who does the same bloody thing. Can't you pack it in?'

'And who do you think would bury the dead if I didn't?'

'They won't be piling up just because you decide to do something else.'

'They would, you know. Anyway, Georgie I don't want to give up my job. I like my job. I don't want to give it up. I like it.'

Preston had taken to death. It had excited in him a hunger for scholarship. He could trace, with precise chronology, the shift from burial to cremation, broken down by gender, race, nation and social class. He had begun to follow the hit parade of causes – heart disease in at the top (up three places from 1900), good rises for cancer and stroke but a poor effort from the former top three: our old friends pneumonia, tuberculosis and diarrhoea and enteritis. One of Preston's little jokes was to point out that, actually, we all die of the same thing: hypoxemia, inadequate oxygenation of the blood. Preston was a keen collector of amusing incidences of killer number five (accidental injury – thanks to the car crash with lifetime odds of eighty to one), and blackly intrigued by the steady rise to number nine of suicide, above chronic liver disease these days. A very good show since it had ceased to be illegal in 1961. One to watch, bubbling under: HIV infection, rising fast. War and strife kept falling down the list though famine and pestilence were keeping their end up. Preston knew the death rate and life expectancy of every developed nation and took a keen interest in nativity and morbidity rates. He could explain at length the difference between morbidity and mortality (it was a world of difference for him, with the consolation that one always led to the other). At one hundred per cent of the time, his own morbidity rate was constant. He liked to say that, though life expectancy had increased from forty-seven in the 1890s to seventy-seven in the 1990s he would get them all in the end. The total numbers of deaths, after a brief but worrying fall in the first quarter of the century, had rallied and, as the end of the century came into view, was back to 1900 levels. Since the beginning of time, seventy billion people had snuffed it. Preston reckoned they were still going, around the world, at a rate of about six thousand an hour. If only Preston had not been so dedicated, Georgie might have found him easier to love. Apart from work, he had never really done anything to turn her off him. Preston had never slept with any clients (his clients being the relatives rather than . . . that kind of rumour can ruin an undertaker). She had no evidence about Susan Platt.

13

It was just gossip. The Operatic and Dramatic was an incubator for hearsay.

Bobby had heard all the tall tales. He knew most of the people. It was funny to be in the shows with adults he knew so much about. His mum made him act in the show. He was always in the pantomime too. He was in the boys' chorus and he did a spot with his grandma. She was the ventriloquist and he was the dummy on her knee. It was easy. He had to pretend to be very heavy and fall off her knee. The audience always laughed even though they'd seen it before. He hated it. It made him feel stupid. He lost concentration for a few moments, thinking that he would have to go through the same charade again soon when the pantomime came round. The ventriloquist act was in every one. All the people at the theatre patted Bobby on the head and laughed at him, saying what great fun it was. None of them asked what he thought. Not even his dad or his mum. Or his grandma. She said don't be silly Bobby it's just a bit of fun. But he hated it. Maybe he should go to bed now. He had to be up early in the morning. It was Remembrance Sunday and they always went to church on Remembrance Sunday to think about granddad Fred. That was his dad's dad. His dad's dad had been killed by Germany in the war. They always beat us at football. Bobby didn't care. He was rubbish at football. He should try to go to sleep. He'd be tired otherwise and he had to go to church. His dad didn't like church normally but he always went on Remembrance Sunday. They had to wear poppies to remember granddad Fred.

Then his mum started shouting about his dad's shed. His dad liked going in the shed to get away from his mum shouting.

'You spend more time in there than in our bed. If you could do it with the flowers I reckon you would.'

'I'd have more luck.'

Georgie and Preston had had a marriage of religious purity. Sex had been for reproductive purposes. They had both just preferred not to, neither having learned to fancy the other. Preston and Georgie were not skin-deep beautiful so a little

14

searching, a little learning how to fancy had been necessary. But neither had put the hours in.

There was a break in the slanging. Bobby thought again that he should go to bed. But he knew it wasn't finished. He had an instinct now for the shape of an argument. He could read an interim silence and distinguish it from the end of the show for the night. There was more coming in a minute and he had better stay and listen. He could come this far with the argument and there was some new content hidden in there among all the dross and the usual rubbish.

His mum started again. She was talking about going away somewhere. 'I have to do it, Press. I've always regretted not doing this years ago. I thought the chance'd gone. I've always wanted to play Dolly.'

'You can play Dolly. Nobody's stopping you playing Dolly. Why don't we do it at Heywood? There's no need to go to Bolton for it.'

'It's a professional show, Press. I'll get paid for it. It's a proper theatre, the Octagon. And I'll play the main role, I don't know why you can't be pleased.'

'I am pleased. I don't mind about *Hello, Dolly!*. That's only in Bolton. It's the other stuff I don't like. You can't go off to Ireland. Who's going to look after our Bobby?'

'I won't be away for ever. It's only a couple of months. You can cope.'

Bobby wanted to be involved. He always wanted to join in when they were talking about him. They often talked about him and there was always something wrong. He was always doing something wrong, according to them. But they never told him to his face. They talked behind his back, when he was asleep. Or when he wasn't. He wondered what they said when he was asleep. Probably sometimes he didn't hear everything.

'I was going to take Bobby with me.'

That sounded more like it. No more school. He hated school. There was this kid who hit him. And the teachers hated him too. And the girls. He didn't admit he liked girls but he did. They didn't like him much though. They never talked to him

15

so he'd stopped talking to them. Bobby didn't talk to anyone very much. It wasn't worth it.

His dad had upset a glass. That's what it sounded like, anyway. His mum shouted at him for being so careless and look at the carpet, it was ruined. His dad said not to fuss. He said that a lot, his dad. He didn't fuss, Bobby's dad. He was calm. His dad was always telling him to stay calm when things were horrible at school. He said there was no need to make a fuss. Nobody else seemed to listen though. Everyone else seemed to be making a fuss most of the time. The teachers were making a fuss all the time. So were some of the children. There was only Bobby in the whole class who wasn't making a fuss and it didn't exactly seem to be working. Maybe his dad wasn't as clever as he thought. Maybe his mum was right when she called him stupid.

Then it got worse. His mum said she was going to go to Scotland if his dad didn't give up his business. Then his mum said she didn't like the fact that he was so obsessive about everything being clean and he said that she would be like that if she worked where he did. And his mum said why could they never go on holidays and why did he always think that he was ill when he wasn't really, he was just being soft. And then his dad got really angry and bashed the wall and slammed the living room door and Bobby had to scurry off the third stair down back on to the landing out of sight as his dad came into the hall and out of the front door. Bobby looked out of his bedroom window and saw his dad opening the gate on to the allotments. His dad often went gardening at night, when it was dark.

3
The Spreading Roots of a Tree

Soon after dawn, Preston stretched out of the bed he kept in his shed. He wiped condensation off the window and looked out. The allotments on the south side of Nightingale Street were waking too, stretching out over a hectare to the wood that separated Heywood from the border of Rochdale. Allotments weren't measured in hectares, Preston pedantically insisted. Allotments were measured in rods. A hectare was four hundred rods which were split into forty ten-rod plots. Preston tended two of them at a cost of £2 per rod per week, an annual cost of nearly £2,000. Georgie thought it was a very expensive hobby. Twenty rods was, indeed, a big one. And he had a big shed full of tools too. Preston always sounded inescapably sexual when he talked about gardening: fertility, growth, plant a seed; the two shared a language.

Preston had a flower-garden at the front of his plot and a vegetable patch at the back. The two ten-rod segments were cut by three lines of higgledy-piggledy trees planted by Preston's predecessor but three or four or five. That was one of the things that Preston loved about his allotment: the chain connection, the ancestral inheritance. The trees afresh. He loved to sit alone here, where nobody was looking at him, where he had no need to hide his face or sit with his left profile invisible. Preston tended a remarkable, eclectic mix. Standing in dominion at the very back, guarding the border between flowers and food, he had a giant oak. It leant arrogantly against a resplendent maple, in all ways except character its equal. In

17

front of them, pleasingly arranged like the smaller boys in a school photograph, were the medium-sized trees, the paperback maple (younger brother of the elder), the maidenhair tree *ginkgo biloba* and the ornamental thorn, the prunifolia. In the acidic soil in front he had a flame-tinted liquidambar and a Persian ironwood. On both edges of the assemblage (like the boy who had run around the picture to get on at both sides as the old wind-up daguerreotype took a few seconds to flash across) were Preston's loves, his top trump trees. The talented Katsura tree was, in the season, giving up its pink and yellow leaves in the shape of a human heart. It left a smell on the ground like toffee apples. And then, in the very front row, the infant boys trees, the deciduous azaleas and Japanese maples which were in the process of their brilliant autumnal change from green to red. The traffic light trees, Preston called them. He'd read that in a gardening book but he had made it one of his little jokes. At the edges of the wood, the boundary between flowers and food was now porous. Against the foliage Preston's berries, crab apples and hips showed up, slotted in among the species roses, the *rosa rugosa*, the cultivars with the intriguing provenances and names: John Downie, Profusion, Golden Hornet. Also, what he called the knobbly fruit of the ornamental and edible quince and the fire red of the spindle bush. And all over, a horticultural quirk, the increasingly rare Chinese lantern. Preston walked through the flowers, through the trees, through the scrub, touching the plants and flowers, talking to them as they spoke to him. He went into his shed, closed the door behind and made a restorative cup of tea. He had it all in here. He could live in his shed. He was dog-tired at the moment. Undertaking was quite a business. Relentless. It was killing him. He closed his eyes and drifted off.

He had been asleep only fifteen minutes when Bobby woke him by fiddling with the loose latch. Preston started as if he were trying to conceal the fact that he had been looking at pornography. He upset his tea, which leapt out of the cup on to his hands. It was only lukewarm, though. Bobby wanted to be excused church. Bobby was cute. He always asked the parent most likely to offer a permit. It caused another row but that was one more straw to the collection. It made no difference to the haystack. Usually, Preston would consent to Bobby's wailing that church was dull. Preston agreed. Church was one of the fault lines between him and his wife.

Mary had passed on a loose and dilute belief-set to Georgie: gentle Anglicanism. St Stephen's church was a social club for the head with loose and unrestrictive rules. It didn't need elaborate ritual. Church was just a voluntary society, ladies coming together to make jam, sanctioned at some remote distance by reference to an ancient scroll. Preston had very little time for it all. He had his own spiritual retreats, just not a creed that required such a regular attendance. Preston had taken up many causes, none of them durable. Not believing in the usual menu, Preston was apt to order peculiar and exotic side dishes, some of which he had cooked up on his own. He had been looking into the stars lately. November, he had found, was the month of Scorpio, the sign of sex, death and regeneration. That was like the garden, he thought. He liked that much of astrology but he didn't care for the predictions they thought they could do. How could all the newspapers be right at the same time? This thought mobility put Preston at a disadvantage in his marital fight: he never stuck to anything for long while Georgie was a lapsed Anglican (the starting position) all the way through. For that reason, and also because she cared more, Georgie had won their battle over whether Bobby should go to church. On this sole occasion in the ecclesiastical calendar, Preston sided with his wife against his son.

Preston's father, Frederick, had died in the Second World War. Like Walter, his own father, Fred had been a mason. He had described himself as a writer of biographies. Fred Burns had chiselled words out of stone. Though they had been conventionally employed by builders to complete their stone work, Walter and Fred had made an extra honorarium in the employ of the Heywood municipal cemetery, back in the days when the council looked after the dead as well as the living. Their hands it had been that had chiselled out the names of the deceased. All the memorials in the graveyard that dated from 1895 to 1945 (and it was a boom time for entrance to council cemeteries) had been written by Walter or Fred Burns. But then the younger Burns had to go to war. He had died at the age of twenty-five. His body had been shipped back as Preston's mum was carrying their first child. She had to go on the train to Preston to sign the form to say that she recognized her husband's face. Meanwhile, Walter carried on, for three more years. He retired in 1945, at the top of the market. He completed his fiftieth year as a writer during his final illness. Walter had been a hypochondriac all his life (a condition that Fred and, in his turn, Preston had inherited) and, as he had often predicted, was proved right in the end. His granddad had a saying that Preston repeated too often: *every pimple is a portent of the inevitable*. On his fiftieth anniversary, Walter had been given a clock. But it only had somebody else's time left in it. Walter left his clock to Preston. It now adorned the mantelpiece of Preston Burns Undertakers. Every hour it chimed out its hypochondriac song: every pimple, Preston, just remember that. *Memento mori*. There is no time left, there goes another hour. Wind up the clock but wind down the time. Preston explained to Bobby that this was the only way to remember his granddad. He took a poppy and a pin from his work desk and fixed it on to Bobby's shirt.

Preston went into the house to have a bath. He passed Georgie on the stairs but neither was ready to conciliate yet. Six doors down, they called for Georgie's mother. These days Mary Lees was, to use Dr Knox's technical term, mildly demented. Mary disagreed. Just a little forgetful these days, that was all. The doctor's diagnosis had been late because Mary had for so long refused to let him in. The ramifications had only registered with Georgie and Preston when Dr Knox had used the name Alzheimer and the words 'progressive dementia'. It had sounded like an immediate death sentence but Dr Knox had assured Georgie that most patients did not progress – strange word, he said – beyond the early stages of the withered hippocampus or the entangled neubrofils which he, the physician-poet, had described as like the spreading roots of a tree. Preston immediately concluded that Mary ought to be moved into institutional care. Georgie, naturally, disagreed.

The four of them went to church together. Georgie and Preston, sulky teenagers, did not speak directly to one another . but Mary had plenty to say. She wanted a full report and accounts from Georgie on the embroidery stall. She wondered what show they were planning to do next – *Aladdin* said Preston and then probably *Oklahoma!* She wanted to know when rehearsals started and Georgie said they were just about to. She looked forward to the next time she would be on stage with Bobby and back through all her turns as the leading lady at Heywood Civic Hall. Throughout her monologue, Mary mixed all her names up. Georgie was often as not Isabel (Mary's mother's name) and she referred to Bobby as Tommy (her great love, Tommy Gaffney, had been one of the first casualties of World War II). This misnaming had been going on for six months now. At first, Georgie had corrected her mother painstakingly but she had lately been lazier. Preston was glad to arrive at the church, in the Market Place in Heywood. Chatter went on around them. Georgie even acknowledged friends and acquaintances. There were plenty of people in both categories and Georgie nodded and smiled and said hello. Georgie ensured that Mary and Bobby were settled and then found herself a pew.

The Family Eucharist began but Georgie did not listen. The service was her jumping-off point. The words, in the sense of their literal meaning, didn't matter so much. No, it was more that Georgie found in the unignorable silence some essential solace. There was a clarity in this freezing old barn. It was a touchstone. When the door of the church thudded shut, Georgie gazed around the scene – looking at the rafters, the grimy blackened radiators, the cold stone floor, the elaborate lectern. Over the years that the Lees family had lived in Heywood, Middleton and Rochdale, the claims to truth that were aired in this house had ceased to be the principal point of their attendance. The solace was the reason. The cold air was a stimulus to thought and to clarity.

21

Preston waited stoically in the cold for his moment. He let the words go. They were not for him, except for when the deceased of the two world wars were memorialized. The dead of the parish were named. Tommy Gaffney, never found, presumed dead. Frederick Burns, died in action, 1942. Georgie looked at Preston and something of the kindness he had to offer showed in his face.

In the front row, Georgie watched a man she did not recognize reach out to take the hand of a woman she did not know. The woman smiled as their fingers touched. They were old, in their sixties. Georgie stared at the altar and found herself to be very clear. Her marriage to Preston was over. She looked at Bobby, the reason to lurch on. She had tried that but it hadn't worked. She wasn't happy. Neither was Preston. There was nothing terribly wrong, nothing so debilitating on its own. Georgie had a strong scent of mustiness. She whispered to herself, far too loud not to be heard three rows in front and behind. And far too loud not to be heard by Preston, by her side. Georgie held her hand to her mouth and shrugged her shoulders, admitting guilt but no remorse. She realised, with a start, that she had just spoken out loud: 'I'm sorry Press but I have to go. I'm sorry love.'

4

In the Black

With a quixotic serendipity that Preston was apt to describe as fate, Georgie's choice was complicated first thing on Monday morning. She woke later than she needed to, too late to catch the best of the pre-work traffic past the stall. It had been a tough night, arguing with Preston in a more acrid, more permanent way. Preston had a habit, after an hour of recrimination, of walking out and spending the night in the shed. For once, he had stayed and fought his corner. The dispute had stopped only when Georgie went out to the toilet and discovered Bobby listening on the stairs. Bobby had come down to join them and revealed that he knew as much about their private lives as they did. Preston had gone up to bed at four in the morning. Georgie had drifted off for three hours on the sofa. She woke at seven, disorientated, her body clock telling her that she was late. She threw on her clothes, feeling grubby without the shower for which there was no time and ran down Nightingale Street to catch the seven-forty-five to Middleton.

As Georgie sat on the bus, willing it to move more quickly down the narrow, windy hill, she looked out of the window. Heywood is a town, between Bury and Rochdale, built in red Accrington brick which had recovered its colour slowly after the expulsion of the factories' ashes. It was a town of machinery and tall chimneys from which smoke no longer trailed. The black canal had been cleaned up and the river had lost the colour of purple dye.

The bus stopped in Middleton. It was a place that had

23

been planned to death. The original marketplace had been surrounded, colonised and conquered by road building. It was now overseen by illuminated signs pointing somewhere else. The concrete precinct – in grey to complement the weather – beckoned very few back. The Middleton market started to hum to the tune of a Monday morning. Daily routines were exchanged in greetings now so common that they had ritualistic force for the participants. The pleasantries had no function of information other than to say, wearily and comically, 'Still here then? Yeah, me too. Anyway, better get on.' From out of the choreography of the morning, a familiar figure returned. Mary Lees turned up at the market as if she had never been away which, today in her head, she hadn't.

Mary Lees had been the union representative of Middleton market for twenty years between 1960 and 1980. Like the leading lady of the Heywood Amateur Operatic and Dramatic Society, it was a hereditary position, now occupied by Georgie. Mary had been born and brought up in the White Horse, the pub in Heywood which she had later run with her husband, Jack. In 1950, Georgie Annie Lees had been born there. Five years later, Jack had suffered a minor stroke and so had changed careers. He had started his term as an undertaker convinced that he was himself on the way out. As it transpired, within five years he had bought the business and went on to serve the dead of Heywood for thirty years more. After selling out of the White Horse, Mary had picked up her dormant artistry for embroidery. With the small capital sum they had taken from the pub, Mary had become the proprietor of 'Tommy's', her stall on Middleton market that had, since 1955, sold her own embroidered garments.

Mary Lees had always supposed that 'Tommy's' would be the warm-up for a shop in Heywood, then an embroidery chain across the North West of England. Throughout Georgie's childhood there had been expectant talk of opening a shop. It seemed to be perpetually on the horizon – always visible but always in the distance. Georgie had picked up the slender thread. A couple of good winters – bad winters, cold winters in

24

other words – would bring a run on the jumpers and she would be that little bit closer to a warm shop in the precinct. For a year now Georgie had stood on the stall alone, but since retirement Mary had begun to struggle as chief supplier. Sewing, knitting and purling was taxing her more every night, especially so as she needed to accelerate. A new factory, called the Mill, had opened in Radcliffe. Their machines, located overseas in a once imperial cotton town, span more expensive wool quicker than Mary and spat out cheaper garments. The free bus up to the retail park was packed every morning. Georgie, the new chief executive, had taken the difficult decision to buy in new sweaters and tablecloths, from a factory run illegally from out of the back bedroom of a Mrs Sharma in the tower blocks that overlooked Rochdale Town Hall.

All of this was lost to Mary as she greeted the stall-holders in the way she had when only a Sunday separated them.

'Hiya Vinny, morning Geoffrey. I'm a bit bloody late this morning. Can't get up these days. I must be getting old.'

Vinny Able, the cobbler with a club foot, and Geoff Webb, the overall manager of the market, were the only survivors from the day that Mary Lees used to run Middleton market. Geoff was a self-styled grotesque of no nonsense, known to all, with no adornment, as Geoff. Only Mary Lees had the temerity and authority to call him Geoffrey. She said it with a camp upturn of emphasis on the second syllable. Geoff Webb loved other people's business. Or, rather, there was no such thing as other people's business as far as Geoff Webb was concerned. If it happened anywhere near Middleton market, it was Geoff's business. He had had a dispute over ten years about the siting of Vinny Able's stall. Geoff wanted to move it ten feet to the left to make a corridor between stalls with a straight edge. Vinny Able had stood firm where he was for twenty-five years. He was a cobbler of the old school, resisting all temptation to learn how to cut keys. Mary had once revelled in the obvious joke that his conversation was connected to his business. She tried to remember this gag which was buried in her head somewhere.

'What are you doing here Mary, anyway?'

'Don't be so daft Geoffrey lad. What do you think I'm doing? Do you think I come here for the good of me health? I've got a living to make like we all have. We've not got so far to go until we get a shop. We'll be inside before you know it. We've most of it saved already. And I've squared one of them sites in the precinct they're building.'

Geoff Webb looked at her funny. The precinct had been up for fifteen years, at least. It was a shame it wasn't still being built. He could have advised them to stop. Geoff Webb assumed Georgie was on her way and wandered off to interfere with somebody else's peace and quiet. Mary looked at the bare tressel tables. She couldn't remember where the stock was. She had a faint recollection that there was a store somewhere. Instead of asking, she followed Vinny Able around until he went to collect his cobbling equipment and part-soled shoes.

Mary recognized the work of her own hand. Mary Lees remained a creweller of great repute. She could do a Jacobean Leaf sampler in cross-stitch, an Iris in blackwork, a tree bark in silk shading. She specialized in trammed tapestry and cross-stitch, faithfully covering the designs of the great Moira Blackburn, the closest that embroidery comes to a superstar. Mary told stories through the eye of a needle and yarns that had them in stitches. Long ago was now up close to Mary. That was how her memory failure was working. She remembered as the day before yesterday the time Tommy Gaffney said they would be married when he had finished giving Adolf a bloody nose. She had a crystalline recall of her childhood, pulling pints in the White Horse. But she was long-sighted; objects up close were out of focus. The identities of her daughter and grandson were pixelated and obscure. Mary had a sense that she ought to recognize these characters but sometimes she found herself wondering just who they really were.

Mary struggled with a box of tea towels from the store to the stall. Vinny Able the cobbler and Gareth Adams the smelly fishmonger took the burden from her and placed it on Georgie's stall. They were both confused by Mary's presence but knew enough of Mary's fearsome temper not to question it.

Mary confused them further: 'Vinny Able you scoundrel, where's our Jack gone? He were here a minute ago.'

Vinny looked at Gareth for guidance. Gareth looked at his fish, for the same reason.

'Jack's long gone, Mary love.'

'Where's he gone?'

'It's a matter of opinion is that.'

'Same place as these lads here,' said Gareth, pointing to his haddock.

'He's probably gone to see the solicitor. Did he say he'd be coming back?'

'Not unless he's cleverer than we thought. Jack never worked here, Mary. He was an undertaker was your Jack. He worked in the shop across the way, you know the parade before they put the precinct on the back?'

'You've never made any sense, have you Vinny Able. Bloody cobblers, that's what they always said about you. Bloody cobblers.'

'Are you sure you're not looking for your Georgie? I've not seen her this morning. She's usually in by now.'

'Vinny Able, are you being funny on purpose or what? What do I want with a little girl?'

Vinny gave up on Mary. He didn't know what she was talking about but she was not in a mood to argue. Mary had never been in a mood to argue. Vinny went back to the order he had received for a hundred pairs of shoes to be reheeled by the following morning. They all belonged to the same man and they all needed reheeling at once. In all the annals of cobblers . . .

Mary was very quickly back in the old way, flapping jumpers open and placing the more expensive items in prominent positions on the stall, re-arranging the garments so that colour rather than price was uppermost. She started to beckon customers over. Nobody came. Mary spent five minutes shouting at shoppers, to no avail. She noted that there was a steady trickle of customers behind her, passing Vinny Able's cobblers and Gareth Adams's fishmongers. She had a revolutionary but literal idea for the stall.

27

'Turn it around,' she said out loud, to herself.

Mary lifted the stall and carried it ten yards to the left. Then she replaced Georgie's chair and cash till on the opposite side and turned all the stock upside down. Within ten seconds a young mother hidden behind plastic bags had been enticed away from Vinny's shoes to have a look. A minute later a lady with candy-floss purple hair and Edna Everage glasses asked if things could be made to order. Mary promised blithely that she could sew a likeness if the lady brought back a passport photograph. We'll never get all that hair in the picture though, she thought. Mary looked at the uninterested, sparse crowd filing past and decided they needed a preacher. She climbed creakily up onto the stall and started to bark demands at the shoppers from on high. She had a voice in-between alto and tenor, man and woman, which carried on the waves. Her words were orders, not advertisements.

'Hey you with the hat on, come and have a look at this. Come here, I won't bite. Honestly, you'd think you could catch something the way you lot are walking past with your bloody noses in the air. You mister, don't you wear jumpers in your house? Do you walk round with your skin showing? Come on, it'll not cost you a right lot. At least have a look . . . oh have it your own way you miserable old sod.'

Before long, passers-by were converted into interested parties and then into buyers. Mary was chummy and pub-talking to the men who came by. She persuaded them that their wives would be suspicious, astonished but most of all delighted, if they took home a made-to-order sweater. Well, not made-to-order as such but who would ever know? With the men, Mary flirted as if thrust into a single-again crisis after years of being married. She was told she was a saucy young woman, or words to that effect, five times in as many minutes. She offered discounts, suggested trades with old women wearing hats like liquorice all-sorts and tried to barter an eiderdown for an old lady's poodle. She held up a tank-top embroidered with a house out of the baby's drawing book on the front.

'Come on you all, they're back in are these. Tank-tops. Never went out of fashion.'

A family of three stopped to look, followed by another and then, contagiously, a crowd began to gather. All the young staff on the adjoining market stalls left their stations to listen to the old woman they had never seen before berating the people of Heywood and Middleton from Georgie Lees's pitch.

Mary played to them. 'Folk don't have any need of knitwear round here do they? It's like the bloody Bahamas round here isn't it? Look at everyone, off sunbathing. On their way to the beach down by the ship canal. Only cotton tee-shirts needed in Middleton, every fool knows that. Why did the good Lord bother with all them sheep in the Lake District when, down here in sunny Middleton, we've no bloody need of wool for anything?'

A man at the back spoke derisively. 'Go on then love, I'll take one off your hands. We can't have an old bird starving.'

Quick with wit, Mary was inspired by her return to the stage. 'I'm not a bloody charity case you know. If you want a good sweater for your wife . . .' Mary spoke aside, behind her hand, like an actor in an old comedy of mistaken identity. 'What am I saying your wife? No woman'd put up with you. Look sunshine, I've got one here your mum'd like. You'd better buy her something. She'll not pretend to like you otherwise.'

The man looked as though he was tip-toeing away.

'Come back you slippery cad. I was only joking. That'll be nine-ninety-nine. Give us ten and we'll say no more about it. Good on you lad, you'll not be wanting for owt when it's below freezing. Right, who's next?'

The next in line was the current proprietor, Georgie Lees. Georgie had been too disturbed by her discovery of Bobby to sleep well. As she got closer, she saw what was now, to her puzzlement, the back of the stall. And standing on the top, the unmistakable figure of her mother, holding a crowd that looked up at her in wonder. Shouting went back and forth, some of it producing orders for goods. Georgie fought her way through the crowd, whispering as she pushed that she needed

29

to talk to her mother. In the maelstrom, nobody paid much attention.

Georgie shrieked when she reached the front. 'Mum.'

Mary stopped and looked at her blankly. This strange interloper who had came out of the crowd to claim lineage.

She turned a few phrases in Georgie's direction. 'Bloody hell, that's fame for you. Sell a few sweaters and people start thinking you're family. Sorry love, I'll do you a nice pattern if you like but I'm not starting adopting.'

Mary held up a small beige cardigan finished with cream piping in silk. It was about the size of a ten-year-old. Georgie looked aghast at Mary, a reaction that Mary misread as a comment on the work.

'No love, it's not for you. It's for a little girl. Or a lad if he's that way inclined.'

'Mum, get down.'

'Yes love, I'm your mum aren't I? Like I'm the Queen's mum as well. And Mrs Simpson's. And who's the fella off the telly, the one with the white hair and the cigars? Well, I'm his mum as well. Come on love, let me interest you in a sweater. What have we got on this one? Oooh, look, a duck and some swans. Or are they geese? Does it matter? Does it buggery. Geese, swans, who can tell the bloody difference? To you love, seeing as you're my daughter, it's going for a song.'

'Mum.'

'And this is the song.'

Mary sang the first two lines of 'Happy Talk'.

'Seeing as you're family . . .'

Mary used her speaking aside trick again. It was an entirely different audience so it worked. 'She thinks she is more like . . .'

Stepping in and out of character, Mary used Georgie for her audience's delight. 'Seeing as you're family, I'll do you a special family price. Normally ten quid but to all members of the family, and I wouldn't say fairer to my own mother, a special price of twenty.'

'It's Georgie Mum, it's me. Georgie.'

By now some of the crowd were beginning to transfer their

30

bet on who was hallucinating. Georgie looked at Mary to plead for recognition which did not come.

From out of the crowd a male voice spoke excitedly: 'All right Mary love, come on get down, I think the show's over now.'

Preston jostled the crowd out of the way and reached up for Mary's hand. Her burning, raving fire went out as quickly as it had raged.

Georgie grunted her thanks to Preston. Rather than acknowledge the greeting, Preston began to behave oddly. He waved frantically in the direction of Geoff Webb, who was bringing a problem into Colin Smethurst's previously clear day on the butcher's stall. Geoff came over.

Preston refused to speak until Geoff joined them: 'Show them the paper, Geoff.'

'Press, what the bloody hell is going on here?'

Preston took two minutes to say anything meaningful. He was very excited about something. It had to do with a shop in the precinct. Georgie gave up the ghost on Preston and wrung some sense out of Geoff Webb. It transpired that one of the units on the parade of shops, the one next to Preston Burns Undertakers, had become vacant first thing this morning. Preston had been called by Mrs Bilston to attend to her husband the florist who had fallen face down into his cornflakes.

Preston had to conceal from Mrs Bilston that his feelings on her husband's demise were decidedly mixed. Georgie could now have a shop. The plan had already formed in his head. Preston would re-mortgage some of his assets – he was a bit sketchy on the details for the moment – and he would buy the new unit. He had been trying to force Bilston the florist out of business for years. There was a cross-selling opportunity for Preston. Funerals meant flowers. The only supplier in town had been Mr Bilston and Preston had never managed to cut a good deal with him. So, his plan: to buy the unit, to cut it in half, to set up Georgie as a florist-cum-wool shop, embroidery shop, whatever she wanted to call it.

This was Preston's ingenious way of locking Georgie in. Supplant one dream with another. Tread clumsily, for you offer me all my dreams. It was also, into the bargain, the only possible way that Preston could expand. He had been looking for a way for the business to grow. But the death trade does not grow easily. The only lever he had was price because volume is pretty much fixed in advance. There is no genuine demand (well, only a little). There is no way of persuading us to do it more than once. We don't come away from Preston's service wanting more. There is no prospect of increasing sales, no way that death can be branded to attribute magical properties to the same old sorry notion, so if turnover – a Preston joke, reminding him of spinning in the grave – if the top line was to grow, the bottom line was that the bereaved would have to pay more. Preston liked his clients to leave behind wealthy relatives. If the left behind were on benefits he was limited to the £600 that the DSS thought he should have to play with. Once the minister (that's church, not state), once the minister took his slice – for what, exactly, wondered Preston? – and once the bits and pieces were taken care of, there was nothing left. In order to give the poor their due, and Preston treated his clients (the dead – Preston shifted in his definition of his clientele), he treated his clients all the same as that was how they treated him. He had to put prices up for those who could afford it. What else could they do? Preston knew his market and he knew that death was the end of choice, even for the left behind. So, keep the supply coming, the work would never dry up. Preston had the demise of the baby boomers to look forward to, which would keep his parlour, as it ever was, in the black. Preston used to tell Georgie that he should rename his business In The Black. In The Black, do you get it? No, he was no comedian, Preston. It had been his ambition once. He had been on a course but he had discovered that you cannot teach people how to be funny. Preston now knew a lot of jokes, but that was different. Very different. Anyway, it didn't matter all that much. He had always been frightened of clowns anyway. He had found a word for it: coulrophobia and discovered a doctor who specialized in it. Preston had discovered that there was good money to be earned in death – other people's death anyway – and the cost of dying with Preston Burns Undertakers (yes, he saw the joke and relished it) had gone up by fifteen per cent in the last financial year alone. The closer the patient to death the more expensive they became. And then when they finally went . . . It was an expensive business, dying.

The shop, the show. Mary's feeble grasp. Bobby on the third stair. The marriage, its only apparent connection to the choices of shop and show. Georgie spent the day on the stall, now the other way round.

5
The Unignorable Silence

'Trick or treat. Trick or treat. Trick or treat.'

'Treat.'

Trick or threat. Unless we are recognized, we who have been dormant so long, there will be mischief. Preston held a heart of dough and a puce bowl of cherries and strawberries. He handed them over, to propitiate Bobby who was dressed as a luminous skeleton (a Bobby dazzler indeed). From out of the conifers on the garden path, the pantomime cast of the Heywood Amateur Operatic and Dramatic Society emerged. Georgie stepped forward. She was wearing a long black cape. She had an ugly spot on her upper lip and a Rice Krispie wart glued to the end of her nose. In one hand she held a broomstick. In the other, she held up a goblin's face carved into a pumpkin. Illuminated by an interior lamp, a guardian against the spirits that were abroad this ghostly night, it sparkled against the metal on Preston's little round glasses.

'Come witches and warlocks. Let us take this man into our land.'

The children's chorus moved forward, choreographed as one. Preston covered the birth marks on his temple with his hand. A body of skeletons, bones in white chalk on black felt, moved towards the threshold.

Georgie spoke, stifling her laugh. In the black, she sounded menacing: 'Trick or treat. Trick or treat, Press.'

The treats were all done. This was a threat: an offer he could not refuse. Preston reached into the pocket of his gardening trousers. He brought out a handful of dust and offered it to his wife and son. They took this as a request for a trick. Stanley Atkinson (all in black, including a top hat) and Graham Collins (chief warlock, so grand in a starred coat) lurched through the pack and held Preston still.

Stanley spoke his prepared line with great deliberation. He was a truly terrible actor. 'As you have failed to meet our needs Mr Burns, we are taking *you* to meet your clients.'

See how he liked it. Three boys – a filmic corpse, a grey-haired ghoul and Bobby Burns – stepped forward carrying spades and feigned to penetrate the turf. Preston cackled in pain. Not his lawn. Anything but the lawn. Take me but spare the ground. They desisted and, instead, three junior hobgoblins fired their pistols. Preston pinioned himself to the door, wailing to be saved. The children laughed and fired until their water ran dry. Preston was one of the pantomime's funny guys, never more funny, in fact, than when he was strapped to the threshold being drenched piss-wet by hobgoblins.

Preston broke the spell with a huge peal of laughter. When the victim laughs the fun is over. Georgie called the spirits to order and they set out further down Nightingale Street in search of a further harvest. Preston grumbled to himself that he had strained his forearm wrestling with Stanley. As the children made their way back on to claim their next victim, Preston noted that the last of them was dressed as an infant Elvis Presley. Immortality, of a kind, and scary with it.

The cast paused on the pavement where, led by Georgie Lees, they could not stop laughing. All, that is, except melancholy Bobby Burns who stared at the rest as if the opening of their mouths, the baring of their teeth and their breathy noise were the force of an alien intelligence. Bobby had never really laughed much. Even as a baby he had rarely offered more than a wry smile. His grandmother had ascribed this reluctance to laugh to a high intelligence. He was laughing inside, at the rest of us, she had said. In fact, Mary had turned out to be diametrically wrong. Bobby had quickly developed difficulties in learning and had spent all his school career in what was dispiritingly known as the 'remedial class'. The remedial children were not so stupid that they didn't wear the lack of learning very heavily. As time went by and there was no sign of an enduring remedy to Bobby's basic stupidity, Mary and Georgie began to blame the men in the family. Not genetically: his granddad Jack's taciturnity had concealed an interested, eager brain and Preston had proved to be entrepreneurial and scholarly, after a fashion of his own. But the men may have nurtured Bobby's melancholy. This misery was not in their chemistry but in their trade. Bobby spent a lot of his childhood with wooden boxes and people who had gone to sleep. Mary convinced Georgie that this contact with the next world had caused a deep melancholy to enter Bobby's soul which no special class would ever remedy. Whatever the cause, it was a peculiarity that separated Bobby Burns from his peers and he stood now, as he always did, there and yet not there. With the group, but apart from it. When he refused to join in, Bobby was teased and bullied, along with the other remedial children. Those who were only struggling took a glowing satisfaction in tormenting those who were institutionalized beneath them.

Georgie gathered a banquet around the houses and brought it home to the party. For the past eight years, she had marked every Hallowe'en in this way because 31 October was the day her only son Bobby had been born. It was, every year, the first outing for the costumes for the Christmas pantomime, which Mary hand-made specially each summer. Mary refused to allow the cast at Heywood to wear the same dress twice. Olive Platt, the producer, had written a standard underworld scene that, every year without variation, allowed the costumes to double as Hallowe'en spirits. It had been quite a task to write the undead into *Cinderella*. In Olive's script there was more to the ugly sisters than meets the eye. This Christmas, Georgie's Widow Twankey was to be her valedictory, her final show as an amateur. Rehearsals started for *Hello, Dolly!* in January and the tour began in Edinburgh on the last day of April.

In the living room, Georgie laid out the treats in a circle on the table: strawberries, bread, grapes, red apples (the horrible russet type that Mary and Bobby hated even though they were,

36

apparently, 'good for you'), oranges, dirty potatoes, four tubes of Smarties (the old man at the end house, the rubbish hoarder, gave them those), more strawberries, more cherries, a bag of the round blue-beaded ones from liquorice all-sorts (it takes all sorts) and several shiny tomatoes that kept running off the table. No sooner could Georgie lay them out than Bobby was helping himself. Despite his mother's good-natured scolding, he soon began to bleed strawberry juice from his gums. It coursed over his straight white teeth, catching in the cracks like stage make-up. Bobby gathered the team of skeletons and whispered a plot: run behind me into the kitchen, leap out from behind the door and frighten my grandma. Mary was pressing the ninth and final candle into Bobby's birthday cake. Unable any more quite to distinguish between the living and the dead, Mary screamed blue murder and smashed her fist into the fragile icing. Frightened in turn by Mary's excessive rage, the skeletons scattered.

Preston boxed Bobby's ear. 'Bobby, stop scaring your nan. You know she's not well.'

'I'm not doing anything. You made me wear this stuff.'

'Grandma doesn't realize it's you.'

'Why not?'

'She just doesn't.'

Mary came back in and, as if to defy Preston on purpose, called Bobby by name to join her in the living room. She instructed Preston to bring in the shattered cake.

Mary put Bobby on her knee, called for quiet and addressed the Heywood Amateur Operatic and Dramatic Society. 'Now then everyone, I've brought young Bobby out to see you.'

'Don't Grandma. I don't like doing this.'

Mary moved her lips uncomfortably, impersonating someone who was trying to keep them still. 'Don't be like that young Bobby. Say hello to the people.'

'Stop it Grandma. I didn't mean to scare you. I'm sorry.'

The dummy struggled to be released from the ventriloquist's grip. This was the substance, the only trick in fact, of the act that Mary and Bobby had done for the last two pantomimes and which was about to go on stage again in six weeks' time. As the ventriloquist fought for control, the rebellious dummy slithered and slid. That was good for five minutes of entertainment. Mary usually pretended to be bereft of strength. The act required the dummy to have the upper hand. But, this time, she showed formidable strength to hold Bobby in place as she conducted a chorus of 'Happy Birthday'.

'Happy birthday to you, happy birthday to you, happy birthday dear dummy, happy birthday to you.'

The song ended with a generous round of applause from the audience. Mary released Bobby's skeleton cape from her grip and he jumped up from her knee and ran for the door. Judging the distance poorly under the pressure, he crashed straight into the door handle. It looked like a stroke of dummy-comic genius.

'I hate you. I hate doing that.'

'Bobby Burns don't you dare be so rude.'

Bobby turned to his mother and gave her the two fingers. Preston leapt from in between a warlock and a ghoul, fell over a stray broomstick and just managed to land a slap on Bobby's backside as the caped skeleton escaped. Preston caught him in the hall and stung his bottom. As he dragged his feet heavily up the stairs, Bobby pointed to his temple, giving the sign that usually denotes madness but, in this instance, drew attention to his father's birth mark.

'Get upstairs you nasty little . . .'

Bobby spat back, deliberately loud enough for all his birthday guests to hear: 'I'm not staying here. You can all get lost you stupid idiots. I hate it here. I hate it.'

Preston failed in a second slap and went back to join the odyssey of the undead.

Georgie killed the spirit with her first remark. 'What on God's earth do you think you're doing, Preston? I've told you not to hit out. That's where he gets it from.'

Preston looked around, genuinely shocked that Georgie should address him so harshly in public. In private, he was accustomed to it, but not in front of all their friends.

He replied vaguely, 'I don't think you can just let him off.'

Stanley Atkinson intervened to take Preston's part. Clumsily.

If it was anyone's fault, he said, it was Mary's for sitting Bobby on his knee and making fun of him. She wasn't making fun of him, she insisted. *He*, Bobby, was making fun. There *was* a difference though she, Mary, couldn't expect a village idiot like Stanley Atkinson to understand. Olive Platt joined in. Olive loved a good row. She always had a number of points to make which she liked to enumerate by counting patronizingly on her fingers. As if nobody could understand the transition from one to two to three without Olive doing it in mime as well. In remonstrating with Olive, Graham Collins seemed to jostle Colin Smethurst the butcher. To be precise, Colin accused Graham of deliberately stepping on his orthopaedic shoe. The skeleton-children backed away to the perimeter of the living room as the adults shouted at one another. Georgie suddenly saw the absurdity of a coven of witches and warlocks starting a brawl and began to laugh. Her levity was contagious and Stanley Atkinson interrupted Olive Platt's enumerating the options by tickling her under the arms. The party limped on, more convivially, for another hour.

But when the guests had gone, when Preston had escorted Mary back home, six houses further down the same side of Nightingale Street, a deadly marital silence settled on the house. Georgie and Preston had married late in their lives, thirty-six and thirty-nine. Most of their fragile ten-year union had been glued by their only son, Bobby. Preston Burns had been introduced to Georgie by her father. Preston had been one of his regular pall-bearers. In time Preston had come to show a flair for the trade and, when Jack had finally succumbed to a painful and protracted decline, it was to Preston that he had dedicated the business. Georgie had been fond of Preston from the start. But nothing more than that, if she was honest with herself. They went to bed, together. Preston went in to check on Bobby and, by the time he cleared Georgie out of his space in the bed, she was already feigning sleep. He tried to lift his wife's leg but she did not yield. He kissed her face but she turned away. He poked her hard with his knee. Still, Georgie did not stir. But, aware that she was not asleep, Preston started talking.

'I wish your mother'd drop that bloody ventriloquist act. It causes more trouble than it's worth. I don't want him doing it in the panto.'

Georgie did not reply so Preston repeated himself. And again.

'He's not doing it in the panto. I'm glad you agree. We'll take that as settled then. I'll tell Olive in the morning she'll have to find a different filler.'

'It's booked now.'

'Oh I see, so you're not asleep then?'

'I said it's booked now. Mum's said to Olive that they'll do it. It's in the running order.'

'It can come out of the running order. There are plenty of others who can do a turn instead. He hates that bloody act your mum makes him do. It's not fair on a young lad, getting everyone to laugh at him like that.'

'They're not laughing at him. Don't be so soft Press.'

'I don't want him in the panto any more. I'm taking him out.'

'You're not.'

'I am.'

Oh no you're not. Oh yes I am. Oh no you're bloody well not. I bloody well am. Oh bloody no you are bloody well not, I'm telling you, and there will be hell to pay if you do. Oh yes I fucking well – there's no need to swear Preston – am and there is nothing you can do to stop me. Oh yes there bloody well is something I can do, I can walk out of this house this minute, pack up my bags and disappear on tour that's what I can do. You wouldn't do that. Wouldn't I? Just watch me, You wouldn't. I would. Wouldn't. Would. Oh no you wouldn't. I just have. I want you to warn me children when the ghost of separation walks on to the stage. Make sure you shout. When I say 'Where's your marriage? I want you to shout at the top of your voices – behind you. Where? I can't see it. Behind you. These words had been said in anger many times. Either the exchange becomes a ritual, secretly relished by the participants and part of the landscape of the relationship. Or the gravity

40

increases slightly every time. Georgie and Preston had rowed their way through a ten-year marriage but their cleavage over belief, Preston's obsessive duty to work and the gradual erosion of that small portion of attraction that glued them together in the first place, were all leading inexorably towards ... It didn't need spelling out. It was time she acted. The thought, the decisive thought confirmed and settled, saddened her, made her feel more fondly towards Preston. Georgie turned the light off and feigned sleep again.

6
Bobby Dazzler's Dummy Run

Mary Lees struggled out of the wings to a great cheer, dragging a heavy suitcase behind her. She flicked it open and Bobby Burns dropped out. He had been made up in the wings to look like a doll-clown, with a big red nose and peculiar cat's whiskers daubed across his cheeks. He was the Bobby Dazzler. Mary tried to pull Bobby up on to her knee but he resisted, affecting to be too heavy. This was really the beginning and the end of their ventriloquist act, its only scripted joke. Mary did not like to be hemmed in by too much prior thought and her memory was failing her alarmingly these days in any case. Mary had played thirty pantomimes and none of her scripts had ever been the same as another. Jack had always prevailed over the Giant, but the route up the beanstalk had varied every performance. Cinderella had always made it to the ball but never in the stage-coach as planned. It had all depended on Mary's journey around the stage. Mary had always refused to commit her lines to memory, preferring instead to stick them to the back of the furniture. She had turned an old theatrical saw on its head. Mary Lees didn't know what she was saying *until* she bumped into the furniture. The cue she had offered depended on whether she was looking at the back of the armchair or the underside of the kitchen table. She had tried pinning a note to Bobby's back but her script was too minute for her fading sight. She put it down to getting old. Not that she felt eighty-two. Or looked it.

Bobby sat in a doll-like seizure, his features stilled into a travesty of a small boy, a faithful cover version of a child. He understood his privilege: he had a licence for impertinence, and even for violence. The strange transforming power of comedy allowed Bobby Burns to do something that would have been unthinkable otherwise: he was allowed to defy his grandma, even, if the part warranted it, to inflict physical pain on her. As Mary introduced her dummy, Bobby Dazzler, to the audience he began to elude her grasp, to slip slowly down off her knee on to the floor. The art of ventriloquism really didn't come into the show because the act was almost wordless apart from Mary's muttered swear-words as she struggled to lift Bobby back on to her knee. The act worked precisely because it was not an act. Mary really *was* trying to lift Bobby up again and he really *was* refusing to be lifted. It was a gothic horror in which the dummy usurps control from the hand in its back. Bobby lay flat, playing dead.

Finally, Mary made a virtue of Bobby's recalcitrance by leaving him inert on the floor, standing up and shouting: 'You little bugger. Stay there then.'

Mary reached down, sniffed Bobby's hair, took his pulse, pressed his heart, pinched his skin, which cruelty he heroically withstood. Like an ancient necromancer casting a spell, summoning death, Mary stepped away from Bobby and looked up at the audience: 'Little bugger's dead. No wonder he's gone a bit quiet. I've been flogging a dead dummy for years now. Here, there's an idea. I think I will flog him. He'll fetch a fiver. Anybody want a little lad? He'll make a good doorstop like one of them sausage dogs.'

'Grandma . . .'

Bobby stepped out of the world of pretend. 'I'm sorry Grandma . . . Don't sell me grandma.'

'Tell you what, I'll either flog you or flog you. That's your choice.'

Bobby was flummoxed by the options until Mary drew back her hand to smack his bottom. He jumped up and started for the wings. Mary stretched out to prevent her dummy escaping and they both went crashing to the stage floor.

As ventriloquist and dummy wriggled, the audience was

slayed by Mary's muttering: 'I'll kill you, you little devil, when I get my hands on you.'

Bobby got up and ran to his mother, who was watching, with a charmed smile on her face, in the wings. Georgie swept her little dummy into her arms and laughed at him. He looked straight through her, no relish in the joke at all.

This complex counterfeiting of life: faking as a doll, dummying to be alive but suggesting a death that was impossible unless the onlooker granted the dummy life in the first place. And order disrupted again by the come-back of the dead – the dummy's abusive retort. To his own grandmother at that. Somewhere in the non-linearity of the act, an important transaction took place between Mary and her audience, the currency of which was laughter. If this was a safety-valve, it never felt like it. As Bobby hit the stage floor with a thud, the last thing he would do would be to make it feel safe, neither for the audience, nor indeed for himself.

Mary bowed to the applause. Bobby refused her invitation to share the appreciation. He crossed in the wings with his mother who, against convention, always played Heywood's main woman. There was nothing like a dame the way that Georgie Lees strutted across the stage. She looked somehow painted into her habitat: thick slashes of lime eye shadow and cheeks reddened like a harlequin. She commanded the stage, drawing every eye in a crinoline dress garnished with large green segments of velvet fruit. Georgie tried out her full repertoire of womanly moves as she stretched a washing line across the stage and hung out ten pairs of comedy underpants to dry. To the children in the audience at Heywood Civic Hall there were only comedy underpants. Widow Twankey's first gesture was a furtive glance, askance, over her gold, small-moon glasses (borrowed from her husband's extensive collection without his knowledge). It registered a mood of camp disapproval. The audience laughed and Georgie treated them to her second and final gesture: an exaggerated lift of the bosom, full of imagined maternal warmth and plenty.

The chorus of *Aladdin* filed on stage. Georgie winked at her son as Bobby (face only partly scrubbed clean of his doll-paint) took his place to dance.

Georgie took a massively exaggerated breath and launched into: 'Food, Glorious Food' out of which they segued straight into 'American Pie', continuing the consumption theme. Excess, the carnival spirit of pantomime, was observed beyond the point of appeal by Olive Platt. Olive liked to interfere with the scripts, to insert, along with the obligatory chthonic scene, a series of songs and inverted comma jokes on a *leitmotif* irrelevant to the central narrative. Olive's *Aladdin* was all about food. There was no reason for the connection buried in the plot. Olive thought simply: everyone likes food; let's talk about that. And so, for that non-reason (food for no thought), the cast was led by a double act of Preston Burns and Graham Collins as Sweetie Pie and Mushy Peas. Each successive verse of 'American Pie', and they went through all six, was sung by a new principal member of the cast. When the villain Abanazar (played with all the threat of a soggy leaf by Stanley Atkinson), when Abanazar took his verse then truly, the music died.

The dancing was like death warmed up too. The ladies' chorus doubled up as the dancers, there not being enough of them for different disciplines. The youngest was twenty-one and the oldest fifty-eight so, like a wedding speech pitched at the religious old dear most likely to take offence, the choreography was aimed at the most fragile. The dancing was so simple that anyone who saw a single show at Heywood Civic Hall could have joined in before the evening was out. As Preston described the jester who sang for the king and queen, the entire chorus walked through the Heywood dance, pioneered and taught to their mothers and fathers before them by the great choreographer, Agnes Mills. It was a four-step. Step one took the dancers a single giant stride forward, step two was a clean move to the right, step three was a second leap, backwards this time, and step four was one short move to the left. It was known as the oblong dance. Once back where you started, repeat until the music runs out or until the dame finds her next line on the sideboard, whichever is the sooner.

45

Georgie and the chorus gave way to the comedy duo. Preston had auditioned for the part of the dame's second son, Wishy Washy, and for the Genie of the Lamp. The comedy part (not taken seriously enough as usual) was offered to him as a consolation prize. Preston stumbled alone, with breathless, uninfectious enthusiasm, on to the balcony, the only function of which was to set up a gag. He slapped his hands on his thighs, clicked his fingers and cuffed the top of his own head. Preston was another mime act, but a loud one.

Down below, Graham Collins appeared and spoke to Terri Buckler, the principal girl who was acting lost on the stage. 'My, you're a pretty thing.'

'That's very mushy Peas,' said Preston, clapping his hands, stamping on the floor and opening his palms to the audience.

Graham paused for the laugh and turned *Aladdin* into a script by Pinter in the process.

He looked up at his partner in crime and said: 'Oh look kids, it's Pie in the sky.'

Outside, the wind whistled. Preston ploughed on, head against the current. His next move erased the distinction between player and audience. Preston turned his back and mimed having a piss. He then jumped around and drenched the front four rows with water from a comedy flower in his fly. The point should be that the audience adores its own abasement, that taking the piss and taking it in the face are just as much fun, the one as the other. But Preston had a way of turning solid metal into soft material. There are some people who can take unfunny words and make them funny. Preston wasn't one of those people. He could do the opposite. And then there are people who are so unfunny that their very unfunniness itself becomes funny. Preston wasn't one of those people either. He was irritating. No matter what the comic rule, Preston Burns was the exception. He was always the butt of the joke.

'Now then kids, do you like poems?' asked Mushy Peas.

The overwhelming silence might have been interpreted as an enormous no.

'I always eat peas with honey, I've done it all my life. They do taste kind of funny, but it keeps them on the knife.'

Preston Burns and Graham Collins were the only comic double act in history to feature two straight men. They were like a routine by Tommy Cannon and Syd Little, only nowhere near as good. Graham was a passable foil. It wasn't really his responsibility to be funny. But Stud, as he appeared in the programme for extra comic effect (Preston – Press – Press Stud), was spectacularly, terminally, unfunny. To the point of being annoying unfunny.

'A man goes off on a business trip, right, and he gets his mate to look after his cat. A few days later he rings up about his cat and his mate says the cat has died. The poor man's right upset and he says to his friend, "Couldn't you have broken it to me more gently? The first time I called, you could have said that the cat was on the roof. Then the next time I called, you could have said that the cat had fallen off the roof and wasn't looking too well. And then the time after that, you could have said that you didn't fancy his chances and so on." Right, are you with me children?'

Silence. Broken by the sound of small children crying.

'Anyway, when he got home this fella got himself a new cat. But then a few weeks later he went off on another trip and left the cat with the same bloke. After a few days he rang up and said, "How's the cat?" and his mate said, "Your cat's all right but your mother's on the roof."'

In their first long scene, Stud and Graham raised only a single laugh, when Mushy Peas emptied a glutinous brown chocolate mud into Sweetie Pie's yellow trousers and jammed it in until it squelched through the elasticated bottoms. Reaching for scatology in his laughless desperation, Preston plunged his fingers into the sticky custard the colour of shit. He licked them clean and pulled a tortured face. Preston found his only material in his own materials, like intellectual compost. A nervous chuckle of laughter/disgust came from the older children, frightened to betray to their parents that they had got the point.

Not a silent moment too soon, this tragi-comic act gave way to

47

Widow Twankey and the boys' chorus who moved disjointedly into position to demonstrate how Agnes Mills's oblong dance could be adapted to the tempo of the Inkspots' 'I Like Coffee, I Like Tea'. The song was supposed to anchor the setting of the show which Olive Platt had relocated from a Chinese laundry to a Heywood tea shop, Twankey being, as she superciliously pointed out, a once popular brand of Chinese tea. Also, it fitted the food theme. Well, almost. Food, drink: much the same. The boys linked arms and made themselves into a machine. They moved as one to the front of the stage and then round the sides of the oblong, tentatively, in a daring collective variation on Agnes Mills's great contribution to choreography. Each lever of the machine had its own individually oiled function without which the whole disciplined oblong would have collapsed into shoddy shapelessness. But one little blond lever was dancing and singing in a soft echo, just very slightly out of step with the rest. After the refrain of 'a cup, a cup, a cup, a cup, a cup, aaaah!', Iris on the piano stopped.

The dance proceeded with mechanical inexorability and the spotlight fell on Bobby Burns. He put his finger to his lips, thinking hard to recall what he had to say to his mummy, and then asked Widow Twankey, with a childish lithp: 'Can I have a cup of tea pleathe Widow Twankey? Put the kettle on will you?'

Iris started again but was drowned out by the laughter. The little boy had reached the audience. He had raised a laugh where Sweetie Pie had failed. He had asked for a cup of tea where Sweetie Pie had asked for a laugh. Georgie said that of course he could have a cup of tea. She folded Bobby into the fruit of her dress. He resisted, pulled away and ran into the wings. Why did they laugh at him? It was school over again. He was only asking for a cup of tea. What was so funny about that? Why did these faceless clappers in the black bully him with their nasty laughter?

Bobby locked himself in the toilet, pretended he was being sick, and refused to reappear for the curtain call. The applause rose gradually as the principals came forward, hitting the peak of the crescendo for Widow Twankey. Bobby heard the cheers from his seat, where he was sobbing at the cruelty of the audience who loved his mother but hated him.

As the men lifted tables on to the stage for the cast party, Georgie tried to coax Bobby out of the toilet. He refused to open the door and a queue was forming of men reluctant to use a urinal with Widow Twankey looking on. Georgie went to fetch Preston. He was standing in front of the tea shop scenery drinking a flat pint of lager.

'Our Bobby's still in the loo. He won't come out.'

'Let him stew in his own juice.'

'Preston, don't be disgusting. He's in the loo. I want to take him home.'

'Leave him to sulk Georgie. He likes the attention, that's all he wants. If you ignore him he'll come out eventually.'

'Press, I want to take him home. Will you go and get him out please?'

'Can't you do it if you're that worried?'

'Stanley's in there having a wee.'

Preston laughed.

'It's not funny, Press. Why don't you take it seriously? Bobby's not well. He needs to go home. Now will you go and get him or do I have to ask someone else?'

Preston put his beer down and grudgingly went to the men's toilet. He came back five minutes later, said bluntly that Bobby would not open the door, that he had not been able to break the lock and that there was not enough room to climb over the top of the wall. Preston picked up his beer where he had left off, having proved his point. He promised to keep checking on Bobby, which he did, every ten minutes throughout the party, as did Georgie. But Bobby kept up his vigil on the throne.

Georgie joined in the cast's celebrations but, despite an appearance of jollity to the contrary, she felt detached from the proceedings. She stood on a table to sing, she shared the in-jokes. But the ghost of herself in the pew in church, talking out loud, sat on her shoulder. The party went on around Georgie. Preston bored people with tales of work. Bobby came out of the toilet. His eyes were red raw from where he had been rubbing away his tears. And eventually the party had wound down, taxis had been ordered and Georgie had found herself opening the door at home for Preston (drunk) and Bobby (sullen). The wood in the door had expanded a little. It was stuck and needed a push but not the violent thrust that Georgie gave it. When the door did not give to her first attempt, Georgie made the glass panelling shake with the end of her fist.

'Bloody door. I'm sick of it. Can't you get it fixed?'

'Stop hitting it like that. You'll smash the glass.'

Georgie hit the door harder and it gave way. As she stumbled over the threshold she had an image of Preston struggling with his suitcases, going the opposite way. She stopped in the doorway and held out an arm to Bobby.

As she looked at Preston, from the left, his less flattering aspect, he seemed older than forty-eight. The vivid stripes on his temple caught the light. Preston's thick, tightly curled brown hair looked incongruous framing the Michelangelo-perfection of his round face. Preston had skin like used blotting paper: pale yellow with splodges of inky red on his cheeks, the end of his nose and the marks of his coming into the world on his temple. It was the man inside that . . . Georgie had once thought she would never marry. That had been an important consideration in her marrying Preston. Her father had recommended him. Preston was, Jack had said, a kind man. Nothing flash, nothing untoward. Jack's sketch had been precise. But traits that seemed like attributes, from a distance now looked like flaws. Preston had never soared. He had never lifted Georgie. She had no cause for complaint, no high, no low, no drama, no tragedy. Preston and Georgie had been a flat line.

And then Preston had fallen half in love with his dreadful work. His rival on the Manchester Road in Middleton had collapsed, doubling Preston's business at a stroke (Preston's joke, in poor taste). As the parlour became more and more successful, Preston had been at the service of his clients. He had been an absentee father, never less than attentive when he was there but rarely present when needed. Georgie had decided to leave home to go on tour. You only get one chance . . . It's not a rehearsal . . .

She saw Bobby up to bed and asked Preston to sit down in the living room. She suddenly felt, once again, a surge of pity for him. He had not done anything wrong and he would not understand what she was going to do.

'Press, I've got something to tell you.'

'You're not pregnant again are you?'

Preston knew that couldn't be true.

'Press, this isn't a joke. I'm going to do this show in Bolton and then I'm going to go on this tour. I should have done it years ago but I didn't and I've got a chance to go professional and I want to take it.'

'What about our Bobby? Have you thought about him?'

'I want him to come with me.'

'Don't be ridiculous Georgie. You can't take him out of school.'

There was a prolonged silence. Georgie got up from the sofa and looked out of the window at the allotments across the road. The sight of Preston's great love made her feel sorrow for him again.

'It's not doing either of us any good, Press. I have to take this chance. I'll always regret it if I don't.'

'That doesn't mean . . .'

It didn't mean anything, really. Georgie could have gone on tour and stayed married. She would come back. Probably. She would come back if she wanted to, of course. But she didn't want to. She had decided that she would, of course, come back to Heywood. To her mother. But not to the stall or the shop. And not to Preston.

Georgie guillotined any discussion until the morning. She said she would spend the night at her mother's. Preston said there was no need. He didn't feel like sleeping anyway. He would go on to the allotments. He had some gardening he could do. Leave me alone, I'll be fine. You go on your precious tour then. Preston closed the door gently behind him and Georgie watched him trail sadly across the road and disappear into the trees.

7

In the Dead of Night

The call to collect always came in the dead of night but never before one so distressing. Preston reached out an arm. He could hear 'Oh What a Beautiful Mornin'' from *Oklahoma!*. It was the ringing tone on his mobile. Preston scrambled across the room in the bed and breakfast he had booked into. This was his third night here but he still woke up wondering where he was. Where was everything? He fell over his own shoes. He picked himself up and found his watch on the rickety formica table. It was four o'clock. He found his phone on the floor, under the table. He must have been very drunk. Stanley Atkinson had come round to the hotel bar and insisted. He had a hangover brewing. He turned on the light and it hurt his eyes. Focusing with difficulty, it was his own home number Preston could see flashing. Maybe Georgie was ringing to say that he could come home.

Georgie put so much into her tone of voice. She managed to say, in uttering Preston's name, that there had been a terrible accident. Preston had a vision of Mary. He had known that Mary had been coming towards him, her rate quickening all the while. But, as he started a rambling commiseration, in the hackneyed homilies of at-least-she-had-a-good-innings, Georgie cut through his vagueness: 'Bobby.'

Georgie dropped the telephone. The receiver swung pendulum fashion and Preston's voice faded in and out, as though it were sliding through a radio frequency. Georgie composed herself enough to control the curling, snagging sidewinder wire. Preston's voice carried, dissolving in and out, of sound,

52

of meaning. Georgie ... have you been drinking ... do you want me to come round? ... are you not coping?'

'Press, he's ... he's ...'

Say the word for me, Preston, perform this husbandly intervention for me. Please Press. Be a father to the boy you always wanted, the heir to your ghastly trade.

'He's ... he's ...'

Preston got dressed and left his hotel like a fugitive.

Georgie sat at the kitchen table to wait for him to arrive. Why? Why? Why? Why? Georgie's present from the cast of *Aladdin* – a golden thimble – glistened beside her on the table. The day of the final performance. Was that a clue? It was three nights ago. He couldn't still be upset about that, could he? It was only a bit of fun. He did understand, didn't he? He wasn't *that* stupid. Was he? Thoughts shot at an astonishing velocity. The twenty minutes that Georgie sat alone in her kitchen waiting for Preston were enough to contemplate, all mushed up and yet also in precise and specific detail, the events of the three days just past. In among them was, perhaps, a reason or a clue, a route out of this dream-maze. Packing away the sweaters and blousons on her stall on Middleton market, the four o'clock bus home, as always. Taking Mary a cotton beef sandwich, for fear that she would forget to cook, and leaving it for her to throw away. The four times repeated cycle of Mary's conversation and the acrid fumes of the gas fire that had never worked properly. Mary's unreliable intentions towards the fire compounded by its loose dial: on–off, heat–cold. Back home, the door into the yard open and Bobby kicking a ball as hard as he could against next door's fence, threatening the window pane in the door but never hitting it. The little rapscallion. The little varmint. Those were Preston's words: the thought of her husband at work, as ever, surrounded by misery guts. A flash into the future, into what Preston would now have to do, quickly expelled. A fleeting sensation of loving Preston and the briefest intimation of comfort. Reading the appointment card that Dr Knox had sent for Mary to attend the memory assessment clinic. Knox's ornate handwriting and the insight that, in the middle stages, the patient begins to lose awareness of the condition, the porridge in the head as Preston described it. Character begins to ebb towards caricature. Starts to flatten, was the phrase the doctor had used, like a portrait in embroidery. Patients become their essence: what they most evidently are, only more so. Like one of the funny ones in Dickens, Knox had said. Only not so funny. Sausages, chips and beans for tea. Or peas. Bobby's choice, so she did both. Why couldn't he make up his mind? Because he was like his dad, was Bobby: indecisive. The television talking to no one, cartoons of cats squashing mice who spring back to life again. Snapped off. Bobby attracted back in by the noise of the vacuum cleaner, running in front with his hands over his ears, shouting, trying to drown it out. Enough to waken the dead, he said, a phrase he had been given by grandma. Mary taught him Lancashire dialect swear-words too. She thought Georgie didn't understand them but the words were too good, too onomatopoeic. A great big chewing gum bubble, blown up and popping all over his face. Telling Bobby off, the momentary panic attack of not being in control, of knowing that telling him off wasn't working and that he was slipping away, sitting down to darn a jumper, nervous about the performance. Still shy, still unsure, after so many times. Final polishing of the script. Stage make-up, an erasing of the face, all the features blown up. Mary confused in the dressing room, saying odd things, checking Bobby was ready with his twin roles. Olive Platt frantic, counting out options on her fingers, Stanley Atkinson following her around cracking rude jokes about bodily waste. Graham Collins and Preston acting funny. Not being funny, just acting. Struggling into the dress, fruit falling off. Searching for Sellotape. Going out and killing them. Bobby and Mary, the dummy and the ventriloquist, still flogging the horse. Corpsing when Preston dropped the jelly and slipped in it, dear Stud inadvertently funny, off the script and by accident. Can I have a cup of tea pleathe? The laurels at the end, the life-giving moment . . .

And then after the show, what happened? Preston rattling the door of the gents' until Bobby gave in. A tantrum at the party, the sulky thing. Mary wanting to take Bobby home, will he be all right on his own for a while, of course he will, stop fussing Georgie, I'll tuck him up in bed and see he's fine for a cup of hot chocolate. His mood, sullen and deflated, annoyed at his grandma, not understanding his role in a moment of expurgation. Not humiliation, don't be silly. Or, rather, do. *Be* silly. Mary trying to explain that laughter meant love, Bobby insisting that it didn't. Tales of school, where laughter and love knew nothing of one another. Why didn't she read more into that mood? Could she have done? Could she have read more? No, don't be silly Georgie, it was only a bit of fun. And then Bobby fell out of the tale for a little while. Georgie had forgotten about him. Culpable, surely? How could she forget? How could she have simply gone back to the party, with Bobby contesting such a point? Why did it not matter to her as it had to him? Why had she not seen it coming? Because it was unforeseeable. But why hadn't she seen it? The party on stage, resisting Graham Collins's inept flirting, Preston's anger at Graham. Their argument funnier than the script. Preston's melancholy recognition that something was seriously awry, his pleading that it would all be fine (what a lifetime away that now seemed), the chatter about who is sleeping with whom (their spouses apart). Laughter (our old friend again) at Georgie's wit. What had she said that was so funny? Cannot be re-created. You had to be there. Georgie the life and soul, as always. Standing on a low table for 'I'm Going to Wash That Man Right Out of My Hair'. How sickly appropriate ... Unintended, not even considered at the time, how unfeeling that looked now. Was she that wrapped up in herself? How others might see you. How wrong, how hopeless that judgement can be. The sheer joy of singing and dancing, the pleasure of parading a talent. The thought of singing professionally, once seriously envisaged and then buried in the basement under a pile of good amateur notices. Preston forcing a discussion, it's a party for God's sake, about Mary and when it would be time for professional care. And then home, Preston not wanting to come, the relief of avoiding a repetitive discussion of what was the matter and the spark can come back and, in the end, to get him to let her go, giving way

55

and kissing and feeling something deep for Preston, something like pity.

And at some point amid all this the conviction that she needed to act. To act now. Was it the song? Was it the performance? Was it that powerful? That it could affect our individual action like this. Why not? As good a candidate to move us as the planets, the moon, the stars. We are all propelled along by the mysterious movements of show tunes. Arriving home, punching the door open, a vision of Preston carrying suitcases. Deciding (again) to go. Life's not a rehearsal ... Telling Preston the leave-home truth. Had Bobby heard this? He used to sit on the stairs. He used to sit on the stairs and we never knew. He must have heard everything. We thought we were grown-ups but he probably knew it all. It's just a dream, that's all. Poor Press in the shed again; he lived in there really.

Three days of fog. Omens and decisions. The same decision, to go, to go on tour. Press moving out. Not able to cope any more, he said. Bobby crying. Don't go away Daddy. Don't go away. It's just for a little while until things calm down. Press going into a little hotel, just up the road. But so far. To be not in the shed. How far away is that? Archie Gregson calling, do you know what I'm saying? Not liking him on the phone, somehow smelling a rat. A rat called Archie. Three days of rowing. The image of Bobby on the stairs. Sorry, we should have stopped but, oh Preston, those dead folk, please God why didn't you let them lie? Please God, why? Please God. God only knows.

Arriving home from the stall late. Preston still thinking he could buy the shop in the parade. Getting Bobby's tea again. What did he have this time? Sausages and chips, no that was the day of the show. Why so much stress on the day of the show? Was it more important? Don't know, don't know. God only knows. Bobby home, latch-key children they used to call them but he had his grandma to look after him but he thought she was a bit mental and she was too. Leaving him on his own after tea. Why? Meeting Archie Gregson. A wine bar. Far too posh. What did he want? A rat. A smell. Wanting to go home. The odd sensation, in the wine bar, of thinking something was wrong. Premonition? She didn't believe in that sort of thing. That was Preston's sort of thing. Sometimes, anyway, you never did know with Press. But maybe God gives a warning, maybe that's His way of giving a signal. But if He knows it's happening why does He let it? Why? God only knows. Leaving too late. A strange sense: missing Press. He should be at home. Bobby is there by himself. Why did she not ask Mary to look after Bobby? Why? Because she had said he didn't want grandma to look after him. A tantrum, again. Because she had been in a hurry to get out. Life's not a rehearsal . . .

Arriving home late, too late, gone eleven o'clock or something, the thought that Bobby was a big boy now, did nine-year-old really count as a big boy, he kept saying so but they grow up too quick now, fumbling for the light in the kitchen. First conspicuous object: a folded piece of paper on top of the fridge. On the outside, in Bobby's shaky jagged handwriting, a single word: *Mum*. Opening the folded note carefully and reading the near-illegible message, with upper and lower cases sprinkled at uneducated whim: *dear Mum I'm very Sorry. Every one Laughs at me and I hate it and granmar tells me Off. I miss You from Bobby xxxx*. Running away, Bobby Dazzler is on the run, as he always threatened. But where? To grandma, six doors down? Nowhere else to go. Maybe to his Uncle Terry, Preston's brother, on the other side of Bolton. Might as well be the other side of the moon. How many sides does Bolton have Bobby? Don't know; not the brightest boy. Probably an unfair question though. The thought of calling the police, to intercept a star of stage on the streets, looking for his father's brother. Second object in sight: Bobby's orange school-bag on the floor under the table. And the sudden surge of alarm and the image of something seen and unnoticed – the curtains in the bedroom closed. Why closed if Bobby had run to his uncle? They had been open. Georgie never closed the curtains. The nightly ritual, the tantrum if ever Georgie usurped Bobby in closing the curtains, a nightly exhibition of independence. Maybe she was wrong. Going outside and seeing . . . no, not wrong. Why closed? The abandoned bag, the closed curtains. But no shuffling on the ceiling, no activity.

Maybe he was asleep, false alarm. But where did the alarm come from? From the note. Odd and alarming, that there should *be* a note. Unfolding the scruffy lined paper, feeling the perforated circles at the top where it had been ripped off the iron curls. Reading the words again, out loud. *Every one Laughs at me*. Pause. It was true. They did. And not just charitably, it had to be said. *And I hate it. And I hate it. And I hate it.* The echo of her own voice in an empty room. Urgent and frightened, running up the stairs. Tripping over the final steps, chanting his name. Third salient object: the cheap calligraphic engraving 'Bobby's room' standing out clearly against the cream door. Attacking the paint-splattered silver handle and smashing the door open at full pace.

Time broken by the spectacle in the bedroom. A moment which comes to locate all subsequent events. Georgie Lees had screamed with a piercing intensity that would echo in that little room for evermore, until the house was demolished because nobody was prepared to live in it again.

Finally: Bobby's legs rocking very gently to and fro as he hung by the neck from his wardrobe, suspended by his mother's best silk scarf which he had wrapped around a coat hanger. The iron curl wrapped around the top of the wardrobe door. A scratch on his cheek running out from the base of the nose as though he had drawn a red line with the point of a blunt compass. Gagging for breath, diving towards Bobby to wrest him down but the hue of his neck and the coldness of his skin . . . Too late home . . . I won't be late home love. Too late . . .

Bobby Burns, Georgie Lees's, Preston Burns's only son, swinging there inert, hung to death on a coat hanger before her very eyes. She left him there. Georgie took the telephone off the hook, sealed the doors and closed all the windows, made herself a cup of tea and sat at the kitchen table in silence. The long hand of the clock slid over three numbers. It was a break in time. As suddenly as she had sat down Georgie thought she must ring Preston. It was pitch black outside but she had no idea what time it was.

8

A Kind of Murder

Preston retched at the sight in the bedroom. In the course of his work Preston had presided over some grotesque corpses, usually the upshot of road accidents. He had officiated at a handful of suicides, not a common cause of death on Preston's watch. Every one, he had noted, with scholarly detachment, had been taken by an overdose. Preston had compiled a scrapbooked anatomy of newspaper rippings about strange ways to die: poisoned by a meal of huntsman's breeches in milk, strangled by a man who was asleep, bludgeoned with a plaster statuette of W.C Fields, asphyxiated by a penis in the windpipe, an unfaithful husband accidentally crushed to death by a suicidal wife jumping out of a window (she survived, the bastard even dying to foil her), locked into an old oak chest and lost, eaten by rats when left home alone, electrified by six hundred volts shooting up a line of urine, crushed in the belfry by a giant church bell, suffocated in a pit of manure, dropped down dead after shaking hands with the Queen Mother, choked to death during a ping-pong ball blowing contest, pulled apart in a tug-of-war, turned on by a nasty cow (no, an attack not sexual attraction) (Preston liked to kill his lines with an explanation in parenthesis – even his brackets came in brackets), bloated in a snail-eating exhibition after three minutes and seventy two snails (both velocity and volume beating all-comers), a religious man who tripped over his own beard and fell down the stairs, auto-poisoned by methane, killed by a malfunctioning machine for taking the wrinkles out of prunes (surrounded by broken steel cylinders and half a pound of wrinkled prunes), choked on your girlfriend's edible knickers, killed in vaudeville by a poor knife thrower, brains beaten out by an assailant's (or, worse, your own) wooden leg, a driver smashed into a lamp-post looking like a car on a stick, feet coated with salt and tickled to death by the hungry lick of a goat's tongue, frozen to death in a lorry-load of broccoli, stuck down a well trying to rescue a chicken, spontaneous combustion from the inside out, smeared in honey, hung in a basket and stung to death by voracious wasps, stabbed to death with a wedge of parmesan cheese, sealed inside a barrel and rolled down a hill. For the final tale of his regular act in the Pack Horse after rehearsals, the one that killed him, Preston reserved his all-time favourite: the man who died laughing while watching a monkey trying to pull on a pair of boots. No, nobody alive knew more about death than Preston Burns. Though not formally further educated he had majored at the university of death. Yet nothing in the mortuary trade could prepare Preston to witness the body of his own nine-year-old son.

No method of death drips out so much personal guilt, so much self-apportioned blame, as planned death. Georgie screamed out blame: what had she done wrong, why had she let him play the dummy? Preston insisted Georgie stay out of sight while he attended to the first and most difficult part of his work: the removal of the body from its place of rest into the disposal casket. This was the first moment, in his long experience as an undertaker, that the bereaved could not cope. He found himself asking the questions that he had heard so many times, the stupid questions which had simple and obvious answers.

'What happened?'

Georgie breathed audibly, throwing her shoulders into the effort. The short bursts of air she took in sounded as if she were trying to cool hot liquid. Preston repeated the question but Georgie was a blank sheet, featureless and unbroken pale. Her face seemed to flatten and stretch as she began to hear her own internal technology – heartbeat, breath. The turn-up on Georgie's nose straightened out, sharp white irises and green pupils became slated with grey, the rosy speckles of her cheeks puffed and rounded out into an insipid and hollow yellow.

'Press . . .'

Georgie swallowed and choked and shook her head. She tried a silent prayer but could not complete it. She shook her head again, more violently this time, but at what? In answer to an implied question: heaven and earth, what can help me now? She thought of Mary, her mother, alone and unwell in the family home. She winced as she expelled the thought that this was her fault, if only she, Georgie, had stayed at home, if only she hadn't gone off chasing some illusion, in a wine bar with a horrible licentious dwarf. If only she had insisted her mother had come round, if only she had got a babysitter. If only, if only. Heaven's above. Hell's bells. The same questions circled round again and parked on her brain.

Preston stood still by her, tentative and frosty until he was cajoled by his wife into holding her. He turned aside to her left so that she would not look at his birth mark. Wordless still, Georgie floated, as if above the floor, into the bathroom where the taps came on and flooded hot water on to the dirty, chipped enamel of her bath. Georgie's clothes levitated, paused at the extent of her arm and fell into a heap on the bathroom floor. Preston watched in silence, ready to hand in case Georgie needed him. In turn, a lime roll-neck jumper and a shirt in blue and white marine stripes leapt and dropped. Preston and Georgie stared at each other as she bared herself. She pressed the trampoline of her stomach and felt a childish pleasure in the bounce. She unhooked her bra and her heavy, unscaffolded breasts drooped. Preston recalled the full bosom that had first stirred him when he had seen Georgie Lees dancing in the chorus line in the Heywood Amateur Operatic and Dramatic Society's production of *Cinderella*. Life and soul, it had been said of her even then. He saw again Georgie's features at the age of sixteen, etched into a blank face. Georgie with the dancing eyes. Her father had christened her that because of the egg-shaped craters dug into her 'heavy bones' (again, Jack's coinage). Georgie had a mobile face. It changed shape when she grinned. It was an unreliable face – colder than its owner, a radiator that remained cold to the touch but mysteriously heated the room. It meant that people took longer to warm to Georgie than they might have done. Unblinking and frozen, Georgie unbuttoned her tartan pleated skirt. It sat on her ankles, stiff and firm, upright from the bottom of her kneecaps. A curl of flesh was pushed up over the top of her pale knickers and, in this ungainly position, Georgie Lees stopped. Preston had to come forward the five paces that separated them to persuade her to remove the last of her clothes. Georgie eerily said nothing and Preston was forced to pull the knicker elastic himself. His grip slipped and the elastic snapped against the exposed flesh. Preston removed the last of her clothes. He slipped his arms around the statue and put his lips to hers.

'You're still . . . you know, I still . . . like a fine wine. I think that's the expression.'

Georgie pursed her lips as Preston's hands moved across her naked body. He started and aborted three sentences. Georgie resisted through stark naked inertia. Preston desisted at once and signed off with a gentle kiss to the cold perspiration on Georgie's forehead. He tested the temperature of the water, helped her into the bath and went into the bedroom. He had the thought, which he at once expelled as inexplicably selfish, that this might bring them together. The triviality of the intimation was apparent when Preston went to work.

He made a mark of allotment dirt on the white sheet as he stood on Bobby's bed so that he could take the dead weight of Bobby's body and lift the strain from his neck. Such a tiny movement, so definitively late. Preston stopped, unable to look, then breathed hard and did what he had to. Somebody had to do this. It was a terrible, utterly terrible job, a job like no other. But it had to be done and Preston prided himself that it was his undertaking, his pledge and his promise that the job be done clearly, efficiently and without histrionics. All the fuss was inadequate. Preston had seen the best efforts of the most hysterical and it had never made any difference. This job was about to prove the rule.

Preston lifted Bobby down from the wardrobe, removed the dreadful accoutrements – the silk scarf, the iron curl of the coat hanger – and put the body away. Preston lifted the casket and carried it downstairs to the hearse. As he was struggling down the stairs Georgie came out of the bathroom, still dripping, naked, her full body on display. Preston shouted at her to get back inside. Preston had often been attacked by relatives catching him about his work. The act of taking away the body seemed to them like a theft, or worse, like a kind of murder. But can you thieve what is yours? Bobby was still his. Preston had a momentary inkling of the awful dual role he was engaged in: personal and professional run right together. He put his head down and concentrated on the job. It can't be happening . . .

In tranquillity, Preston made it to the hearse. Years before, he had prepared his own mother, as he had always expected to do. This had once been standard practice until we began to contract visceral experience, to control it to a low profile. Care has become anonymized, the exact reverse of a former tradition. Now we give over the privilege to a parlour, extension of the beauty business. And he had thought many times that one day he would meet Bobby in a professional capacity. But it would be Preston insensate on the slab, attended to by his son who had, on that day, turned Preston Burns into Bobby Burns Undertakers. Now, what sense was there to the idea of them in fact meeting? Would there be a Preston to witness the transition? That was the question. In a sense, he hoped not. A post-mortem could hurt if you were still living. Preston was vague on this. He never was less than certain, though, that it would be him at rest and that it would be Bobby at work. He opened the saloon door of the hearse, gripped the top of the casket as if he were smothering his son's face and, catching his breath, in a choke, embraced the sheer terror of life after death. Suddenly Preston understood the link between death and hysteria that he had witnessed so many times. Georgie followed outside, still unclothed. Preston folded her into a hug.

'Where's the little Bobby dazzler?'

Preston was suddenly clear on this. This was when vagueness ended, at the moment that, for the rest of the world, true eternal vagueness only began. He rose to clarity, for Georgie's sake.

'It's not Bobby. Bobby's gone.'

Preston had a rule that he did not refer to the body by name. This lesson had been left him by his mentor, Jack Lees. Preston had even been there at Jack's end and had, of course, performed that final service for him. So Preston still observed Jack's law: it was Bobby's body but the body was not Bobby. Preston did not believe that his bodies lived on. He believed that his work took place after the fact. The spirit flew, from the body. Preston believed in a number of different spirits, ripped, like his funny stories, from various traditions. Preston was always a sympathetic voice for his clients, because he liked to tell them what they wanted to hear. Preston believed in everything. His latest incarnation was a cover version of the Hindu cycle of life. Preston borrowed liberally and unseriously from established traditions. But he was clear enough on the nature of the body. The body was his business and the body was different.

Terrible things could happen to the body that needed to be separated from the person. Sliced, pickled, waxed, rouged, trimmed, everything short of revived. A body could be chewed up and sold as sausages, boiled down to best dripping or cut up to make tobacco pouches and wallets. Bobby, the boy Bobby, was deprived of spots, stubble, pubic hair, a bass voice, halitosis, the realization that people younger than him were playing for England, significant birthdays, first fulfilled regrets, the shock that his parents were weak and scared just as he was and the verdict on whether he was climbing out of or sinking into his background. But, as for Bobby's body? That could be deprived of nothing now, nothing but his father's care. Preston urged Georgie to dress and to come with him. She murmured that she would be all right on her own. She did not want to go to the funeral parlour with Preston and she couldn't face waking her mother at dawn to tell her the tale. The cast of people to tell appeared in a line before her eyes: Olive Platt, Graham Collins, Stanley Atkinson, Colin Smethurst, Iris the pianist, the ladies of the chorus, the men opposite them. She thought of the people at church. All of them friends, some closer than others, but none of them would soften this. Georgie marvelled at the task of finding the words to tell them all.

Preston left Georgie in the living room hanging on grimly to another cup of tea. As Preston closed the door behind him, Georgie was staring at the picture of their son that hung over the fireplace. As soon as Preston had closed the door behind him she felt deeply alone. In a terror too profound for solitude, Georgie rapped on the window. When Preston did not notice her she bolted out of her front door and begged him not to leave her there on her own.

Preston wasn't ready yet to cope with the autopsy he was charged with performing. He left his boy in the back of the hearse and went, first, to find a sanctuary on the allotment. As Georgie and he shivered on the park bench that Preston had placed in his plot under the azaleas, he demanded that Georgie take pleasure in the plants. He kept up a babbling chatter, explaining where he was in the round of the seasons. Every autumn Preston struggled in a vain battle with natural processes, green fingers against black fingers in a two-step of growth and death, thirst and refreshment. Preston loved gardening in the dark. He couldn't be seen then. The red marks on his temple were invisible and he was reduced to a common shape. He had a theory that the soil was more responsive at night and the stiff, unbending flowers that were his favourites stood to attention in the still air, in their hard, regimental lines. Preston liked to stay in the garden overnight until dawn said good morning and birdsong broke. He brought a torch from the shed and encouraged Georgie to walk through the plants. Straining to see in the dark, she caught herself on an old tree stump which Preston had disguised by training wichuraiana, rambler roses, to coil around its crooked timber. She tried to pick her way through the colour-drained flower beds in the dark. As she went, she crushed yellow and orange tagetes under foot and kicked a clump of soil on to a bed of petunias. As her eyes became more accustomed to the dark, Georgie felt the pure white outline of a deep rose, the Lavatera Loveliness. Preston now came up very close. If the morning had ascended upon the pair of them they would have looked like lovers.

'Georgie love, can I ask you something?'

'What?'

'Will you answer?'

'Press love, how do I know if I'll answer before I know what the question is?'

Preston left a long gap. He returned to the shed, brought out a universal hoe and began to redistribute the soil.

'Have you seen the blade on this one Georgie? You can use it for pushing and pulling.'

Preston went back into the shed to swap tools as if he were demonstrating them before sale. He came out with a sharp-tined fork with which he started to prick the surface of the lawn.

'Some people say you shouldn't do this till autumn but I think the earlier the better. It's like putting little holes in a jacket potato.'

Georgie began to shiver. 'Press, why are you telling me this? I'm not interested in gardening.'

'You like flowers don't you?'

'I like flowers but not gardening.'

'You can't have one without the other.'

'Course you can you daft beggar. What about wild flowers? Anyway, why are you going on about the garden?'

'I don't know . . . it's all I can think of to say.'

Even in the torch light, Georgie could see that Preston was struggling to contain himself. There was a deep silence in the dark.

'He was bullied you know. I should have . . . It never would have happened if . . .'

'Don't Press. There's no point.'

Preston went back to the soil. He began to dig a hole and when the dirt behind him began to block the door into his shed, it became evident that he was digging a grave. Preston lamented (sometimes) the current preference for cremation over burial, even though coffin burial polluted his soil through the breakdown of the solvents, the glue and the finishes and the leaking embalming fluid. Burning only emits dioxins, hydrochloric and hydrofluoric acids, sulphur dioxide and carbon dioxide. That sounded worse than cremation but Preston insisted that it wasn't. Georgie interrupted his increasingly feverish exertions by throwing her arms around his neck and clinging on for dear life. She did not cry – only Preston was capable of crying, but the immobile terror on her face stirred the kindness which was all that Preston brought to his wife.

'Come and look at this love. Come on, come and look.'

Preston sat back on the bench and, carefully planting his arm around Georgie's neck, resumed his description of the seasonal turn, turn, turn of his allotment. Transfixed by his side, Georgie gave in to the monotonous hypnotism of Preston's voice and drifted out of this undeserved day. Preston wrapped Georgie against the breeze, whispered that he would always love her and pointed the way back to the hearse. Bobby Burns would wait no longer.

Preston drove through the empty streets to his premises in Middleton. He heaved the casket in through the narrow door, refusing Georgie's offer of help and left it, rather insultingly it seemed to her, in the ante-room. Preston joked unsmilingly that he always kept the dead waiting. Georgie thought this remark was inappropriate. Preston looked at her blankly and they both had the same thought: so what words would be appropriate? What *is* the correct thing to say in the circumstances? He made a cup of tea and began to witter on, anxious not to allow Georgie a moment to reflect. He wondered how many others, across the globe, shared this departing moment. There are books which list the famous people who share our birthdays. It is probably, he speculated, because we turn away from the fact that there are not equivalent books for us to entertain ourselves over those with whom we are fated to share a date with death. Also, at the time of reading we don't know our own day. And that takes away all the fun.

'Press, what happens? Where does he go, our Bobby? I mean,

67

where do they go when you've done what you do? I've never thought about your work before. Not properly.'

Preston had nothing to say in response to this question. Preston sneezed and complained to himself that the cold night had advanced his illness. The hypochondriac is always right in the end: every pimple is a portent of the inevitable. Georgie told him to shut up. She had heard this routine before. For want of anything else to do, Preston began the reflex of planning the funeral. In the circumstances, it was probably the right thing to say. Without reason, he talked out loud at Georgie, who sat staring at him, entirely bemused and in a different world. His boy would receive, of course, the full attentive service, the one he called the Traditional Funeral. It included the works: taking instructions and making all necessary arrangements, obtaining and preparing statutory documents, liaison with the cemetery or crematorium authorities, the hospitals, the doctors, the coroners, the clergy, all the attendant grave-diggers of the sub-plot. Transportation locally from the place of death was thrown in (service already performed), so too use of the office and mortuary, the full attention of a registered Funeral Director and Operative (his assistant, Liam, no not Liam, Lucy) on the mournful day. Preston's advertising brochure announced that he was available in the week preceding for advice, assistance, support, associated services and correspondence. That one always got him – why had he put correspondence? What was this, an exchange of letters for publication? Dear Mr Burns, with regard to your latest epistle. You may well consider my preference for burial over cremation to be rather old-fashioned and, whilst I appreciate that space is at a premium in the Milnrow area, what with that new superstore and everything, could I none the less request . . . Well, they could write if they wanted to. In addition, Bobby's body would be embalmed and cared for in suitable conditions (whatever he meant by that), laid in the Chapel of Rest and provided with a gown. Then, when he was ready to go, he (no, it – remember the rule, it was Bobby's body but not Bobby. It's not to change just because it's Bobby in there – well his body anyway, you know what I mean, oh be quiet

Preston). Anyway, where was he? It (yes, it) would be given the polished hearse and there would be a six-seater limousine for the mourners. Which seat in the car would Preston sit in this time? This whole package usually retailed at £999 plus coffin and urn. Veneered coffins added a grand, solid wood £500 more and urns came in anywhere between £25 and £100. There were other bells and whistles: a horse-drawn hearse for £800 or the same for a floral hearse (Preston's speciality – he picked the flowers himself, mostly white lilies). The prices don't matter this time, said Georgie flatly.

Preston completed his monologue as abruptly as he had begun it. He showed Georgie into the staff room so that he could start his work. He opened the casket and began the futile process of arresting the flesh's decay. This much was for appearance's sake, because although the corpse remains indifferent to the show (its motto: whatever), the faces of the dead still matter to the living. The features need to be set in that calm smile of anti-movement that no living person can ever wear. The dead wear a less reliable smile than Georgie Lees. It is as if they are allowed one final strut to imitate the living and their effort resembles life. The naturalism always fails, of course. Left to themselves the dead would slump down but people employed Preston Burns because they wouldn't have their dead being seen dead like that. That was why he always took great pains to scrub under the fingernails. He didn't comprehend why but people wanted their loved ones to be clean for cremation. Whatever: it was Preston's motto too. Inside and behind the ears and underneath the nails; the women always checked. They usually wanted to dress the body too. Preston had fitted a body out in a red cap at a rakish angle, a full three-piece chalk stripe with polkadot cravat, Hallowe'en spirits, a Rochdale United kit, full Elvis drag, Princess Di dresses and so on, all the way into indignity. Many societies, he thought, like to cram their caskets full of prodigal goods. He wondered what he would give Bobby to take with him: his football kit, a ball, his trainers. Not much really. And his bike. To go on a journey. And a gun, to shoot the devil.

After half an hour of tendering, Preston took a break. He

69

had a shiver which was beginning to frighten him. The job was not too hard, he thought. Once he got into it, he found it strangely easy to concentrate. It was an it, not a him, after all, still less a Bobby. He went to check on Georgie. She was sitting in the ante-room, waiting. Not knowing what else to say, Preston couldn't stop talking shop, about the unlikelihood of all this, how few child deaths there were these days compared with a century ago and how few of them take their own lives.

Georgie murmured, Why, Preston? Why are you telling me this? Why am I sitting here? Why me, why this, why?

He went back to talking about the prices. He had forgotten to mention the super-charged funeral, with even greater attention, better cars (hired on demand) and *cordon bleu* at the wake. It all had to be paid for, he said. Except if . . . at the bottom of the page of his brochure there was another lonely sentence: babies and children up to sixteen years of age can have simple funerals free of charge. It wasn't such a generous offer. Time was when Preston's predecessors, the directors of the Middleton Funeral Parlour, buried tiny caskets once a week. One in every fifty of babies for Elizabethan Prestons died before the end of their first day, one in twenty before a week was out and one in seven within a year. By the time they had attained Bobby's age more than a quarter had gone. Out of every ten babies at the turn of the nineteenth century, one and a half went in infancy. Preston loved that half. But it hadn't been like that for him. The communicable diseases had been tamed, not to mention those with death in their names. Now one hundred and seventy-two and a half live babies were needed for a single one. A death at Bobby's age was a one-in-ten-thousand shot. Suicide at that age took the odds off the scale. It just didn't happen any more.

Oh thanks Press, that's just what I wanted to hear. Why is it so, that's what I need to know? Why? What do you say to that then? What's your answer to that?

Preston went back into the operations room. By now the young corpse on the slab, the it in front of him, had already acquired a blue tint around the ears and very early rigor in the eyelids, jaw, neck and shoulders. Bobby's body was dying bit by bit – a process Preston had observed more times than he could recall. The blood begins to settle now that it is not being oxygenated and the skin takes on a reddish purple colour: hypostasis or post-mortem lividity. Preston had eight hours or so until this condition reached its height. He lifted Bobby from the slab and saw the grey patches where the blood had been squeezed away. Meanwhile, the bacteria were gathering in the gut, preparing to eat through the lining of the digestive system. But on the surface, all was still. Preston had not known what stillness was until he saw his first corpse. Once, as a boy, his mother had taken him to a Remembrance Day service in Rochdale. The unworldly quality of the silence had left its impression on a young Preston. He had never heard the hum subtracted from the din before. He felt like that now about bodies. They had a calm he saw nowhere else, as if all the unnoticed noise had finally been quietened. At peace, like people said. Preston thought people said a lot of rubbish to make themselves feel better when someone had died but that one was true. Preston was also struck, as he was every time he performed this operation, by the whiteness of death. Though death was always subsequently draped and memorialized in black, on the slab, under the sheet, the body's pallor was written in white. Like all bodies, Bobby's had achieved stillness. It was the body's only accomplishment and Preston found it to be universal. They were all bags of bones by the end, no matter the stratum, the caste, the class of origin. The dead came in a single rank.

Preston looked at Bobby's body intently and realized that he had got it wrong. *It* was wrong. It wasn't *it*. The separation, of body and Bobby, was wrong. Now that he was the bereaved as well as the officiator, he saw that the body and Bobby, if indisputably not the same thing, could, for all that, not be separated. Preston wanted something that respect could be paid *to*. There was no doubt about this one thing: the body was indubitably *there*. The same could not be said of Bobby although Bobby bore some obvious relationship – a family resemblance – to his lifeless body. What is this relationship? Preston's experience counted for nothing now. He had no idea. Wasn't this the question that Georgie was screaming out repetitively in reception?

Preston completed his preliminary duty. He had done his job. It was held by the Egyptians, ancient Greeks and Romans and Orthodox Jews today that an improper handling of the remains could prevent the dead from making it to the other side. Preston didn't believe in the other side but he believed in making preparations for the journey. He turned out the lights and drove Georgie home as the rest of Heywood was coming in to work. His staff, Gundappa, who had added to the parlour expertise in Hindu and Muslim rites (Gundappa was an atheist but he could play both parts) and Lucy, just sex-changed from Liam, would find the body when they arrived at eight-thirty, as many mornings they did. But of course it wasn't usually a youngster and it wasn't usually . . . Preston trailed off and took Georgie back home. She sat on the sofa and sought for depth in philosophical questions that we lock away, to flash up at times of danger.

9

The Facts of Life

Bobby Burns was fast-tracked by his father through an inquest (the verdict, suicide, was not heard by either parent nor, indeed, by anyone else) to a burial three empty days later. Preston arranged for the funeral service to take place at St Stephen's church, Heywood, and invitations, at Georgie's request but to his chagrin, were not issued. Georgie gave the first signal of sinking; her withering denunciation of the therapeutic value of the funeral shocked Preston and Mary. Georgie claimed not to want a funeral. She could not make any sense of her feelings but she had a sensation that she did not want to do anything to help Bobby on his way to his destination. More than that, she didn't feel she deserved a funeral. Preston pointed out the obvious: that it didn't matter what she deserved (not that she didn't of course). What did Bobby deserve? That was the point. And, furthermore, he thought, it might be what you need, whether you know it or not. Georgie did not want a funeral retinue or anyone looking at her, thinking it was her fault. She only went along with the funeral arrangements at all because Preston took over and because she was forced to concede that there is nothing else.

On the way there in Preston's hearse, Georgie fiddled with a loose tooth she had been ignoring through months of gradual decay. She plucked at it, trying to pull it out and only making it hurt. When they arrived, it was clear that Georgie's wish for an unnoticed funeral, for an ignorable silence, had not been granted. The foyer of St Stephen's church teemed with respectful friends.

'Preston, I told you not to tell anyone. I didn't want anyone there. I don't want all of these people here. Looking at us, wondering . . .'

'You can't keep secrets like that. I had to tell someone. It was in the *Observer* anyway, in the obituaries.'

Preston had written a short notice for the local newspaper. He had lately added this scripting function to his professional offering. People liked being in the paper, though most of them managed it only by being born, by having a birthday and then by dying. The notices of the local paper were like a pithy philosophy: you're born, you have birthdays and then you die. Preston's obituary for Bobby was very short, like an epitaph on a gravestone: 'Dear Bobby Burns, 1987–1996. He lived not long enough.' Georgie had seen it. She had cut it out and put it away in a drawer. She hadn't yet managed to read it. The hearse pulled up outside the church.

Preston turned to his ex-wife and pleaded with her, with heavy stress on his third word: 'Georgie, I *had* to tell someone. Don't be upset with me. This is hard enough . . .'

Hand in hand, they walked through the crowd. Preston stopped as they crossed the threshold. Though he was much less well known here than Georgie, it was Preston who greeted Mr Brace, the massively fat vicar whose robes were always splattered with the remnants of his last meal. Georgie was accustomed to enjoying church. It was a place where nice things happened to her. A place she could breathe in, where things always got better.

The service began with the great words from John xi. 25, 26: I am the resurrection and the life saith the Lord: he that believeth in me, though he were dead, yet shall he live: and whosoever liveth and believeth in me shall never die. Georgie perked up. She began to listen to the words. Not to hear them, as she allowed the words usually to wash over her, but really to listen. To listen, to think and to analyse. To examine: he that believeth in me, though he were dead, yet shall he live: and whosoever liveth and believeth in me shall never die. This, thought Georgie, was the whole point. The biggest and most contentious claim of all, right at the very beginning. This was the practical contribution that belief was meant to supply. Immortality of a kind was pledged even when the fact – the fact of death as opposed to the facts of life – was there in the church along with you. The Lord gave and the Lord hath taken away. Forty years of Sunday schools and Eucharists had drenched Georgie in a way of thinking. Now, for the first time, she asked for something back. She looked at her mother, who was calling up a down-payment on her own faith. Mary had forgotten saying (as she had the day before) that the order of the burial ought to be denied to those who had laid violent hands on themselves. It said so in the book. The priest read from I Corinthians xv. 20. The sequence about the resurrection of the dead sounded insultingly more than hollow: it is sown in corruption; it is raised in incorruption; it is sown in dishonour; it is raised in glory; it is sown in weakness; it is raised in power. Georgie thought about the death of her father. After the passage of a decade it still came on her suddenly, Jack's long prelude in illness with a sudden death, expected and yet surprising. She put her hands together in supplicating prayer.

She asked and found nothing there. The implication had been clear. There had been a definite promise: this will help, when the time comes. Georgie had accepted the terms in good faith. Georgie looked at the rafters, looked at the stained glass, looked at the floor. She did not find her answer there.

Georgie looked across the other way at Preston. Poor all-over-the-place Preston, curly Press Stud, little Stud who never quite knew the time of day. He had been someone worth holding on to these past three days. Preston had taken Georgie through the embalming process, in excruciating detail. He said that he had wanted to make her cry. On the first day of the rest of her life he had compelled her to choose the clothes that Bobby was to be buried in. Preston had insisted that Bobby should be smart. When Georgie objected that Bobby wouldn't care, Preston snapped back that his father certainly would. On the second day, Preston made Georgie look at the body. Three details penetrated her numbed consciousness. Preston had managed to get the dirt out from underneath Bobby's fingernails. She hadn't seen him with clean fingernails since he had been a baby. Since then, the little monkey had never stayed still long enough to allow his hands to be scrubbed. His ears, inside and back, were raw clean, no longer fertile for potatoes. And she noted again that red line, fading quickly, from the blunt scratch of a compass point. Preston had either not tried or not succeeded in erasing the mark. It made Bobby (Bobby's body; it) look more like his dad, like the family scar. But Georgie had not cried, as Preston had hoped she would. The shock had dried her tears. Without explanation, grief, which is the body's recognition of the loss, was on hold.

Preston was sobbing into a handkerchief that Mary had made and that Georgie had given him as a wedding anniversary present. Georgie wanted to cry like Preston. She had the thought that Preston was crying in a controlled way, that he was crying just about the right amount. What was that, she wondered? She was intrigued to find herself dwelling on the strength in Preston. Odd, too, that she envied him his tears. Though Preston was a sceptic, he was finding solace somewhere. You never knew where with Preston. Something Buddhist, something reincarnated, something reheated and warmed up, something just invented for the purpose. But *something* was working for him. When he had called it up for comfort he had found the required combination. Georgie looked hard at her husband. Once upon a time Preston's prowess in the garden, his solid prospects at work and his stolid decency had seemed enough. What had Preston done since then to turn her away? Bored her with gardening, infuriated her with contradictions, involved her in his macabre collections and obsessions, suffocated her with kindness. Georgie dropped her hands out of prayer. She took Preston's kindness gladly now. Without him she could barely contemplate being here. Now, there's an idea . . . Georgie tried again to pray. She asked desperately for comfort but found instead, as she looked around the church . . .

Georgie suddenly understood what Preston meant when he said that most funerals were ordinary. She noticed that the funeral made all the mourners look the same. Vividly individual expressions appeared to be compressed by a show of grief. Everyone there wore a death mask. She was troubled by a toothache like a long monotone. Preston had told her many times, in different variations, that the memories, the acts, the idiosyncrasies were always buried in the box in the ground. The point of the funeral was the grounding communion, the sameness, the touching base. It was already clear that there was one exception: the funeral of a child. The funeral of a child is not at all part of the communion for the child has been crucially deprived of life; of stubble, of spots, of a new perspective on his parents, of so on and so on. For the joy never had, for the time never torn off, the hopes never modified, the funeral of a child is extra-ordinary. In the rite to mark his death, Bobby Burns was separated from the common herd by so much that the word funeral had a derisive echo in its application to both.

Such a deep terror washed upon her. Death had had a walk-on part all her life: Jack had sometimes mentioned it, though he did not like to talk about his work outside the parlour. Then she had married her father's apprentice. She had lived most of her life on the proceeds of inevitability. But Georgie had no gratitude; she had always been terrified of death. She had inherited this fear from her mother. Her father had tried to calm them both down, to instruct her that there is nothing to be done in any case. But Georgie could never manage Jack's stoicism. Her mother Mary had provided a better answer: the consolation of the church. The terror was made bearable by the certainty. But as she looked around St Stephen's church, Georgie had her mother's terror without her certainty and her father's fatalism without his stoicism. The worst of mum without the best of dad.

Suddenly Georgie was struck with an overwhelming desire to laugh. All these merging faces, replicas of one another, excited the need for a release. It could have come through grief or weeping. It came out instead as laughter. All these familiar people, standing in twos, in pairs of twins, multiplied and covered in black. The pairing of replicas is oddly funny, the comedy in the twinning as neither face is at all comical alone. Georgie opened her teeth and began to laugh. It was an expression of grief, a defence of individuality and a protest against its destruction by all the mourners at the graveside who had come dressed to bury themselves. Would that they had been clowns, in spots and stripes, with caps and bells to mock the grave and the provident. Or Hallowe'en witches and warlocks. All heads turned as one. They all saw a woman who was understandably hysterical. For laughter they heard a scream.

Georgie will never have a recollection of moving out of church and into Preston's hearse for the journey to Heywood cemetery. Preston held her hand tightly in the back of the hearse. At Heywood cemetery, the road rose to a steep fall at the end of a long gravel drive. It was like the approach to a secluded country house. Two chapels face one another on the mount. They look like wrestlers about to lock into combat. Below them, down below, the plots, cut up by asphalt drives on which relatives are parked, talking to their old friends. The scene has woodland to its right and sterile fields to the left and Heywood Mill stands out in the valley. It is a splendid necropolis on a hill, as of old.

The full congregation had followed in their own cars. Once there, they re-assembled on a patch of grass. Georgie, Mary and Preston had to work their way through the well-wishers to the tiny plot where an urn would be buried in remembrance. Preston insisted that Georgie stop and thank their friends for coming. Preston wanted to break Georgie's dry, tearless hysteria. Preston had compiled a mental encyclopaedia of grief over his years in the dismal trade. There were a number of identifiable types: those who washed away the pain with tears, for whom grief supplied the need for meaning; those who found a silent consolation in faith; those who presented a philosophical and stoical face; those who found strength in assorted other creeds and notions (astrology, nature, hedonism, alcohol, reincarnation, spodomancy, love, work) and those who, like Georgie, evacuated the world because the horror it disclosed could no longer be spoken of or acknowledged. Those who, like

Georgie, imposed a social exile of mourning upon themselves. All the comforts had fallen away at once. The carnival frolics and tender stage bonds of the Heywood Amateur Operatic and Dramatic Society. The beauty of the hydrangeas on the allotment, the physical sensation of patterns in embroidery, the dream of a shop, the warmth of a familiar embrace. But, above all, the invisible dimension, found wanting at the vital moment. As she stared down at the turf, Georgie Lees put her hands together and, uncomforted, withdrew. She nodded solicitously at the grave, as if confronting the altar, bowed her head and walked away. Away from the enfolding arms of everlasting consolation, Georgie's life was now set on a different recourse.

Preston brought Georgie back to the graveside. He held Mary from one side and Georgie from the other. Man that is born of woman hath but a short time to live and is full of misery. He cometh up, and is cut down, like a flower; he fleeth as it were a shadow and never continueth in one stay. Even the cruel precision of the words did not connect to Georgie. There was no blessing and no spiritual transference took place. She walked in a vain shadow, disquieteth herself in vain.

Mary offered the comfort in which she was herself enfolded: 'There's a reason for all of this you know love. Your dad used to say that, even when he was hurting, that it was all for a reason. He was in pain was your father but he used to say it was all for a reason.'

Georgie did not reply. Mary began to delve into memory, phrasing it in the present tense, where she thought it should still be.

'Is Bobby allowed to come to the stall tomorrow? He does love doing the money. I'm sure he's going to be something to do with money when he grows up, that lad.'

'I don't know about that Mum. I'm not sure they have money where he's gone. Wherever that is.'

'He can count up with the best these days.'

Preston did not approve of Georgie allowing Mary to live in a perpetual present. Mary gave her son-in-law short shrift.

79

She bared her yellow teeth at him. 'When I want your opinion Preston Burns, I'll know I've lost my marbles.'

Mary seized Preston's wrist and pushed him back three paces. 'You've always been a funny one have you, Preston Burns. It's your mum's fault. She used to knock you on the back of the head when you were a nipper. But that's no excuse.'

Preston dismissed Mary with a weak flick of his wrist. His blemish burned and he could feel its impress on his head. The priest said the famous words and Bobby's ashes were covered over with dust. From dust to dust. As the dirt hit the brass there was a collective gasp. Every one of the uninvited mourners had the same reason for being there. The loss of so much life is a greater tragedy than death at a natural term. If a funeral is a celebration of life, as it is often said to be in comfort, then the life of Bobby Burns had to be honoured, precisely because he had only just begun.

Preston led the way back to the hearse. As they shuttled back down the drive, Georgie noticed a sign on the exit: 'Drive carefully. Please leave quietly.' Do not disturb the residents. Mary comforted her daughter to let her know that lucidity had returned.

'He's gone to a better place love.'

Georgie had never believed this less in all her life. At just the moment that she was supposed to be within the fold of eschatological consolation, the belief had gone missing. In its place came a wordless terror. When the coffin had been lowered, when the mourners had filed away from the grave, Georgie stood with the last enemy. Throughout all of this Georgie Lees stood like a street entertainer whose trick is to remain unnaturally still. Even her breathing made no movement. Georgie Lees had frozen. Georgie Lees had stopped. The stationery and handkerchiefs had acquired a black edge, the antimacassars and teapots were covered over. The explanations Georgie had taken for granted but never had to confront seemed to lack all power. She felt she was falling through a hole in the ground, dropping straight, endlessly into nothing, no sound, no words, thoughtlessness. Just the alarming realization that, in this void, the fact was that life, as the phrase rang in her head, has to go on.

10

An Iron Curl

After the burial had been endured and another journey had
been lost, Mary dragged her frozen daughter into the Masons
in Heywood to recuperate. Georgie was oblivious to the conversation. She winced at the stuffed head of a boar that was
watching her from above. Georgie hated animals' heads in
pubs. She thought they looked creepy sticking out of the
walls. Mary went to the bar to order two prescription whiskies.
While she was getting served, a mother and daughter with
matching bleached wedgès, each with a cross of St George
tattooed on a bare shoulder, muscled past Georgie to the
adjoining table and inquired coarsely whether the other seat
was taken. Their heavy plastic bags brushed against Georgie's
leg as they squeezed through the small gap. The plastic curl of
a cheap shop coat hanger caught Georgie's shin as the bleached
daughter tugged it by.

'Can you move your leg love?'

'Be more careful will you? That hurt.'

'Shift your bloody self then.'

Georgie jumped to her feet as if she were about to attack but
instead pushed past and staggered out of the pub. Mary came
back with the first drinks that had come into her head: a gin
and tonic, a glass of advocaat and a can of Special Brew. The
bleached pair snarled that Georgie had left. Mary nodded her
thanks and drained the three glasses.

Georgie ran dementedly through Heywood town centre. The
image of the iron curl had scarred her mind. The texture of

the plastic coat hanger, its very softness, had brought back the glint of that harsh metal. While Preston had been treating the body, Georgie had sat in Bobby's bedroom holding a coat hanger, tearing violently at the iron curl which she blamed, in the absence of any sense, for the death of her only son. In desperate anger, Georgie had ripped all the hangers from Bobby's wardrobe, spilling a heap of half-man sized clothes on to the beige carpet. She had run downstairs, coat hangers falling jaggedly, dangerously on to the floor. Twice, on her way down the stairs, Georgie had stood painfully on an iron curl which had forced itself up through her slipper, causing her to yell in pain that screamed out for the loss of her little Bobby dazzler.

Georgie ran past shabby independent shops. Heywood cried out for established brands which, elsewhere, are said to herald the end of character. She ran into Dorothy Perkins and through the shop, knocking over a bundle of dresses as she went. She pushed in at the front of the queue. 'Have you got any spare coat hangers?'

The cashier reacted as if Georgie had told her to empty the till and put her hands up. 'Errrr . . . what do you want? I'll get the manager.'

A lanky, gawky man, whose early twenties had not yet conquered his acne or his bum fluff, came out from the office at the back. He walked over reluctantly and spoke to Georgie in the trained manner, as if she were retarded: 'What can we do for madam?'

'Have you got any coat hangers? Those plastic ones.'

The manager's look revealed his contempt for the request.

Georgie mistook his sneer for miscomprehension. 'I want some of those plastic coat hangers.'

The young man brought out a large pile of spare coat hangers that bred in the back office and laid them on the floor of the shop. Georgie had by now gathered an audience. It was not abnormal to want coat hangers but it was very odd to need them so *urgently*. Staff and shoppers watched expectantly as Georgie rummaged through the heap. The flab on her bicep flapped like a sheet in the wind as Georgie lifted coat hangers to the light. Though she barely knew what she was doing or why, Georgie had anthropomorphized coat hangers, metal coat hangers with iron curls. She took out the two iron hangers from the plastic cluster, rubbed her index finger over the iron curl and threw them down violently. The hangers bounced up, clattered together and parted like a hand-clap. Two startled young women shoppers jumped on either side of Georgie, in a pleasing symmetry. Georgie snorted at the staring people in the queue and left. They didn't know whether to laugh or applaud.

Armed with a large bag full of sky-blue plastic coat hangers, Georgie strode purposefully next door to Boots where she presented her mother's prescription. Dr Knox had stressed that drugs were useless except, perhaps, to help a slight slowing of the rate of dementing. That was his phrase, *the rate of dementing*. In any case, he had said, the patient is liable to forget to take the pills. So it was just as well they didn't work. When effective drugs are developed the sneaky condition will have seen them coming, playing forgetfulness to block the remedy. Dr Knox had suggested some non-pharmaceutical placebos: *gingko biloba* or melatonin. Georgie didn't bother with those. She asked for three bottles of aspirin (a long shot: only useful if inflammation turned out to be a causal factor). She handed the doctor's sweeping scribbles to the pharmacist who read the prescription and began to offer an interpretation. Georgie repeated her order impolitely, at which the pharmacist disappeared, grumbling that he was a trained professional who had been to college, into the back of his premises. He came back holding a cholinergic which, he said in order to prove his point, stimulates the production of acetylcholine wash, the brain transmitter that sharpens cognition. Georgie turned to go but then went back and asked for some strong sleeping pills. They came in a small bottle of tinted glass with a child-proof screw-top. She told the assistant, needlessly, that the pills were for her mother whose sleeping now obeyed no pattern. The pharmacist handed over the bottle with a remark to the effect that he could as well be replaced by a machine and no doubt soon enough would be.

Georgie went back to the Masons, where her mother had drunk the first round and assembled a second. She went to the bar herself where she complained about the reindeer's head over the door and bought the desired glass of whisky, with a pint of lager chaser. The bleached, tattooed couple had left. Mary was alone, apparently asleep on the grubby mauve sofa-bench, jerking to and fro as if she imagined she was in her comforting rocking chair at home. Georgie hid the coat hangers under the table and lifted a clump of her mother's greasy black hair off her forehead. She kissed the top of her forefingers and brushed them over the exposed skin.

At this lightest of touches, Mary was startled back to life. 'Hello love. What you doing here?'

'I had to get your prescription. I just went to the chemist.'

'Here, who's looking after the shop?'

Six months ago, Mary had opened up an occasional embroidery shop in her head. It had been her lifetime's ambition realized.

'You mean the stall. No one is. It's closed today.'

'No love, I've got a shop. I've got more than one in truth. I need to get someone to look after them.'

'Mum, I look after the stall and it's closed today.'

'Don't be silly, you can't do it on your own. You're only a young girl. It's a proper tough job is running a shop. We've worked ever so hard in that shop have me and Jack.'

'Mum, you're thinking of the pub.'

'Your dad'll be opening up. We should get back. Do you want to help me with the glasses?'

'I never worked in the pub, Mum. That was you when your mother and father owned the pub.'

Mary looked at the door as if she expected her mother to walk in.

'Where is my mother? I've not seen her for a while.'

'Mum, she's dead.'

'Don't be bloody daft. You spend too long with that husband of yours, that's your trouble. Our Bobby needs watching love. He's been slapping Susan Platt's young lad. I caught him the

84

other day. He's going to get in proper trouble if you're not careful. I've told you before, you're too soft.'

Mary scared Georgie when she brought people back to life. She scared her even more when she killed people who were living. Georgie feared that she would be next. They drank round after round, discussing their progress towards a shop, until the customers were being cleared from the tables as the chairs were stacked around the straggling drinkers.

As Mary and Georgie stood in the cold, waiting for a bus, the clock in Heywood Town Hall sounded midnight at the edge of the audible distance. Georgie gazed in silence into the dark streets. A group of boys with square bodies and aggressive hair were shouting to mark out their territory. The last 471 of the evening came by, carrying the dirty-stop-out young children back to Heywood, long after they were expected home. It was a school night. The children on the bus were not much older than Bobby Lees. But Bobby would never get off the bus, late, on time, never.

Georgie had decided to stay the night in her old bedroom, at her mother's. She might have to stay here for a while. For ever, perhaps. She had no idea what this meant for Preston. The tour had gone. Archie Gregson had called, not knowing anything. Georgie had enjoyed shouting at him. Back at home, in the kitchen, she poured herself a whisky. She took her bottle of sleeping pills in the tinted bottle from her handbag, lifted up the full vessel and read from the instructions: 'Adults: take one pill before bed. Do not exceed the recommended amount.'

Georgie had never had trouble sleeping. Georgie did not need a bottle of sleeping pills. It was a tinted glass carton of keepsakes, entry tickets to Bobby dazzler's new world. Georgie stared hard at the bottle and screwed off the child-proof top. She poured out a handful of pills and shook them as if she were playing the maracas. She opened her hand and looked at the collection of white capsules. Sleep in a bottle. Georgie thought of Preston, of Bobby, of Mary, of the Heywood Amateur Operatic and Dramatic Society and then, again, of the sleep in this tinted bottle.

Shivering at midnight in the kitchen, Georgie resolved that she would find a use for the sleep contained inside these pills, the moment Mary's decline was complete. Georgie made a silent vow to herself that the day that Mother no longer recognized her own daughter was the day she was no longer needed. Preston would understand, she thought. He had a mature attitude on this – on only this. So, as soon as Mary was finally incapable of recognizing the difference between her mother or her aunts or some stranger and Georgie . . . Georgie would give Mary three chances. If, on three consecutive occasions, Mary spontaneously, on sight, could not place Georgie correctly, then the arrangements for care would be made and then there would be nothing . . . Nothing worth finishing. Don't worry Bobby lad, I'm coming soon. I won't be long now, just got to check that your grandma's OK. I'm sure your dad can look after himself. No, he will be, he'll be OK.

'Georgie. Who you talking to?'

Georgie was startled to find that she had been talking to Bobby. It was a comfort. At least, it was better than anything else so far. Georgie held out her palm and let the pills slide, like water over smooth rock, into the bottle. She opened the glass cupboard above the fridge and put the bottle on the shelf inside. Shorn of the consolation she had expected to find in the language of the burial, Georgie conceived of this memorial. One day she would honour her boy's act in the repetition. To join him soon was a classically honourable course. One day, not too long away . . . This time, she thought, indeed she told Bobby as much, this time she'd let it go.

11

Bloody Mary

Life lapses, time elapses. Preston found a sanctuary on the Nightingale Street allotments with a host of Heywood husbands: nature's guardians also forgetting their everyday. Transfixed beside the gas fire, Georgie and Mary watched the leaves fall to the floor and the trees slowly refresh themselves in the drink of the winter. There was nobody in 32 Nightingale Street now. Only Bobby. Georgie too refreshed herself. In the drink of the bottle. She closed the door to the comfort of friends, who all came offering a shoulder to cry on and kid gloves to caress her with. Georgie craved anonymity not sympathy. It was less shaming. The doctor prescribed happy pills but Georgie mistrusted their placebo promise. The few remaining potatoes and ripened onions were lifted and the tomatoes were brought in. Cauliflowers were protected with a portable cloche and rhubarb, hardy and permanent, was planted. The caterpillars crept over the cabbage leaves and left their eggs on the undersides. But, for Georgie, to think was to be full of sorrow. Come with me to the memorial. Come to the graveside, pleaded Preston. He went weekly to visit Bobby as, in the lavish cemetery, the wheels of the cycle whirled around.

Apples and pears were harvested and small off-cuts from the gooseberries and the blackcurrants were made safe from the murderous winter. The beds were hoed and weeded, compost moved and all the tender plants brought under hibernating cover. Mortal summer flowers were cleared away from the beds which were forked and replanted with spring herbaceous flowers. Hyacinths, anemones and narcissi were planted. The leaves were left in a heap, just damp, to decay. Meantime, cuttings were taken of the antirrhinums, hollyhocks, petunias, pentstemons and peonies, delphiniums, oriental poppies and irises. The border plants and the spring bulbs were planted, offering a promissory note for the new year to come. Georgie drifted away glacially from Preston. Their staggered and uncomprehending movement: a parting in slow motion, split into two hundred stills, each a day apart.

As and when rain relented, Preston touched the gate hinges and latches with oil, coated the greenhouse doors with paint and repaired the pergolas and espaliers. Humus formed on the compost pit and was packed into trenches on the vacant ground. The fruit buds began to swell to prove that the trees never really go to sleep. The gardeners reappeared into view to dig deterrents to weeds and pests. They aerated and sterilized the soil and lay the fuchsias and the pot plant relatives temporarily on their sides. Almost as soon as they had reappeared, the gardeners retreated inside to make plans for Christmas and for the New Year. If any passer-by had listened closely he could have heard long, precise (even Preston) conversations about rotation, fertilizer, insecticides and seeds. Georgie stared, in blurred focus, as, in the greenhouses, under cover, onions and sweet peas were sown in boxes and leeks and parsley hung on a frame. The ground was prepared for the sowing of the seeds in March. Artichokes and shallots were planted on the plot. The first days of spring encouraged the early-flowering perennials.

And so Georgie Lees saw nothing for it but to go back home to her mum at the age of forty-six. She made the one-hundred-yard journey up Nightingale Street to find her mother Mary waiting for her on the doorstep of number forty-four. It was as if she had simply stepped out twenty years before for a packet of fags and come back to a fathomless future with a husband in tow.

As Preston cursed with their suitcases, Mary stood, arms crossed in judgement: 'What you doing here? Here, you. Preston. What you doing with those suitcases?'

Georgie ignored her mother. There was little point in explaining, again, that she would never go back into her own house. Preston had put it on the market but did not expect it would ever be sold. They could take a bulldozer to it.

'Mum, get in will you? You'll catch your death of cold.'

'Where's your Bobby?'

'Get inside mother. It's freezing out here.'

Preston lugged the suitcases into the front room, the living room these days, now that Jack was no longer here to make a coal fire every morning. When Georgie had said that they had to leave their home, Preston had not demurred. He had simply asked, politely, whether she wanted him to come with her. He didn't want to live in the house any more either. Georgie had surprised him by gently saying of course. Georgie had not made a new decision. She had decided not to decide, pending . . . well, pending she did not know what. Preston had assumed command this past week. She wanted him next to her. So Preston had emptied the wardrobes, Preston had packed the suitcases, Preston had led the march down Nightingale Street. They had nowhere else to go, apart from the shed on the allotment. Preston only had his brother Terry (they didn't really get along) and Georgie only had her mother. Preston promised to find a house to rent. But, in the meantime, Georgie went home to her mother.

As soon as she followed through the back door, Georgie's heart dropped. The deep and rich smell of roasting meat filled the kitchen air. Mary had got into the habit of cooking Sunday dinner, every day. Her day's routine had become invariable. It was just all in the wrong place. She got up in the middle of the night and came downstairs to stare at the allotments and listen to the radio. And then she wanted to go to bed at three o'clock in the afternoon. She got up at ten and started cooking a roast because it was, once again, Sunday. So, Mary's cooking a roast was not explained by the once-in-seven-days fact that it was Sunday, as indeed it was today.

Mary disappeared into the steam. Her protuberant shoulder blades looked like two pointed fins in her lean, unmuscular back.

Metal pans full of boiling water covered the hob and the smell of roasting beef had wrapped itself on to the surfaces in the kitchen. Mary jumped into the midst of a chaotic chemistry experiment, light on her feet like an infant, turning from one brew to another, stirring here and shaking there. She dipped a finger into a mint sauce. It had been improved with a suspicious hint of toothpaste. A pan full of boiling water suddenly ejaculated. A white film poured down the sides of the cheap steel and doused the short flame.

'Bloody hell Mum, who are you doing that for? It'll not get eaten.'

'Course it will. Your dad'll want a proper tea when he gets in. It's hungry work burying dead bodies.'

Mary had begun her preparations for the family, by which she meant her parents and aunts as well as her husband, her daughter and son-in-law and their new-born little baby boy Bobby: eight pounds six ounces, he had his mother's rounded eyes, his father's curls, his grandma's angry spirit. A grandchild had been looking unlikely when Bobby had come along in the late morning of Georgie's life.

The presence of the whole family located Mary's mental position very precisely in time because there had indeed been three days in 1987 when all these people now here had been alive together. Halfway through cooking, this original motivation had gone missing and now Mary was surrounded by an army of pointless soft vegetables. Georgie swore at her mother and bought her off with a glass of whisky. It was Sunday lunchtime, it was fine. Preston found the carrots and cauliflower already soggy in the pans, the potatoes boiled into wet mash and the beef in the oven a charcoal husk shrouded in fog. Mary began a cup of tea while Preston turned off all the gas rings and dumped the watery greens in the bin. Mary shuffled about in the kitchen, getting in the way, mixing a new substance out of the bags and granules she found in her pots. A little of this, a lot of that, add water, milk, sugar and salt. Preston cleared the kitchen while Mary took Georgie a cup of mongrel coffee-tea.

Georgie pulled her face at her first mouthful. 'Mum, what the bloody hell's that?'

'It's tea.'

'It's not tea.'

'I mean coffee.'

'It's not coffee either. It's bloody horrible whatever it is.'

'Oh stop being so bloody miserable. It's hot drink isn't it? A hot drink's a hot drink. Just get it down your neck and take that face off. You can't keep moping about the place, we've got a business to run. Here, give me that glass, you shouldn't be drinking at this time of the morning.'

Georgie bade her mother sit down by the gas fire. At once, Mary jumped up again and bounced a suitcase on the brand-new, bright cerise sofa that only someone with her failing sight could have appreciated. She beamed a toothy smile, to show how much she enjoyed scolding people.

'You're a dead loss you are Georgie Lees. I don't know what you're doing leaving your own house. Unless it's that husband of yours. I argued with your father about taking him on in the first place. I said he wouldn't be able to cope. I said he'd go a bit funny. But you shouldn't leave your house just for that.'

'I haven't left the house for that. Don't be daft.'

'You shouldn't have brought him with you anyway. I don't mind you staying but I don't want that miserable beggar.'

'Mum, he'll hear you.'

'I suppose you have to take what you can get. Look at that Olive Platt with her daft hats. She's been looking for a fella since Adam were a lad and nobody'll have her. I thought she was courting with that one off the telly not so long ago.'

'Who, Olive Platt, someone off the telly?'

'That funny-looking bloke, oh what's his name? He smokes a cigar.'

'You mean Jimmy Saville.'

'That's him. He wears a funny tracksuit like Billy Crispin used to sell on the market.'

'Bloody hell Mum, you're obsessed with Jimmy Saville. Olive Platt's not going out with Jimmy Saville. Don't be so stupid.'

'Well who do I mean then?'

'You're thinking of Stanley Atkinson from the show.'

'Am I? Does he wear one of them tracksuits?'

'No. He smokes a cigar.'

'Well it's probably him then. He's not on the telly though is he, this fella you're talking about?'

'Course he isn't. Mum, you know Stanley Atkinson. He's been in more pantomimes than you have. He played King Rat.'

'I've never heard of him. Anyway, what's he got to do with the price of eggs?'

'Nothing Mum. Olive's married in any case. She's got kids.'

'She came round looking for you earlier.'

'Who did? Olive?'

'Yes, who do you think I meant, the Queen of Sheba? She's looking for a Bloody Mary. Her leading man's buggered off too, so I gather.'

Mary got up to turn the fire on. Georgie told her to sit down and did it for her.

'Did you go to church this morning Mum?'

'It's not church today.'

Georgie held up a copy of the *Mail on Sunday*.

Mary could not read the small type.

'You should have told me, I'd have come with you.'

'I didn't go. I don't feel like it at the moment.'

Mary sprang up and took the Bible from the window sill where it had always sat. She began to recite from the Book of Psalms but memory soon gave out and she had to screw her eyes, to use up her dwindling eyesight to make out the tiny script.

After six lines Georgie interrupted. 'Mum stop it. Please.'

Mary carried on.

'Mum. Please. I don't want to hear this. I don't want you to pray for me. I don't want any prayers.'

'It'll make you feel better.'

'No Mum, it won't. It'll make *you* feel better. It won't make me feel better. I've tried it and it doesn't work.'

'Do you want a cup of tea love?'

'No thanks. I've done nothing but drink tea for days. I'm

sick of drinking tea. Everyone seems to think a cup of tea will cure this.'

'You want to have a word with the parson.'

'That's worse than a cup of tea.'

Mary asked Georgie to kneel. She did, as it was easier for her to comply than take on the argument. Mary extemporized in prayer. Georgie switched off and did not hear. The words sounded desiccated and withered. They were interrupted by Preston who wanted to know which wardrobe to hang his shirts in. *Non sequitur* was the sole advantage of Mary's condition. Georgie took the opportunity to change the subject. She folded her black cardigan into her midriff and shivered gently. 'You want to put fire on Mum.'

'Fire is on.'

'It's not.'

'Is it not? Well it's turned itself off then. I've had it on all morning. Turn it on if you want.'

Georgie did. The gas fire shot a portentous burst. Every time she had ever turned this fire on – at the age of seven it had been her first adult act – Georgie had imagined the house brought to rubble. The grey dial had become semi-detached from the fire and had to be pressed back in to make it turn. As a consequence, the numbers on the dial bore no relation to the temperature. There was no thermostated warmth; the fire was either on or out. Georgie perched on the unfamiliar sofa and airily grunted no to Mary's asking (again) if she wanted a cup of tea. Two minutes passed as they listened to Preston's feet on the floor above and then Mary asked again. Georgie clarified that she was quite capable of making herself a cup of tea if she wanted one and no, she did not want one just at the moment thank you. Tea and prayers, two common nostrums. Once Georgie had believed in them both.

A third source of comfort knocked at the door: Olive Platt. She had come round to beg and plead that Georgie Lees and Preston Burns come, with only ten days before the opening night, to the salvation of the Heywood Amateur Operatic and Dramatic Society's doomed production of *South Pacific*. Olive had a tale of terrible woe to tell. Her original Ensign Nellie Forbush, Rita Murphy, had run off to Manchester with her aerobics instructor. Until she did that nobody in Heywood knew she *had* an aerobics instructor. Susan Platt, eldest daughter of the producer, had been upgraded from playing Liat into the lead role. Susan had been replaced in her turn by Beryl Collins, who was only in the show in the first place because she went to wine-tasting classes with Iris Chivers, the pianist. Iris was trying to resign because she had just received confirmation from the hospital that she was deaf. This had been obvious from her playing for many years. Stanley Atkinson, the leader of the men's chorus, called her Beethoven. Or Ray Charles, because her sight wasn't up to much either. Then Beryl Collins's husband Graham, in his first lead role, as Luther Billis, had collapsed to stage fright at the thought of singing 'Honey Bun' in a grass skirt, a mop wig and a brassière made of two large coconuts. In the original Broadway production Myron McCormick had made the ship tattooed on his stomach pitch and roll by flexing and releasing his muscles. With a forty-four-inch gut Graham was worried that his ship wouldn't do any more than wobble. Olive had convinced him that if he jumped up and down it would look just right from off stage. Olive would say any old rubbish sometimes. You had to be a cock-eyed optimist if you were the producer of the Heywood Amateur Operatic and Dramatic Society.

And now Olwyn Jones who was playing Bloody Mary (it should have been Georgie's role) had run off with Colin Smethurst the butcher who had been playing Emile de Becque, the male lead. The loss of Bloody Mary was bad. But to lose Emile de Becque was terminal. The major plot of *South Pacific* deals with the romance between Ensign Nellie Forbush, a nurse from Little Rock, and the middle-aged, dashing French planter Emile de Becque, a widower with two Polynesian children. Emile's vast knowledge of the South Pacific makes him valuable to the United States forces and he agrees to go on a risky expedition knowing full well Nellie's prejudice, which is her unspoken reason for rejecting him. While Emile is away Nellie grows fond of his children, ethnicity and all, and realizes she is in love with him. Emile arrives home safely and the rest is flowers and loveliness. In short, it's not much of a show without him. Although Olive was the first to concede that Colin Smethurst was a better butcher than he was a romantic tenor, and he wasn't an especially good butcher, his loins being a bit streaky, he did at least know the part. Her only hope was that Georgie and Preston had the time and the desire to learn the main roles from scratch in little more than a week.

Preston listened to Olive's breathlessly delivered story and told her politely that Georgie and he were not exactly in a mood for the show at the moment. It's not exactly a matter of life and death is it? Olive pleaded again and Preston assured her that they would think about it. Georgie said nothing throughout. She had a frisson of excitement at the thought of the stage which had disappeared when Preston took the sensible line. She saw Olive out and promised she would call the next day to say yes or no definitively.

When Georgie came back in Preston knocked her stone dead with a statement of pure clarity.

'I can't believe you're even thinking about doing the show. Do you realize that our son has killed himself? You do realize that?'

Georgie took the petal of a lily from a vase on the table in front of her and crushed it between her thumb and her forefinger. She turned her back and started to walk away.

Preston stretched out and grabbed her back. 'Don't turn your back on me Georgie. You're always turning your back on me but not this time. I'm sorry to have to say this Georgie but someone has to give it to you straight.'

Georgie shrugged at the irony.

'I want you to talk to me. What's going on between us? What are we doing? I get the impression that as soon as you're back on your feet you'll not have any more need of me looking after you. I'm not doing that Georgie. Either you want to make a go of this or you don't. And if you do then we'll do it properly, on my terms. And that means telling me what you're thinking. I can't stand this silence.'

95

Georgie felt a wave of revolting despair. 'I don't want to talk about it Press. I just don't. We're fine as we are.'

'I'm not being used like this if you won't even take my advice. I won't stand for this for ever, I promise you. I do know what I'm talking about you know. I've seen a thousand people like you and I've seen what they need to do. But if you don't want to listen.'

Georgie turned to leave.

'You can't run away for ever Georgie. That little bastard will haunt us for ever, you know that don't you?'

Georgie waited for the thought to pass, as though a short silence were enough.

'Why Georgie? Why us? He seemed such a happy kid . . .'

'Shut up Press.'

'That little selfish bastard . . .'

Georgie did not respond.

'Do you hear? I called him a little bastard. He's ruined my life that little bastard . . .'

Preston's sentence cracked. He spoke clearly, on this one topic. 'You haven't even cried.'

There was an accusation in this report. Georgie replied with the simple poetry of barely describable pain.

Her mother offered her a way out, the one other possible source of hope. *Non sequitur*. A salvation. 'Oh Georgie, look at them begonias. Georgie, come and have a look.'

Georgie went over to the window. The perimeter of the allotments was lined with a wall of begonias. They were twenty yards away, directly across the road.

Mary was looking over to their left, at the fence and the stile gate. 'Mum, the begonias are over there.'

'I know where they are. I can see for myself.'

When Mary turned to face the begonias, Georgie saw that she had tears covering her fading lantern emerald eyes. Mary's sight was closing in on the end of her nose. As Mary got visibly older, she was becoming more transparent. Her face made cartoonish revelations these days. The lines on her forehead creased when she was anxious. Her eyes widened when she was content and

96

narrowed when she was thoughtful. Georgie held out her arms and let Mary fall into her. Her mum only reached her chin these days and the hair on the top of her head was thinner than it once had been. It was still full of golden dye, though, and the smile on Mary's full red lips scattered twenty years away. With the begonias in mind, Mary ironed her furrowed brow. She knew the begonias were over there. Preston had described them to her so that they would be in her mind's eye every time she stood up in her front room.

'Can you do me some spring onions for my tea, love? I've got some in the pantry. Preston brought them for me. He's a funny beggar Preston, but he grows nice vegetables. I'll give him that.'

'All right. You sit down and don't mess about with the fire.'

'Thanks Isabel, love.'

Georgie stopped in the doorway. 'You what, Mum?'

'Nothing love.'

'What did you call me?'

'I didn't call you anything.'

'What's my name?'

'Georgie, what do you think it is?'

'I'll make you some spring onions.'

Georgie went into the kitchen where she smashed a knife through the spring onions, stared at by the tinted bottle of pills in the cupboard above the fridge. She had never felt so deeply lost. But even the strong onions did not make her cry.

12
The Moth-eaten Indigo Brocade

Georgie slept like a woman haunted. The scene was the stage at Heywood Civic Hall. The boards were littered with metal coat hangers. They covered the entire floor, some wedged in the pile and standing up, arrogantly to attention. Bobby was there. He was still alive but he was a dummy sat on her knee. He did not know he was dead and the refusal to submit was keeping him alive. In the dream, if he knew the truth it would kill him. There was thus a conspiracy of silence thrown around him to ensure that he was not informed of the fact of his own demise. Georgie was woken by Mary whose intuitive sense of time, honed over years on the business-watch, enabled her still to recognize the moment that work was due. Georgie moaned through another hangover from congealed tinned alcohol and reluctantly got up to contemplate the bus to work. Preston had long gone. He was back at work, as if he had never been away. Georgie kicked about the house for half an hour, her boredom overcoming several parries – television, newspaper, embroidery, cutting the grass, romantic novel, Mary fussing around that she needed to go, that the stall would not wait. She made another cup of coffee from her hidden store that Mary knew nothing of. Mary could persist with her experiments in a mix of tea leaves and chicory grains. Georgie sat in her mother's chair facing the window. She fiddled with the fire, tried again to read the *Daily Mail*, peeled an orange. She had nothing to do, nothing to keep still for. She got up to open the leaf-green curtains halfway.

At nine-thirty, Georgie poured the day's first measure of

whisky into a dirty glass. After three large mouthfuls, she began to drift away. Georgie had been an irregular presence on Middleton market in the six months that had now passed since Bobby's death. She rarely rose before ten and thus missed the bulk of the day. The business end of the day on Middleton market was first thing in the morning, before work. Then, in the second wave, between eleven and two-thirty, Georgie was, more often than not, slaking the thirst of indolence in the Pack Horse. Georgie had lost interest in snow-scenes, in sweaters and knitted kittens, in the moth-eaten indigo brocade on the stall.

Mary lost patience and forced Georgie out of the house. She arrived at the stall at eleven-thirty. She stood still and silent, greeting none of the familiar market faces. Behind Georgie, two lines of cars formed, one pointing at Bury, the other at Rochdale. Middleton gradually came to life towards the lunch break as if the scenery were being shifted on to the stage. Georgie turned away from the primitive waft of Barry Wilson's delicatessen stall. Opposite, somebody was unwrapping a crate of cheese that had sat overnight, gathering smell. Georgie listlessly unpacked Mary's red wool with green brocade, her cute collection of cat cushions, her découpage portraits, her Impressionist tea towels, a cross-stitch that called to mind Seurat's 'Bathers'. She struggled to recall the recent past when she had cared about the art of these garments. Georgie had not long since ceased to control the politics of Middleton market. She had been the stallholders' representative to the borough council and had been such a forceful and voluble spokeswomen that her adversary in the bureaucracy had suggested that she might like to join the political group. Georgie had led the stallholders' campaign to overturn the planning restrictions that prevented an old stinking toilet being demolished. It had also been the moral force exerted by Georgie that had stymied Vinny Able's plan to smash the offending brick shithouse by night. In her few spare moments that were not consumed by office politics, Georgie had also run a highly profitable stall. She had been an entrepreneur. But not now. Momentous events had overtaken sweaters and needlepoint.

An argument began behind her. Vinny Able and Gareth Adams were shouting at Geoff Webb. As Georgie approached she began to make out the subject of the dispute. The shop in the parade which had fallen vacant on the death of Mr Bilston the florist still had not been allocated. When Preston's hope of realizing Mary Lees's dream had collapsed (from the beginning), Vinny and Gareth had both put in their bids. Neither had been successful. Geoff had decided that cobbling was not a prudent investment and that, though a fish shop was eminently plausible, Gareth wasn't. He had awarded the lease to Colin Smethurst. The parade needed a butcher (apart from Preston Burns, he had said cruelly). But now Colin had disappeared, leaving a note for Geoff to the effect that he wasn't coming back. The shop on the parade was up for issue again.

The argument depressed Georgie. The desire to own a shop to sell Mary's embroidery had been a source of inspiration for both mother and daughter. The stall had been turning over well for many years now. The costs of the business were not high. Mary took a share of the profits so required no dent in the immediate cash flow. She made the bulk of the merchandise. The rest, from the Rochdale factory, came absurdly cheap. The overheads of the stall were meagre. Ground rent and a contribution to the union of stall-holders were also cheap. But, that said, Georgie needed to sell sweaters to cover the £400 a month she needed to break even: twenty sweaters in her £20 bracket. Five a week, one a day with a bare day on a Saturday. It wasn't much. It was good business, with a good margin. The tee-shirts, tea towels, tablecloths, handkerchiefs and so on all fell straight through to profit. There was a small store of money in the bank. And, twice, the opportunity had arisen to take on a lease. On the first occasion Georgie had been overwhelmed by the other dream stirred by Archie Gregson. Now that the butcher romantic tenor had run away with one of his leading ladies, the chance had come again. But, this second time, well, there was no point now . . . The argument depressed Georgie because she only so fleetingly, so listlessly considered that she might realize the long-held desire. Geoff greeted Georgie, inviting her to join

100

in the argument, to settle it by expressing a desire to be included in the judgment. Before Bobby had gone, Georgie had been the envoy the market-traders sent to sweet-talk Geoff who acted on behalf of the company which ultimately owned and managed the site. Georgie had been a redoubtable negotiator, a veteran of the labyrinthine planning blight of one of the borough council's least ingenious departments (some competition) and a subtle tribune to the officious authorities. But Georgie had been quietly, temporarily, replaced by Margaret Reid (stone wash jeans, some with piping, some with embroidered lettering running up the femur bone). The planning questions of Middleton market were at a crucial stage. The empire-builders of the borough council were germinating grand plans for a European *piazza*. Sir, with the greatest respect, this is Middleton, Georgie had said. She didn't care now. Take the bulldozer to it. Georgie's business had declined precipitately. Georgie had not been turning up. She had spent six months staring out of the window, gazing at the changing trees and flowers across the road.

Georgie told Geoff to discount her from his deliberations. She left the men to their argument, for want of anything else to do and because there were no customers in sight, went to see Preston. She passed the empty shop as she walked along the covered parade. A group of young boys were playing on the pavement outside, trying to hit the kerb with a bouncy ball. When they missed, which was most of the time, the ball bounced into the window of the empty shop. The ball bounced off the window and hit Georgie on the back of her calves. Georgie turned around, to face the window, to see what had hit her. As she picked up the ball, she had a shock. The window acted as a screen on which an image, poorly tuned, shifting and sea-sick, was faint but visible. All the young faces were stretched free of distinct features. Their faces came together into one. They were all Bobby's friends. They had all liked Bobby's mum. She had always given them Coke and chocolate digestives and sent them to the shop for a quarter of banana whirls and sports mixture. Bobby had liked the cricket bats, especially the red ones. They had played with Bobby but they had never really known him.

Georgie turned round and her eyes arrowed in. One boy emerged into her line of sight. Georgie looked at him and saw a ghost. He was a dead ringer. He was Bobby's divided self, his mimicking clown. He had a scratch on his cheek from the easternmost point of his nose to the mid-point of the cheek where, one day, soft flesh would give way to stubble. He was a little rounded in the puppy tummy and the cat flick of his hair was uncut and ruffled. Georgie gasped as she saw him and took back the first letter of his name which came, without meditation, to her lips. Georgie threw the ball away, accidentally hitting the kerb on the other side of the parade and receiving an ironic cheer from the children. She pushed the clown-mimic away and ran into Preston Burns Undertakers.

She found Preston comforting a lady of sixty who had just lost her mother. Comforting others had become Preston's own consolation. He had not been successful in cajoling Georgie to accept his help. Preston was becomingly increasingly anxious that she had still not cried. To all outward appearances, Preston had kept up his professional detachment. But for those who peered close, like his two assistants Gundappa and Lucy, it was apparent that he was slipping. For all that he remonstrated with Georgie for not talking about the death of their son or not accompanying him on his Sunday visit to Bobby's grave (which she absolutely felt unable to do), Preston was struggling in secret. His legs were kicking beneath the surface. He was becoming more aware of his birth mark and had taken to curling his hair around his index finger most of his waking hours. It allowed him to obscure his birth mark with his forearm.

Preston had carried on working after the death of Bobby. Indeed, the intensity of his obsession increased. But he was changing, slowly, caring less. Preston had always prided himself on a number of employment principles of which the first and most crucial was the following: never let your private life interfere with your professional life. Keep home and trade apart. It was the most world-weary of the shibboleths that he preached at Gundappa and Lucy, always prefacing it with 'Have I told you this?' and proceeding anyway through their frantic nodding. The work piled up after Bobby. And undertaking is not work that can be left aside. The living tend to be importunate on that issue. So do the dead, at least in the matter of decay. But pile up they did. Gundappa and Lucy noticed that Preston had started to ignore calls, the sort of calls that need an answer. One of the important services rendered by Preston Burns Undertakers was answering that call. People need to speak to someone at once when a lover, a friend, a relative has left them. Preston's mobile number was general issue. His own stricture on the division between trade and home fell away at once.

Preston's slight loss of responsibility and his lack of interest were quickly apparent. Undertaking is a magnifying service. It deals with people at their extremes. Not the dead – who are extreme in a sense – but their bereaved. It also involves the extremes of human belief, the outer limits in the market of human explanations and, less profoundly, the extremes of the senses. A corpse was like nothing else to the eye, to the touch, even, in the squelching of operations, to the ear: to the tongue, to taste, we now prefer to avoid, except in extremis. But the dead were especially an assault on the nose. The back room of Preston's parlour was coated in the odour of embalming chemicals. Gundappa, who had been a Funeral Operative only for six months, had not yet trained himself how not to gag on entry. It was getting worse for him because Preston was not cleaning up after himself with the required care. Preston had always prided himself too on the throwaway claim that all bodies were the same. Bobby – was it Bobby or Bobby's body, he was no longer at all sure – had thrown his belief system out.

Preston's penultimate apophthegm of undertaking was to keep the office tidy. Twice daily he was prone to say, whether it was needed or not: look at the state of this place. This was part of the code of keeping up appearances. Clients liked to see streamlined austerity, rigidly cold order when they visited to arrange the disposal. Too vivid colour, too much vivacity of any sort was strictly forbidden. But Preston was slipping just a little. A thin film of dust settled on a book of jokes open on the front desk, brochures crept on to the floor, upset urns coughed out their contents on to the desks, slabs of masonry were untidily distributed along the lines of the skirting board, leant against open coffins awaiting fillers. The back room of the parlour, where Preston did the mortuary work, a place not usually open to visitors but indicative all the same, looked as if a not-very-determined burglar had given up ransacking it halfway through.

Clean surfaces and vacant spaces in the office began to be taken. The office became littered untidily with the Catholic paraphernalia and mementoes of passing away: chasubles, birettas, albs, missals, chalices, cinctures, stoles and maniples. Preston had lately become denominationally imprecise. It was a falling short from his own standard. Another prided principle for Preston: never be caught short, theologically. Never mix your greens and your oranges. It tends to bother the believers. It's the kind of issue on which they are apt to divide. Preston knew the doctrinal differences between the Unitarians and the Baptists, the Methodists and the Anglicans, these days too the Hindus and the Muslims and the Sikhs (the slot for Gundappa the ecumenical, more flexible, as atheists tend to be). Theological scholarship was the undertaker's version of 'know your customer'.

Preston's final principle was the culmination, the combination of all the others. It was his manifesto of undertaking: at all times be as serious as a unique tragedy warrants. Remember at inappropriately funny moments (what else is funny except inappropriate things?), remember that this is the only communion for this person. If you laugh at them now you laugh at them for ever. The final principle – the uniqueness of this event – was in direct defiance of Preston's most common observation: the sameness of the event, the oneness of the body. But this was his purpose, he thought. To send the individual into the communion and to charge the latter with the unique imprint of the former. That was why it was vital to recall the uniqueness, the fingerprint of each occasion and, above all, to accord it seriousness. And so working for Preston Burns was a matter for concentration and focus.

It was the violation of this alpha axiom that betrayed a change in Preston's attitude. He had suddenly acquired a sinister levity at work. He was beginning to detect in himself a germ of the myth he had always countered – Mr Sowerberry, the cramped and shrivelled cynic. Among friends, or in the pub with Gundappa and Lucy, Preston had always been an unfunny comedian but he had been peremptorily clear that humour could not pass over the threshold of the parlour. Comedy was a private matter and this was a public space (cross-reference to the first principle, the one to which Preston only vaguely adhered). The dead, said Preston in one of those pronouncements that might have been profound if someone else had said them, belong to us all. They live in public, they lie in public. There is no cause for laughter, to be released from binding categories. Laughter was for the outside world but Preston had now reneged on both sides of his bargain with himself. He had started to joke in the parlour and, as a related result, had lost the ability to laugh in the pub.

Drinking with Gundappa and Lucy after work, Preston was known for greeting their friends with tales from the mortuary: people sitting up in their coffins, people being buried alive, people too big for their coffins having their feet cut off so that they would fit. Preston was still telling the tales but he had lost his relish. On two occasions Lucy bade him tell his new favourite stories: the heroic bricklayer from King's Lynn who laughed so much at the Goodies doing a spoof *Kung Fu* from Lancashire called 'Ecky Thump' that he had a heart attack. And, his current all-time favourite, the demise of a pall-bearer in Kensal Green Cemetery. The coffin, lined with lead, was carried down a narrow path towards the open grave when the bearers stopped to turn around so as to proceed head-first. Our hero stumbled and fell, causing the other bearers to let go of their heavy burden. The coffin fell on the great man's head and chest and killed him. On both the occasions that he was invited to tell this story, Preston politely, quietly, certainly, declined.

Yet during his hours at work Preston began to lose his gravity. One morning six weeks after he had seen his son away, Preston had called Gundappa and Lucy into the back office and read to them from a book he had just got out of the library. Pausing only to laugh edgily and without joy, Preston read out the cases: the coal dealer who was frightened to death in 1714 by a ventriloquist, convinced that a demon was speaking from inside a coal sack. William Huskisson who was run over by Stephenson's *Rocket*. John Merrick, the Elephant Man, the weight of whose neurofibromatosis dislocated his neck as he did what he had, all his life longed to do: lay his head down on the pillow. Emile Zola, a precursor of Mary Lees, who died of carbon-monoxide poisoning from the fumes cranked out by his heater. Pope Adrian IV who was choked by a fly. Aeschylus who was killed by a tortoise dropped on his head by a passing eagle. Edward II of England who had a red-hot iron thrust into his fundament. Tiberius who was suffocated under a pile of bed linen. The dean of Westminster who died after swallowing Louis XIV's preserved heart. Lucy wanted more on this one – it begged too many questions to be true. But Preston knew nothing more. He was just reading them out. As soon as he was asked for more detail he wondered what he was doing.

Georgie demanded to be taken home. Preston left the day's business to Gundappa and Lucy. He was doing that regularly now, in any case, as he often had to rescue Georgie from the Pack Horse. In any case, he didn't feel at all well. Influenza was courting him. At least influenza, it was probably worse than that. When he asked what had happened, Georgie was all but mute. They got into the hearse in silence. As Preston careered sleepily down the dip of the hill from Heywood town centre towards St Stephen's church at the end of Nightingale Street, he could have sworn he saw Mary Lees, dressed in only a thin nightgown, by the family and staff entrance to the White Horse. He stopped the hearse and realized, to his horror, that he was right. While Preston was looking for a parking space long enough to accommodate his absurd vehicle, Mary ran at the locked door. She bounced back and crumpled down on to the dirty pavement.

Georgie ran over to her and, as she approached, Mary cried out in anguish: 'Let me in. My Jack's in there. He's dying. I need to rescue him.'

106

Preston took his overcoat off and wrapped Mary in it. 'Mary. Come here love.'

'Excuse me young man, can you help me please? I need to get inside. My husband's in that pub. In fact he owns it. But he's not well. I need to get to see him but they're not letting me in.'

'Mary, it's me. Preston . . .'

'I need to get inside but they won't let me in. But he's in there. And they're in there. He's dying. They said he was going to die today and they're in there with him.'

'Who's in there?'

'The doctors. And our Georgie.'

Georgie pleaded that she could not be in the pub because she was here, pleading. There was not a glimmer of recognition in Mary's eyes.

'Mum. It's me. Mum, you've got to recognize me. Mum, you don't know what . . . Mum . . .'

Georgie repeated her plea until Preston intervened. Georgie was so distressed she almost cried. Mary consoled Georgie, but as she would a lunatic in need of help, with no particular fondness, but with an impersonal care for human likeness, a sentimental recognition of suffering. Then, just as suddenly, Mary jumped up and managed to scratch a fingernail against the window. The landlord came out and threatened to call the police if Mary did not leave. He explained to Preston and Georgie that he had been forced to throw this old lady out of the tap room three times that afternoon. Mary screamed as Preston pulled her away. She looked at him and suddenly appeared to know who he was. He lifted his hands to hold off an expected attack. When it came it was purely verbal.

'You'll not get me you know. You'll not get me like you got our Bobby. You'll not . . .'

'Mary, come here love.'

'Get out of here. I know who you are. It was you wasn't it?'

'What was me Mary?'

'You killed my Tommy didn't you? What had Tommy Gaffney ever done to you, eh?' Mary's first love, Tommy Gaffney, had never returned from Italy. He had been lost in combat and never found. The loss of her fiancé was bad enough but the absence of explanation had made it worse. Mary had longed to be given a reason but a reason had never been supplied.

'It was you wasn't it? You think you've got away with it but you've not. They got our Bobby as well. But you're not getting me. You've always been a funny one you have Preston Burns.'

'What did I do Mary?'

'It's wrong to be so bothered about folk dying.'

'What did I do Mary?'

'You're a murderer you are. A bloody murderer. Are you listening?'

Preston took firm hold of Mary's wrist. 'You shut up this minute mate. We agreed. We agreed with your Jack. He was in pain. He'd had enough and you know that very well.'

'You're a bloody scoundrel you are Preston Burns. I've a good mind to tell the police.'

Preston and Georgie took Mary into the White Horse and persuaded the landlord that they would control the lady who had been besieging the place. They bought her a drink and sat down to deliver a sermon. Preston told Mary (what they all three knew already) that he had spent a great deal of time at Jack's bedside during his final week. He went through Jack's final days, in which the pain of cancer of the lung had been added to his mental decline. Jack had complained bitterly about the restrictions this imposed on him. He had never wanted a painful, abstemious epilogue to life. He had wanted his extra time full of beer and fag pleasure. Preston reminded Mary that Jack had set limits to his suffering and then surprised himself by going beyond them, about his faith that life was sacrosanct and his conviction that even his own anguish had a purpose. At night-time especially, he had found the pain close to insufferable. Jack had been one of the very few for whom death had come too late. It was, said Preston with complete clarity, a blessed relief when the end had come. Georgie nodded and held her mother.

Preston noticed that Mary's bare feet and ankles were blue.

He bent down to look at her legs. Her varicose veins were like red and blue felt-tip slashes across crinkled white paper. The flaking, shrivelling skin on her calves looked like small droplets of ice about to melt as they thawed. As Georgie held her for warmth Mary was shivering. Mary did another mood somersault. She spoke now with profound resignation. She seemed to have some understanding of her condition, as though she knew that she was confused, as though she were aware that she had acted incomprehensibly during the last half an hour. Mary whispered her answers so softly that the fight seemed to have disappeared. She suddenly consented to being directed home.

As soon as they arrived Mary's obstreperousness returned. Preston opened the trellis gate but Mary refused to go in.

'I don't live here.'

'Course you do.'

'Do I hell live here. I live in a pub. I told you, my husband's the owner. I don't know why you've brought me here. Can we go to the White Horse please? My husband will be expecting me. He'll be opening about now.'

'Come on Mary, it's fleeing out here.'

'You go in if you want. It's not my house.'

Georgie opened the front door but Mary refused to step in.

'This isn't my house. It's my auntie's. I'm looking for my mum and dad.'

Preston had a bright idea. 'No, it's not your auntie's house Mary. It's my house.'

'Press . . .' said Georgie under her breath, 'what are you talking about?'

'Have you got a better idea?'

Georgie relented. She had *no* idea.

'This is my house Mary. We're just stopping off to pick up a delivery before we go to the White Horse. Would you like to come in and help me choose?'

'What you choosing?'

'Some drinks. We've run out of bottles. I've got some in here. Shall we go and have a look?'

This seemed an eminently good idea to Mary. At last some-body was being reasonable. Mary stood back, waiting for Preston to lead her into his house. Georgie opened the door on to a full morning's sweat of mess. It was astonishing what Mary had achieved in the short time she had been in the house alone. The floor of the living room was lost under a layer of detritus. Copies of the *Rochdale Observer*, tracing paper, abandoned bits of haberdashery, an uneaten roast dinner, daguerreotype photo-graphs, a light blue kagoule, a pan with a rim of abandoned soup around its middle, a box of scrumpled tissues. That was just the crust.

Preston began to clear up while Georgie made them a cup of tea (with supplementary coffee for Mary) and went to find some clean clothes. Oblivious to the mess, Mary started to overturn the kitchen looking for bottles of beer. She opened the fridge and took out a slice of fetid ham and a cultured yoghurt. She rooted around between the cooker and the damp wall and disturbed the debris on the floor of the back room. Mary trailed barefoot through the shit in the hall trying to balance a half-full bottle of HP sauce, one full of salad dressing and a brown bottle she had recently emptied of Holsten Pils. She offered them pathetically to the young man who was coming down the stairs carrying a bundle of petticoats, skirts, tights, jumpers, blouses and knickers, all clean. Georgie dropped the clothes on a chair, took the bottles and smiled as if Mary had been a very good girl indeed.

'Where are your shoes Mum? There's none in your wardrobe. What have you done with them?'

Mary did not know. Georgie looked in every room for shoes. There wasn't a pair in the house. From the back-bedroom window she saw a pair of wellington soles wedged in by the dustbin lid. Underneath them she found ten pairs of shoes, three pairs of slippers and a week's completed embroidery.

As Preston and Georgie waited for Mary's antique kettle's whistle, Preston drew an evident conclusion: 'She really ought to be in a home, Georgie.'

'I've told you Press, she won't go. She's lived here for donkey's years. I mentioned it the other day, trying to make a joke of it and she went up the bloody wall.'

'You can't use that as an excuse. We'll get someone to come in. There are volunteers you can get to come. I was talking the other day to someone whose great aunt I was burying and she said she'd had a volunteer service come round and they were a great help. I'll get the number off her, it sounded very good.'

'We'll see Press. But she won't have it. You know that. We've had people in before.'

Mary had seen off a succession of visitors from social services, deploying a range of household implements to do so. She had once aimed a vase of water at an approaching home-help. The water had hit the home-help on the top of the head. Unfortunately for her, it was still in the vase at the time. She was also convinced that visitors were stealing her bed linen.

'She'll make a bit of a fuss, she's bound to but she can't stay here for ever.'

There was a definitive explosion from outside coming into the room.

Mary stormed in and rapped her fist on the Singer sewing machine that was on top of the chair-side low table.

'It might be the best bloody option for you two scoundrels but I'm leaving here in a wooden box. You're not getting me in one of them homes while I'm living and breathing. They're corpses in them places most of them.'

'Mum, we were only . . .'

'I know what you were doing Georgie Lees. Trying to get rid of your own mum.'

'Oh you know what's going on all right now don't you?'

'It's for the best Mary.'

'And you can belt up and all you weasly old devil. Georgie, did you invite this morbid scoundrel in here? You're a shady one Preston Burns, I've always said so. I know you had something to do with it. My Jack would never have allowed it. I never much liked you. Our Jack spoke up for you but I always thought you were a queer one. I'll stay here until I see fit to leave. Have you all got that?'

111

'Don't get yourself worked up Mum. We'll not do anything before you're ready.'

'I'll never be ready. I've told you: you can carry me out of here. Yon fella can be useful then.'

'Mary, you have to be realistic . . .'

'I'll not be . . .'

'Oh shut up the pair of you. I'm sick to death of this subject.'

Georgie went into the kitchen to make three cups of tea. She stood silently in the draughty hall, looking at the hat-stand that was never used and the address book that had already been falling apart when she had last lived in Nightingale Street, twenty years before. She was disturbed by the wolf-whistle of the kettle and took a can of Carlsberg from the fridge.

Preston's face dropped when he saw the tin in Georgie's hand. 'What you drinking that treacle for? It'll ruin your brain.'

'That's the point isn't it?'

'Leave her alone. She can have a drink if she wants.'

Mary's distaste for Georgie's workaday drinking was overtaken by her animus towards Preston sharing it. Her gift for haphazard reasoning allowed her deftly, unwittingly, to change the subject and the mood. Georgie looked at the cupboard above the fridge. Another day passed, another long night came on. The pills were behind the frosted glass and another morning arrived without a dawn.

13
Give Blood Saves Lives

An eventless week later – by which Georgie now meant that her mother had not caused any major traffic accidents or failed notably to recognize her own daughter – Mary was in the course of one of her conversational loops about going to the hairdresser's when a van pulled up in the twilight outside. It stopped outside number forty-four and Georgie noted that it bore a strange legend that didn't quite make sense: *Give Blood Saves Lives*. Georgie was a little surprised to see a man get out and head for their front door. He introduced himself as Brian Wood, a volunteer from the Florence Nightingale Hospital League of Friends in Worsley, East Manchester. Mr Wood spoke in the flat, almost camp, vowels of urban Manchester. It was a voice always at least on the edge of satire. Mr Wood explained that he covered Heywood, Middleton, Blackley and bits of Rochdale and that a Mr Burns had demanded he call but had been unclear as to when or, indeed, why he might be required. From the look of the person who had opened the door, he said cheesily, he must have the wrong house. Georgie smiled weakly and said Preston was at work but that Mr Wood should come in for a cup of tea.

Brian Wood was a small man, five feet eight in his highly polished black shoes. His skin was rutted from awful adolescent acne but burnished by half a life lived outside. His thin eyes folded into his face like arrow holes in the wall of a castle of slabbed stone. He had a full head of jet-black hair and a thick black moustache which tickled his nostrils at the top and his lip at the bottom. Most conspicuously, his stomach sat contentedly on his belt, from which a Swiss Army knife was dangling, and his forearms were painted each with a violent tattoo: Manchester City and an unnamed woman.

Georgie made Mr Wood a cup of tea and briefed him on Mary's state of mind. She warned him that Mary could be angry at new people and violently dismissive of anyone whom she suspected had been brought in to reduce her independence. She told him about the most common fantastic tales – about still being the landlord of the White Horse Inn, about owning a chain of wool shops across the North West and about her conviction that somebody was sneaking into the house at night and stealing her embroidered sheets.

'Oh yes,' said Georgie, a little embarrassed, 'and she gets very frightened of Jimmy Saville whenever he appears on the telly.'

'Fair enough. So do I, the creepy silver-haired bastard.'

Georgie laughed. It was a strange sensation. To open your mouth wide for the first time in a while. How odd that felt.

'And Terry Wogan makes her go a bit funny too. I don't know why.'

'I do. It's that hairpiece.'

Mr Wood could not have been any less perturbed. He said he would arrange for Mary to have a memory assessment. There were tests that the doctor could do to work out if her capacity had been dangerously eroded. He asked to be given a back-door key in case of emergency and said simply: 'Look love, it's fine. I've met these symptoms plenty of times and the important thing is to relax. If your mother doesn't take to me I'll bugger off and we'll send someone else until she finds someone she can get along with. We're only here to give her some company. I've no plans to tell her what to do with herself.'

The warning complete, Georgie nervously took Mr Wood into the living room where Mary greeted him as if he were an old friend. She thought he was and he was too adept to disabuse her. He did shameless diplomacy naturally: 'Have you had your hair done Mary?'

Mary went to the hairdresser every Friday. She came back

114

every week with her few sad last grey hairs swept up volumi-
nously into a vertical bun, a sort of lollipop on her head. From
the charm of Mr Wood's smile you'd have thought he had a
thing about tall grey hairdos. He immediately gained Mary's
confidence and she began to ask him, with an audible sigh from
Georgie, how well he knew so-and-so. She had played this dull
game a lot recently with her mother. The usual answer was that,
no, she did not know so-and-so because so-and-so had been dead
thirty years. But Mr Wood appeared to know everyone Mary
referred to. He intrigued Georgie the more he drew her mother
in. Was he pretending? Was this a tried and tested technique
to deal with failing minds, to enter into their worlds and accept
the vagaries of illogic, the people never met, the chronological
chicane? His story was that he knew Mary's friends through
his work with the Blood Donors' Centre, from whence came
his ungrammatical van. He must have been lying about some
of them unless he'd worked there a very long time.

Mary began a train of speech that required Georgie's explanation: 'My grandson'll be back in soon. He's playing out. He's
a little devil he is.'

'Well you know what young lads are like.'

'I don't know where they get it from. He loves insects.
Horrible, dirty things. He's always pulling the legs off things
and stamping on them. He's been told at school but he
won't stop.'

'He'll stop. I used to do the same but you grow out of it.'

'Will you have a word with him? He needs a man about the
house but his dad's not around.'

Georgie knew she should intervene but she let her mother
continue. She liked briefly being able to live before the event,
before the fact. It was good to have a stranger in the house
who knew nothing of their circumstances and to whom no
explanation was required. If she wanted to revive Bobby here
then she could.

Georgie left Brian and Mary to talk. She went into the
back room and put her dusty vinyl copy of *South Pacific* on
the turntable. Preston had bought her a compact disc player

and the same sides on a better pressing but she hadn't got used to the new buttons yet. She had the original soundtrack recording on which Mitzi Gaynor sings the part of Nellie Forbush and Rossano Brazzi the part of Emile de Becque. She looked mournfully at the creased front cover. Rossano held Mitzi in a stylized and staged embrace in front of a cobalt sea. Preston had decided that he did not have time to learn the part of Emile de Becque. He had never played it before and it was the axis of the whole show. Georgie, though, had been tempted. She had played Bloody Mary fifteen years before, though at a local church society rather than the Civic Hall. It wouldn't be difficult to re-acquaint herself with the part and Bloody Mary's songs were wonderful. She had decided to see if she could remember the words and make a decision then. It was redundant, of course, if Preston said no. Still, she loved listening to the music. Georgie moved the needle carefully into the groove for 'Happy Talk'. She straightened her back and sang along in a part-Polynesian, part-Rochdalian burble. After three rounds, she still could not get the entry into the last verse. Every time she sang it, her contrived accent got the better of her and she started talking nonsense about counting all the wipples on the sea. She gave 'Happy Talk' three more runs and turned to her dialogue. After acting out her main scenes alone she went back to 'Happy Talk' and counted all the wipples on the sea again.

Bored with Bloody Mary (maybe it wasn't such a good idea), Georgie treated herself to the 'Twin Soliloquies', the latter of which, 'Some Enchanted Evening', was her favourite song ever sung. The first soliloquy is, in fact, a fractured duet in which Nellie Forbush and Emile de Becque separately reflect pessimistically on their chances with the other, though neither can hear each other's thoughts, which would hasten their coming together rather too quickly. Georgie imagined Mitzi Gaynor as she was on the front cover in a still from the film, with the sea at her back, but alone this time; no Rossano Brazzi by her side. She wondered how she would feel, living on a hillside. Looking at the ocean, beautiful and still. She let the dreamboat Rossano sing

Emile de Becque's lines. When he sang about someone young and smiling she imagined that he meant her. Georgie came back in with the fear that the two of them were not alike. She was wary of boring him, Emile being a cultured Frenchman, she a little hick.

Georgie closed her eyes and sang the words as she tried to remember what it was like: she was like a schoolgirl waiting for a dance. Ezio came back in to say that he was like a schoolboy and did he have a chance?

The duet ended and, from behind Georgie, Emile de Becque's soliloquy began. Georgie turned round as a deep male baritone rang out in an impressive whisper. Some enchanted evening. A stranger. A crowded room. Not exactly, thought Georgie but it sounded comforting none the less.

The words got closer. Mr Wood came into the back room with Mary beside him, listening intently and smiling. Mr Wood sounded like he wasn't even trying. As he sang, in a cod French accent, he glanced at Georgie. Catching sight, she looked away, embarrassed as he suggested, rather too intimately, that he already knew that he would see her again and again.

Mary stared at Mr Wood, properly enchanted. Georgie thought this home help might well avoid the vase of water. The sound of her laughter, the most human way to show disregard, sang in her dreams.

Mr Wood looked again at Georgie and smiled. She wasn't used to being flirted with and fluttered her eyelashes awkwardly. I'm a married woman, she thought. The song is conclusive: once your true love is found . . . there is then nothing more to think about. Brian Wood smiled again. Could he mean her? He was a cultured Frenchman and she was just a little hick. Perhaps he was just acting the part. Or acting the goat.

After the careful phrasing of Mr Wood's last words had echoed in the room and gone, Georgie and Mary clapped and Mr Wood took a bow. He revealed that he knew the part well and had played Emile de Becque three times, the last occasion a little more than a year ago, at a church hall in Swinton.

'What are you doing next Sunday?' asked Georgie.

'My word, you don't mess about. I'm free if you've got plans for me.'

'You can come to our dress rehearsal and play Emile de Becque. Ours has just dropped out and we go up in just over a week.'

'I'm a bit rusty. I mean, I know the songs. You never forget them do you? But I'm not sure about the words and the actions.'

Mary joined in as an advocate. 'Go on, don't be such a coward. You've got long enough if you know the gist of it.'

'I don't know. It's a bit short notice.'

The record had played on through 'Bloody Mary' into 'My Girl Back Home.' Mary scratched the needle across the vinyl to the tenth track. She took Brian's hand and fearlessly faced him and argued his doubts away, declaring, as corny as Kansas in August and as normal as blueberry pie, that she had found herself a wonderful guy.

'She can remember the words to that all right,' said Georgie, amazed.

Brian joined in as Mary swept him across the back room in a waltz. They were both as trite and as gay as a daisy in May. A cliché coming true. Outside, the moon happy night poured light on the dew. Mary and Brian danced through to the end to declare I'm in love, I'm in love, I'm in love, I'm in love, I'm in love with a wonderful guy. It was best said in an embrace and Mary would not let Mr Wood go until he had agreed to join the sinking ship in the South Pacific. It meant he had to drink three more cups of hybrid coffee-tea. With this brown gravy, they toasted Emile de Becque.

Five minutes later, Mary had disappeared upstairs and Georgie found herself spilling her memoirs to Brian over a deep glass of whisky each. Brian kept interrupting to ask for the happy times to be included. There *must* have been some happy times, he suggested. Then she told him the final act, Bobby's curtain call. It was a strange, disjointed dialogue between a jovial optimist and a pessimist in black: the glass is overflowing, there is no glass. The conclusion of the staccato tale was that

118

Georgie had decided, after struggling with the scratchy vinyl, that she probably wouldn't bother with *South Pacific*. She was too haunted and pursued to care for Bloody Mary.

Brian listened carefully. He took an unbecomingly noisy mouthful and touched Georgie intimately on her forearm: 'Now look Georgie, it's not my place, so if I'm overstepping the mark just tell me, I mean, I hardly know you, but I hope you'll hear me out first. I think it might make you feel a bit better if you do the show. I know you don't feel like it – God knows, why should you? – but I once had a terrible bereavement . . .'

'Brian, please don't tell me you understand. I'm bored of people telling me they understand.'

'No, I shan't say that. I'm sure I don't. Anyway, I was doing a show and something happened to me, it wasn't really like you. My wife passed away. But it knocked me for six all the same and I packed it in with a week to go.'

'What show was it?'

'*White Horse Inn*.'

Georgie hummed the title track and Brian supplied the lyrics.

'I love *White Horse Inn*. I was born in the White Horse Inn. My mum and dad used to keep it so that was their show.'

'It's a super show. And I decided to carry on. And do you know why? Because my mum told me to.'

'My mum'll not be doing that. She's not sure what day it is half the time.'

'I believe the technical term is that she's losing her marbles.'

Georgie looked shocked at Brian's frankness.

'You shouldn't be afraid to be straight about it, Georgie. It's better you know what you're in for. It can be a nightmare for those who are caring. My dad went bad in his last years. He didn't know who any of us were by the end. We wouldn't have minded if he'd have just sat still but he had right ants in his pants. He kept running away to Italy, the old bastard.'

'Why Italy?'

'He was in Italy in the war. He kept trying to go back but he only ever got as far as Hollingworth Lake. He thought it was

119

Lake Como. Funny how everyone spoke English at Lake Como and how they serve roast beef and Yorkshire pudding in the pub. After a few times even my dad wondered about that.'

Georgie almost laughed again. 'I don't think my mum's quite that far gone just yet.'

'Sorry, I was telling you about *White Horse Inn*. I'd decided to come out of the show and I remember my mum sitting me down and telling me I couldn't let people down. She said I wouldn't be doing anything wrong if I did because everyone would understand but she said think of how big you become if you go on. She told me to think of the end of the first performance. She said think of that moment when all the cast take their bow and Brian Wood steps forward and the audience cheers you to the rafters. And I had a think about that and I decided to carry on.'

Georgie played with the HP sauce bottle.

'And when it came to the end of the first night, it was amazing. I wasn't really that great to tell you the truth but at the end of the performance I stepped forward and the whole audience, every man jack of them, got up on their feet and cheered me. It's the greatest sound I've ever heard in all my life. I'll never forget that sound as long as I live. It made me realize it's good to be alive.'

Georgie lifted her eyes from the carpet. Brain continued at a high-octane level as she began to concede. Glass half . . . well, at least there was a glass. Perhaps nothing in it, but a glass.

'Please don't leave the show. It's not too late. It might seem like the smallest thing in the world but I do believe it helps. It's always helped me. I'm not religious – you might be religious, I don't know . . .'

'I was.'

'It's a silly thing in a way, dressing up and bursting into song but you have to listen to the applause at the end. I have it in my head now every day. That's why I do it. Say you'll do it. You'll not regret it.'

There was a way in Brian's importuning. It was a light touch that pressed down firmly.

120

Georgie nodded. 'All right, all right. I'll give it a go.'

Brian went into the kitchen, muttering that he hoped they had the right ingredients in the house. He came back in and put two celebratory Bloody Marys on the table. As Georgie drank it down in one and went back to the kitchen to mix another she was just that little bit more interested in Bloody Mary and *South Pacific*.

14

This Nearly was Mine

Georgie played and replayed her copy of *South Pacific*. She committed the words to memory and concentrated hard on not lisping all the ripples on the sea. She had no more interest in work, though. Every morning, as soon as Preston had left for the parlour, Georgie turned over in bed and gave up the morning. Thirst dragged her out of bed and, by lunchtime, she had three glasses inside her.

On the day of the dress rehearsal Georgie limped into Heywood Civic Hall full of charm and sustenance from the bottom of the whisky bottle. The show had already been going forty five minutes when she announced her arrival by bumping into the door. With the first curtain due the following night, Olive had been planning to run through the whole show, without prompts or pauses, twice. She had already abandoned this hope by the time Georgie got there.

Olive had already taken the decision to scrap the show when Brian, encouraged by Mary and Georgie, had called at her house, late the same evening that he had first introduced himself. He had sung unaccompanied in Olive's front room while her husband carried on eating his dinner, unmoved. When she had finished choking back her tears, Olive had declared that the show really did have to go on, no matter what she might have said, and that was the end of it. Brian Wood was the new Emile de Becque. After a week of intense and intensive solo rehearsals, Brian Wood knew the words to his songs – 'Some Enchanted Evening' and 'This Nearly was Mine' – but he was still learning Emile de Becque's dialogue and stage directions. Brian was superb as long as he didn't have to speak or move, but *South Pacific* cannot properly be performed if Emile de Becque is pushed around the stage at every twist by Nellie Forbush.

Olive's head tizzied up and down in anger. She drew her lips tight, made a mouth as if she had taken her false teeth out and pulled at the flared sleeves on her mock Regency blouse. Olive Platt did everything theatrically, especially costume and make-up. She wore lime eye shadow and, on top of a head that was far too big for her body, a large green felt hat. Mary Lees always claimed she was called Olive because she looked like one. She pulled her wrist up to her eyes in a long and wide arc. The grace, style and import of the gesture were only partly offset by the fact that she wasn't wearing a watch. Olive shrieked (or whispered as she had it, Olive existing further up the volume dial than most people) to Georgie that they would begin with 'Happy Talk' as a warm-up. The rank inappropriateness of her big number brought a cold, black laugh from Georgie that was too sinister not to be ignored.

Olive Platt marched at Georgie, swore at her, turned her back peremptorily and waddled over to Ronny Rose, the set designer, who was struggling with the ten separate locations that the show requires. Ronny was trying to find a way to turn the island commander's office into the terrace of Emile de Becque's house and then into a beach by altering one painted panel in the middle. This was Ronny's first show as a designer. It showed. He usually did the sound and Olive was starting to worry that two islands in the South Pacific might be beyond his artistic powers.

With an audible and weary sigh, Olive changed her mind about 'Happy Talk' and called on the male chorus to encourage them into a more emphatic rendition of 'There is Nothing Like a Dame'.

'Now you fellas, come on, attention.'

They ignored her.

'Can we have some hush please? I can't hear myself speak.'

'You're not missing much.'

'You cheeky devil Stanley Atkinson. Now, I want to hear you mean it today. You've been shut away without a woman for God knows how long . . .'

'Who told you?'

'And all of a sudden you see these gorgeous damsels . . .'

'Where are they then?' 'Stanley Atkinson looked insultingly at the ladies' chorus.

'You're no great shakes yourself Stanley Atkinson,' said Olive on their behalf. 'Use your imagination Stanley. I want you to imagine you've not been with a woman for a month.'

'That'll be easy,' said Ronny Race.

'Now you'd give it some oomph, wouldn't you if you'd gone a month without? You'd be barking it out, if I know any of you.'

'Do you honestly think, Olive, that if I saw a young woman after being shut up on a desert island, that I'd call all me mates round for a sing-song? If you want oomph I'll give you oomph good and proper.'

Stanley Atkinson was fifty-nine years of age. He had a gammy leg and a dicky heart. He had an Adam's apple so big he looked like a frog. The idea of Stanley giving a young damsel any oomph was positively disgusting. Actionable. He had designs on Olive, though, because her husband, Ted, was a lorry driver and spent three nights of each week between Rochdale and Glasgow delivering frozen food and ready-to-eat meals for one in a packet.

Time was now so pressing that Olive even used Stanley's lascivious flirtation: 'I never thought I'd say it but I want you to send shivers down my spine, Stanley Atkinson.'

Olive winked clumsily in a facial move that made her look as if she were in the middle of an operation. 'Iris love, let's go with tinlad.'

That was Olive's acronym for the show-stopper.

Iris clipped the keys inexpertly, two at a time. In some productions, instead of full orchestration, there is an arrangement for two pianos. Iris had only one upright but it sounded as if she were playing the black keys on one piano and the white keys on another. It sounded like someone playing 'I Got Rhythm' and 'Phantom of the Opera' at the same time. Actually, it was the introduction to 'There is Nothing Like a Dame'. Stanley Atkinson and the male chorus launched into a flaccid version of their big number. For all the sexual vitality that issued from this rendition, there was little mystery about why these US troops were starved of female attention. There was nothing you can name that sounded quite so tame and lame. The final note was still hanging in the air when Olive waved her arms impatiently for the next scene to begin. Iris, meanwhile, hadn't quite finished yet.

Olive decided to go from the top. The opening scenes were played competently without incident. This is not how they should be. They should be full of colour, *acharnement*, fire. There were no dancing interludes; *South Pacific* was constructed, against convention, with the songs as vehicles for characters rather than intervals slicing up the programme. If they had seen the dancing talent available, Rodgers and Hammerstein might well have had the Heywood Amateur Operatic and Dramatic Society specifically in mind. But dancing or no, gusto or no, the production plodded along in the right order with the words and music just about adhering. Indeed, if *South Pacific* did not require a sober Bloody Mary, which it does, then the show might have gone right through, albeit tepidly and undramatically. But Georgie's first move gave the show the pizzaz and distinction it singularly lacked. She tripped over an anchor and banged her head on a plastic palm tree. Her grass skirt rode up her thick legs and the men of the chorus averted their eyes from the creased pop socks and the wobbly rolls of flesh.

Georgie leapt to her feet too quickly to avoid losing her footing and tumbled to the floor again, this time taking Liat with her. Brian lifted Georgie to her feet and nodded to Iris to begin 'Bali Ha'i'. After the first six words it was already obvious that Georgie was too drunk to sing. After a dozen lines, Olive threw her score on to the floor and stamped her foot as if she were parodying someone who had lost her temper.

'That's it. I've had enough of this. Stop. Georgie, this is the dress rehearsal and you still don't know your part.'

'I do. I just can't remember it.'

Stanley Atkinson stepped in to usher Georgie down from the stage. Olive jumped up and down on the spot, angry beyond speaking. Stanley took Georgie into a dressing room to throw water on her and Brian, whom the chorus had seen as an inordinately plucky saviour, put a comforting arm around Olive's shoulder to persuade her that the show could go on (still). Brian had a knack of making his company believe that whatever they were currently doing was the most important thing ever done.

Rather irritated at his tranquillity, Olive pulled herself together. 'Right then, lead in to the final scenes, everyone take up their places please,' she shouted, as if she had remained calm throughout.

The company had still not gone through the show as one in the right order. Sometimes even the exaggerators and drama queens have a point.

Brian went to look for Georgie. He found her in the dressing room being drenched by Stanley.

'Bloody hell, what you doing? Giving her a shower?'

'She's drunk. I'm trying to sober her up.'

'I don't know if your methods are so scientific.'

'I can't do this. I can't do it.'

'You can do it. You bloody well can.'

'It's only a stupid musical. My lad's barely gone cold and I'm wandering about the Civic Hall pretending to be a bloody foreigner. It's not right.'

'Come on Georgie, give it one last try. Remember my mum. Remember that moment at the end. It's worth it, you know. It really is.'

Brain escorted Georgie back into the arena and assured Olive that Bloody Mary was fit to continue. Olive took them all back to the point at which they had left off and demanded a complete run-through to the end. It was, she reminded them without need, the dress rehearsal.

126

Georgie climbed up into position, with the help of Brian's hand, to resume her journey to 'Bali Ha'i.' In the middle of the first verse she froze. She couldn't count up to three. Let alone all the wipples on the sea. Olive angrily took her off the stage, sat her down in the wings and carried on regardless. In a trance, Georgie began to see pictures. The first image to settle in the kaleidoscope was herself. A younger version of herself with the looseness of the skin competed away. Her facial covering still had patches of colour – the gently deepening red from the bridge to the top of the nose, the A–Z of veins just under the surface and rising, beneath her cheeks, her tawny owl eyes shot with streaks of red and a more exaggerated moustache of fine blonde hair on her upper lip. But the overall image was smaller, more slender. Georgie's oval face had been squared and her hair, which she wore to the nape of the neck, the same length all round, had been styled and brushed upwards with a cat-flick of auburn dye. The film in her mind's eye showed the wings of an aeroplane begin to shiver before take-off. She heard the engines announce that they were ready for flight. Cabin crew to doors please. Saturated in tension, seatbelted into a tiny aisle seat, Georgie desperately tried to lean across two young boys so she could see out of the window. The shutter was pulled down halfway, as if the window too were tired and drowsy. On the runway, waving, Georgie could just establish the silhouettes of her parents. The aeroplane took off from a standing start and, as Mary and Jack receded into dots on the floor, the doors were flung open and Georgie heard herself scream as she was suddenly startled by somebody banging on the window. Georgie looked up and saw the dummy-Bobby grinning stupidly, making an unfunny face with his nose pressed up against the pane. He skipped away from the window, and threw himself, gut-first, into the pool of rain that had formed there. Around her, *South Pacific* limped. There was no audience out there, no vindication, no curtain call. Just Olive and Iris at the piano.

After spending the evening alone in the pub (Preston was out at a funeral parlour convention in Manchester) Georgie opened the door at home on to dark familiarity. She saw

127

her mother outlined in the gloom, hugging the chair by the cold fire.

'Who's that?'

'It's me.'

The voice registered no recognition.

'Georgie.'

'Has delivery fella been love? We've no bottles left.'

Georgie sighed as loud as a sigh can be without becoming another noise entirely. She could not disguise the irritation in her voice. 'Mum, we don't live in a pub. This isn't the White Horse.'

Mary grumbled and, as she tried to lift herself from the chair, she looked as though she had aged thirty years in a single evening. After three attempts, she sank back down into her armchair, and referred to herself in the second person: 'Oh sod you. Stay there if you want.'

There were two empty cans on the table. Halfway through her third, all drunk at some velocity, madness and drunkenness had begun to resemble one another. The distinction between made-up and actual was now porous for Mary. She was clear on events from fifty years ago. As long as Georgie asked about her grandfather, about bad Ramsay MacDonald, about worse Stanley Baldwin or about better Ernest Bevin, Mary was lucid and articulate. But she just kept forgetting that none of these people was still alive. The process had not yet spread, as it often does in the later stages of the disease, to the cerebral cortex. This final distress completes the gradual loss of the longer-term memory. Brian had arranged, as he had promised, for the doctor and a specialist nurse to conduct a memory assessment. Mary had not been told but Brian had taken Preston's line on Mary. He had confided to Georgie that her mother might be better off in Woodhall, a care home that Brian knew to be very good.

Mary tried again to raise herself from her chair, succeeding this time. Georgie asked her mother to bring in the headache tablets from the cupboard over the fridge. And then the stench hit her, the lingering mixture of Carlsberg Special Brew and shit caked into stained underclothes. The strong beer always went straight through Mary. After two cans she lost control of her movements. Georgie fumbled along the kitchen wall for the light switch but the bulb blew as she flicked it down. Georgie cursed and scented a surge of odour as she pushed against a damp patch on the linoleum to resettle her balance. Though Mary was only in erratic control of herself she had, this time, realized what she had done and tried to cover herself up. With a drunkard's logic, Mary had opened the window in the kitchen where she had dragged herself to empty out her pants. She had then taken off her underclothes and dumped them in the bin. On her way back to the living room she had noticed the brown trail she had left on her way in, running from the carpet in the hall on to the cold linoleum of the kitchen. Mary had spent ten minutes, step by step, rubbing the shit into the fluffy white rug in the hall and smearing the light blue kitchen floor, convinced that it would disappear.

Georgie panted upstairs and down and brought her mother's last pair of clean knickers and a clean petticoat. She brandished them at Mary like dangerous weapons. Mary had sat back in her armchair, with a blanket over her knees, raging at the half-open scarlet curtains. Georgie lifted her mother from the chair and the last clinging drops of liquidized shit fell down on to the beige corduroy. Georgie recoiled and swore. Mary was genuinely flabbergasted that Georgie could tell so easily. As Georgie changed her mother's knickers, Mary struggled at the indignity. Her limbs suddenly rotated like a bendy baby's and she began to speak in the erroneous present: 'Have you changed your Bobby's nappy? Come on love, you've got to. You've a little baby to look after now. I know it's difficult. I felt down when I had you. It's common to feel miserable when you're not coping so well. I don't suppose your fella's any more use than my Jack was but you've got to keep going. He'll stop crying soon but he's only crying because he needs something. That's his way of telling you. It's a good sign that he's yelling.'

After ten minutes of fighting and out-of-time monologue about forgotten problems, Georgie gave in to frustration and alcohol fuel and smacked her mother's face. As Mary burst into tears, Georgie pulled the soiled panties down and replaced them with the last clean pair. She held the filthy underclothes by their threadbare edge and put them in the sink to soak. She forgot to add washing powder. She went back into the living room to persuade Mary to go to bed. Georgie asked if she wanted to take a cup of tea up with her. Rather than answer the question directly Mary looked straight at Georgie and asked the anticipated, inevitable question that called forth the glint of the coat hangers and the pills in the tinted bottle: 'What's your name again love?'

'You what?'

'I know you. I know I do, but, I don't know, I can't recall folk so well these days.'

Georgie did not reply. There was too much at stake for her.

Mary pleaded with her: 'What's your name love? I'm sorry but I can't remember.'

'It's Georgie.'

The name too registered nothing, at least nothing visibly betrayed on Mary's face.

Georgie tried again. 'You know, Georgie. I'm your daughter.'

'Course you are. I'm sorry Georgie, I forget these days. I know you, you know that, don't you?'

'It's all right Mum.'

'Have you been stealing my sheets? Someone has. I don't know where they've gone, someone's been coming in and taking them away. Is it you?'

Mary got up without waiting for an answer, turned the fire off and went upstairs to bed, muttering that she hoped she had some sheets left on the bed this evening.

Georgie stared out of the window. Was Preston on his way back? Had he said he was staying the night in the hotel? She couldn't remember, for the life of her. For the life of her, ha. Very funny. She couldn't bear being touched. Preston wanted to hold her, to assert himself, to comfort her. Georgie was sorry – she wanted to help Preston, who could not have been more solicitous – but she felt so solitary. There was so very little point in persisting with the pretence that there was any life left in their marriage. Georgie thought about the process of getting divorced. She went through it all in her head – telling Preston, how would she broach the topic, could she really be so cruel, given all that he had gone through? He didn't deserve it, after all. How quickly could it be done these days? It seemed a pretty straightforward operation. People even recovered afterwards to live second lives, even third lives. Then all these operational decisions were overwhelmed by a single, far more decisive and sinister thought: Georgie would not live long enough to make it matter. The pills behind the frosted glass promised a far more emphatic divorce. Worldy divorce was a comma, a pause. The pills were a full stop.

15
A Cock-eyed Optimist

With ten minutes to go before the curtain went up on the opening Monday, Heywood Civic Hall looked like a room-sized join-the-dots picture. Behind Ronny Rose's lumpily painted, under-designed scenery, Georgie was having her eye make-up applied by Lynn Riggs, the cross-eyed florist-cum-artist. Georgie confessed to Lynn that she was more nervous about this show than any other before. The jinx on the show was part of the reason but so, she found herself saying to her own surprise, was her desire to please Brian Wood. Lynn could smell acrid alcohol on Georgie's breath. She inquired but Georgie prevaricated, whispering a slurred, careful pleasantry that answered the question it was avoiding. Olive Platt came in and the collective hubbub gradually faded away. She was dressed in a green quilted mackintosh and a knotted silk scarf in an adjacent shade. She was a one-woman wood of verdant green.

Olive stood on a chair and called for attention: 'Right, I want a good show tonight. You've not distinguished yourselves in rehearsal so it'd better be good tonight. That horrible spotty fella from the *Bolton Evening News* is in the front row and I don't want another review like *The King and I* so for God's sake get it right.'

Brian Wood looked apprehensively at the rest of the cast in their big knickers and underpants. The dressing room of an amateur operatic society is a festival of large underwear which is scaffolding around soft, encased flesh. The air was thick with blusher and stage make-up. The female chorus formed an orderly queue in front of Lynn Riggs, who was applying thick brushes of shadow to their eyes. Brian turned to the room exactly at the moment that his view was blocked out by Georgie Lees's vast backside in a pair of huge grey pants. He took his turn to stand on the chair, called for order and the preparation stopped at once. *South Pacific* looked to Brian Wood.

'Now then everybody.'

The ethos changed as soon as Brian spoke. A warm glow of assurance framed his fat body.

'We hardly know each other, I know, but I want you all to give it your best shot. Remember, concentrate hard, think about the others on stage and, most of all, enjoy yourselves. Let's think positive. You've all got to believe that we're going to knock 'em dead out there. We've got a crowd out front who know nowt about our troubles and we're not going on half-hearted. Right, we'll have a warm-up. Everyone, after me.'

Outside, the orchestra was tuning up. So were the nerves of the cast. Brian cleared his throat and began to sing, at first unaccompanied, that the sky was a bright canary yellow.

'Come on, you buggers sing. "Cock-Eyed Optimist" from the top.'

The ladies' chorus looked around tentatively and stuttered into song, forgetting every cloud they had ever seen.

They were joined by the men, coughing their way into voice. By the time the title of the song came round the company was in full throated unison, cock-eyed optimists the lot of them, immature and incurably green.

That could have been a comment on Olive. The cast of *South Pacific* screeched on through Oscar Hammerstein's instruction that he is stuck like a dope with a thing called hope. Brian turned to the left to see that the only person not joining in the rendition was Georgie Lees, who was sitting, stony-faced, on the edge of the group, gazing out.

As Georgie stared beyond the window to the weeds of the dirt corridor that ran round the Civic Hall like a black felt-tip line, she sensed the presence on stage of the maniacally laughing dummy and of the white pills behind the frosted glass of the

133

kitchen cupboard. The cast sang on in yellow-toothed smiles as Brian took Georgie gently aside. She testily insisted that she was fine before he could ask.

'You can do it. Just remember. Think about the end and make sure everything you do has the end in it.'

Brian pressed Georgie's arm as if he had confidence in a syringe, as if his belief were contagious and he were deliberately infecting his leading lady. 'Come on love. Let's go. They're all yours now.'

Brian was so uninhibitedly genial. He was so comfortable, so assured, so odd. Georgie flashed him the blacked-tooth smile that was Lynn Rigg's interpretation of Tonkinese dentistry.

The show began with the male chorus in fine voice, joining the overture for a warm-up man's version of 'Bloody Mary'. The main characters were established competently in turn: Ensign Nellie Forbush, the unworldly nurse from Little Rock, Arkansas; Emile de Becque, the French planter of dubious provenance (word-perfect so far); the male chorus as the United States Navy and marines, who are waiting for something to happen. And finally, Stanley Atkinson rising to an unlikely romantic role as Lieutenant Joseph Cable. Stanley was worried about cutting his own dash (even he was prepared to accept that he had been cast imaginatively, some would say catastrophically, against type) but he was more worried still about Georgie.

Bloody Mary is the bewitching Tonkinese entrepreneur who sells shrunken heads and grass skirts to the sailors, seabees and marines. Her most precious item is her daughter Liat (played by Angie Rowles, the sex-bomb of the production) whom she hopes will find a good American husband. Bloody Mary's Polynesian accent, in the wrong mouth, can sound like a drunk talking. It certainly did in Georgie's. But then in Georgie's it was a drunk talking. Bloody Mary takes over the show with the first of her two numbers. Georgie was prompted out to sing and began encouragingly in time and in key with the music. But she soon got lost in the middle of a foggy sea. In the background, Liat made hand gestures, performing utopia in the medium of mime. But, out there on her own, Georgie felt she was on a lonely island. It wasn't Bali Ha'i though. Her volume dial went down gradually and, as she entered the refrain, Georgie was mumbling and inaudible. Olive Platt was in the dressing room fussing over an inconsequential tiff between two lady dancers, one having accused the other of fondling her husband in the lavatory. Brian Wood acted decisively. He had observed the whole of Georgie's performance from the wings so he could be on hand in the event of disaster. He ran into the dressing room as Georgie died on stage and pulled the ladies' chorus out with him. The cavalry arrived in time for the second verse. Georgie stood bemusedly in front as the chorus ran through an unscripted harmony. Brian hoped that nobody would notice that Emile de Becque had just turned up on a wholly different island from where he had left the stage a few minutes before. Georgie's mouth made the shape of some words (she couldn't remember the real lyrics) but the sound came from behind her. From somewhere in the remote distance, where the sky meets the sea, a male voice piously wondered on his own special hopes, his own special dreams.

Brian had almost saved Bloody Mary but the atmosphere after 'Bali Ha'i' was eerie. The cast tried to ignore the fact that the show had slipped. Brian encouraged them back stage to believe that the audience had not noticed, that the ensemble piece had appeared to be a Plattian directorial quirk dramatising the utopian dream that inspires all human beings. Emile de Becque's voyage was simply the same one that all utopian travellers took, across the sea, across time, across credibility. He was Bougainville on his journey, Raphael Hythloday taking to the seas. Ah, but his reach exceeded his grasp and the chorus looked at Georgie Lees with devoted sympathy. Olive Platt glared at her.

But the show went on, inexorably. And the show saved Georgie. The next number was the classic gimmick song, 'I'm Gonna Wash that Man Right out of My Hair', in which Nellie Forbush does just that. Olive's one imaginative move was that she had persuaded her husband Ted to install a functioning shower. To an audience used to actors pretending, this was a fabulous excursion into literalness. Susan Platt exuberantly ran a big red towel through her hair while exclaiming that she would not be bothering with that French planter any more, a plot-negating promise that she had, of course, revoked by the end of the song. By then, the shower had sprung a minor leak. A line of water had escaped and had gone for a walk in the cracks and rivulets of the wooden stage. Nellie Forbush came out of the shower to the front of the stage, modesty ensured by a vast bath towel. Lost in the sentiment and in the bouncing music, she shook her sopping hair so hard that she soaked the first three rows of the audience. Brian began to wonder whether he hadn't got the cast rather too fired up.

South Pacific was back into its stride by the time Georgie made her next appearance. Unfortunately her first stride ended in the splits. She took one careless step into the stream from the shower and her ankles lost their symmetry. Georgie muttered an obscenity, decidedly in the voice of Georgie Lees rather than Bloody Mary, and stumbled slowly, painfully, to her feet to sing the by now comically inappropriate 'Happy Talk'. This song has surely never been sung in such a miserable way. Georgie sang about making a dream come true as if every time she closed her eyes she saw dark little creatures dancing in front of her. She left the stage to gentle applause which she barely heard.

Georgie stayed off the stage for the rest of the show. This required subtle changes to the running order, which Brian and Olive did between scenes. The rewriting was complicated by the unorthodox structure of *South Pacific* in which action is continuous and there are no blackouts. But Brian and Olive discovered that the audience can still get the gist of the plot without words or movement as long as the songs are in the right order. The show creaked on to the end when Emile reprised his song of enchanted love to Nellie and he linked arms with her and the two children. The curtain came down briefly and Brian ran off stage to find Georgie, to insist that she come forward and take a bow. He found her staring at the wall, enclosed by Preston's arms. Preston angrily shouted that she was coming.

Bloody Mary was the first principal to ask for appreciation. Georgie stumbled the few yards from Ronny Rose's painted paradise to the front as the dotted audience gave out a ripple of polite, sympathetic applause. Georgie stood out at the front, on a lonely island, listening to the perfunctory, embarrassed clapping. She could see people in the front rows withholding their applause, sitting on their hands. The applause was never live enough really to die away. It faded like a weak colour dissolving towards white and, as it did so, Georgie turned her back on the audience and stared hard at Brian Wood who was waiting in the wings ready to take his own bow. Stanley Atkinson offered Georgie a bouquet of white lilies, one of which he had for each female principal. Stanley linked arms with Angie Rowles (he should be so lucky) and took her on stage to be cherished. Then, as Brian Wood and Susan Platt stepped out and a throaty roar began to rise in the auditorium, Georgie joined them uninvited out on stage, clutching her bouquet. Georgie Lees rang out with more clarity than Bloody Mary had achieved all evening.

'I should never . . . You total bastard, who the bloody hell do you think you are? . . . I should never . . .'

Georgie launched the bouquet at Brian and then threw herself at him for good measure. He dived out of the way and crashed right into a fake coconut tree, taking Graham Collins over with him.

'I didn't want to do this bloody show. You can't expect me to. I don't know what I'm doing.'

Georgie knew she hadn't got away with it. She had persevered in the hope of the life-enhancing moment and humiliation had arrived instead. Georgie stumbled towards Brian, towards the decisive moment of misrecognition, towards the frosty glass and the little bottle.

Georgie was already at the back of the dressing room when the chorus came in to remove their make-up. Olive Platt shuffled round the perimeter of the room to avoid eye contact. Brian removed his unwieldy hat and went straight over to her.

'Stay away from me.'

'It wasn't so bad.'

'It was bloody awful.'

'I don't agree. I was really pleased. Didn't you see the audience? Didn't you see their faces? When in all the rest of your life do you put a smile like that on people's faces?'

Brian was understating it. Georgie had made people laugh out loud.

'I don't think I've ever done it,' said Georgie, bitterly. 'And I know very well I didn't do it tonight. Don't patronize me Brian. I don't know why I let you talk me into carrying on, but I did. And I've done enough shows in this hall to tell a good one from a disaster. And tonight was an absolute mess and don't you or anyone else try to tell me any different.'

'You're wrong. You were very good.'

'Rubbish.'

'It was good to do it anyway.'

'How do you know? It wasn't you they were laughing at.'

'Nobody was laughing at you Georgie.'

'Don't you ever leave it? I don't know why I ever listened to you in the first place. I mean, it's not as if I even know you. Who are you anyway? Who are you to tell me what to do?'

'I'm sorry, I thought . . .'

'Oh be quiet. I've had a bellyful of advice. Yours and everyone's. Look where it's got me so far. I'll do things my way from now on and if I don't feel like turning up tomorrow night then I won't.'

'Don't say that.'

'I've had enough of this nonsense. I couldn't care less about bloody *South Pacific*.'

'You'll feel better if you carry on. It's all you can do.'

'Have you ever thought of joining the bloody Samaritans? At least you could get paid then for doling out the advice.'

Georgie ripped off her Bloody Mary costume and went home to her mother.

The following night the audience, bigger than Monday's, partly hoping for a repeat of the farce, gathered for the second performance of *South Pacific*. They were greeted with a notice on the front door of the Civic Hall: 'Due to unavoidable circumstances *South Pacific* has closed early. Apologies to all concerned. Refunds are available from the box office. For further details contact Olive Platt on 0706–64626.'

16
No Ifs and Buts

A week after *South Pacific* had ended in ignominy on its opening night, Brian Wood, obscured by an enormous bunch of fuchsias, braved another visit to forty-four Nightingale Street. He had promised, before the débâcle of the show, that he would be there when Dr Knox visited to conduct a memory assessment on Mary Lees. Preston had a funeral to conduct and was going for a drink after work – even undertakers do that; perhaps their need is even greater – so would not be around until late in the evening. Preston and Georgie had dwindled into silence. Preston left very early in the morning, before Georgie had woken up, and, most evenings, worked late.

Brian had come to look after Mary. But he also had a plan to put to Georgie. He had devised a peripatetic market stall experiment. He had decided that 'Tommy's' should expand to two sites: one would be constant in Middleton and the other would rotate from Bury on a Monday, to Oldham on a Wednesday and on to the gold in them there Cheetham Hill on a Thursday. Rawtenstall, he thought, was a decent enough market but an inauspicious name. He would buy a cheap van from the Blood Donors' Centre, which was selling off its old fleet, and have the name of the business engraved on its side in place of the ungrammatical legend that amused Georgie. Eventually, in the distant future, by which Brian meant about six months later, when the Lancashire market towns had been conquered, they would gather all the capital together, take on embroidery assistants and rent a unit in Middleton precinct. And then, when that had proved to be fabulously lucrative, as it surely would, they would transfer to a shop in Deansgate where they would slowly put Kendal's department store out of business. Brian would do the interiors, the repairs, the handiwork, the accounts, and Georgie and her mother would make the clothes, for which they could charge silly money as people are snobbish about garments that they buy inside rather than out. Before they knew it they'd have a national chain. Of course this would require more sewers than Mary, helped on the commodified parts by Georgie. They would need to employ a team, preferably in Singapore (Brian was adamant that it would be in Singapore) where the skills had passed and where labour was much cheaper than in Heywood.

As he let himself in during the grey late afternoon, Brian Wood called out Georgie's name. Mary replied to say that Georgie didn't live there any more. In the kitchen a strong stench of gas from a ring on the hob filled Brian's nostrils. Brian put the fuchsias in the sink. On the metal draining board by the kitchen sink he noticed a half-empty box of matches. He turned the cooker off and opened the kitchen window but the smell was overpowered when he went through the adjoining door into the hall. There he found a study in faecal incontinence. Mary followed him through her own house, like a visitor being shown around by an estate agent. It felt oddly familiar to her, like a picture of a well-known object taken from a strange angle. Brian called Georgie, who was on the bus on her way home. She was curt but not unfriendly and Brian realized that the anxiety about her mother's condition would, of course, outweigh their trivial contretemps about the life-affirming response of the audience.

Brian called Edwin Knox, the family doctor, to ensure that he was on his way. He went upstairs to find Mary some clothes. He did some more palliative work on the mess and entertained Mary in the kitchen, where they had a cup of tea and waited for Dr Knox. Georgie burst in through the door very quickly and was a little embarrassed to find Brian and Mary leaning against the fridge, quietly chatting over a cup of tea (and coffee). Mary was lucid and coherent. Unfortunately, everything was factually wrong. She thought that Brian was Jack and that Georgie was her mother. She described Preston the undertaker as little Bobby. She assumed that Georgie and Brian were married, notwithstanding her previous (five minutes before) view of their identities and she assumed that she lived in the White Horse Inn, where she was the landlady. The house she was in belonged to Brian and she had popped in for a cup of tea (which was lovely; he makes a lovely cup of tea) on her way to do a home visit to a few old ladies just up the road. The whole speech was delivered with complete certainty. Anyone not apprised of the facts would not have doubted Mary. She was proving it was possible to be rational and lucid yet entirely wrong.

And yet the moment Dr Knox arrived, accompanied by a nurse, he performed the miracle of making Mary reel forward thirty years into the clear and present day. Mary greeted him with asperity. She only ever saw the doctor when things were wrong. They were a bloody jinx.

'What are you doing here?'

'Georgie tells me you've not been so well.'

'You don't want to pay any attention to her. I'm fine for a good twenty years yet.'

Edwin Knox winked slyly at Georgie, who stared back at him.

'I'm sure you are. Now can you just tell me where we are love?'

'You what? Are you losing your marbles you? You're in my house you numb beggar.'

Georgie laughed. If it had been artful it would have been a wonderfully executed humiliation.

'And what day is it Mary?'

'It's Monday. Bloody hell, what you asking me that for? Don't you know what day it is?'

'She was all over the place ten minutes ago,' said Georgie, by way of apology.

Dr Knox gestured for Georgie to follow him through into the living room. She gasped at the state of the place and apologized again.

'I found the place in a bit of a mess,' said Brian, with obvious understatement.

'She doesn't know who we are. Five minutes ago, she thought I was her mum and Brian was her dad. And she thought she lived in the White Horse. She doesn't know her arse from her elbow. And then as soon as you turn up she's fine again.'

Dr Knox smiled affectionately at Georgie. His family had treated Mary Lees a long time. It had always been a treat of sorts for them.

'Don't worry. That's very common. As soon as she feels under scrutiny she starts concentrating.'

Dr Knox explained that Mary's symptoms of delusion were like a page from the textbook. He said it wasn't yet known for certain what caused the problems. It could be the ravages of transient ischaemic attacks or thyroid underactivity or a cause located in the brain such as an abscess or a benign tumour. But it was the symptoms, he said, that were difficult for the loved ones rather than the causes. Dr Knox had brought the nurse with him because she was a specialist in conducting a fuller memory test. It was clear enough to the doctor (and to Brian and Georgie for that matter) that Mary needed to go into care at once. The bureaucracy craved its form though. Dr Knox introduced the nurse to Mary. Although Mrs Rooney was a bouncing Irish woman of archetypally rubicund complexion and corporeal girth, Mary sensed at once that she was an inspector, a regulator. Mary reacted like a cat hissing at a stranger as Mrs Rooney asked her a series of simple questions. Dr Knox jotted down the answers as coldly as if he were wandering round a factory recording production quotas.

Mrs Rooney took a watch out of her pocket. 'Can you tell me what this is, Mary?'

'Course I can.'

'What is it then Mary? What's it called?'

'It's a . . . oh, what's it called? . . . I know what it's for.'

'Can you say this after me please? No ifs and buts.'

'You what?'

'No ifs and buts. Can you say that please Mary?'

'What for?'

'Mum, can you just do what you're told please.'

'No ifs and buts, Mary.'

Mary could not say no ifs and buts. The inspectors wrote this down.

'Can you spell the word world for me please Mary?'

Mary did not need to spell the word world. She felt insulted at being asked. She didn't understand the question, couldn't fathom why it was being asked. Nor did she want to pick up a piece of paper in her left hand and fold it in half. The final question on the test was to construct a vertical line with building blocks. Brian started her off by setting up the first four pieces and showing her the way. She struggled to connect the second piece. 'It's stuck. It doesn't fit.'

'It does Mary; just take your time, it'll fit on if you're careful.'

Mary tugged at the red piece of lego. She pressed it down harder and harder but block would not go upon block. After thirty seconds of agonized pushing and pressing Mary lost patience. 'Bloody thing. It's broken.'

She smashed her free hand into the adjacent line and brought the tottering edifice down.

Mary had lost her composure and her concentration. Mrs Rooney asked her to name Georgie. She couldn't. Mrs Rooney asked, if she could not recall the name, what relationship she had to this young woman. Mary didn't know.

Georgie asked her again. 'Who am I Mum? Who am I?'

Mary looked at Georgie plaintively. This young woman seemed rather desperate that she be identified. Did she not know herself who she was?

Mary searched through her brain but found nothing that would help. She held Georgie's arm. 'I'm terribly sorry love but I don't think I know you. I just can't say . . . I'm sorry.'

Georgie carried on asking when the inspectors had left but Mary still could not place her. Georgie tried the recall technique that Brian had taught her – to alight on real events in her mother's past, events at which Georgie herself had been present.

It had worked before but it didn't work now. Brian tried to calm Georgie down but she was not listening to him. He was full of bright ideas, most of them ending in disaster. Brian finished clearing up and whispered to Georgie that Dr Knox would recommend her mother for Woodhall, that it should be a formality. Brian said a perfunctory goodbye after Georgie assured him that she could cope. Preston would be home soon, she said. It wasn't true – Preston would not be back until after the pub shut – but she wanted to be alone. Absolutely.

It was still only seven o'clock but Mary declared she was taking herself off to bed. Georgie let her go. She did not inquire how Mary had concluded that this was, after all, her house with her bed in it. Georgie brought the bottle of whisky from the drinks cabinet in the back room into the front. She turned the dangerous dial, slumped in front of the window and peered through the gap in the curtains. In this position, unthinking and nihilist, she drank herself to destruction. The mark of liquid in the bottle gradually fell down the glass as time passed. Georgie suddenly stood up – it was ten o'clock but she had no idea of the time – and staggered up the stairs. She walked jaggedly into her mother's bedroom and began to shake Mary, to shake her as if she were trying to wake the dead. Mary woke, befuddled and frightened. She thought she was being murdered in her bed.

Georgie screamed at her: 'Mum, who am I?'

Mary moaned.

'Who am I? You've got to tell me. Who am I?'

Mary started crying. She wasn't being murdered but she didn't know what was happening. She didn't know where she was and, crucially for it was the question she faced, whom she was with. Georgie kissed her mother's forehead, told her to go back to sleep and walked back down the stairs, holding herself for balance on the banister, with a greater resolution settled in her head. She had but one thought – it was pure and crystalline, consoling and certain.

Georgie took the tinted bottle from the cupboard in the kitchen. She brought through a second glass and poured whisky

144

into one and tap water into the other. She laid all the ingredients down on the carpet, in a pool left by her mother. The end could come so easily, it was contained in these capsules: Georgie tried to imagine what it would be like, half in love with it and half disgusted by it. Outside, the lamp-post was giving out: sickly light becoming dark and flashing to gold again. Georgie went over to the window and stared across the road. Had she been a happy child, she wondered? She had. Lonely, an only child, but she had felt resourceful and confident from an early age. Her mother had given her that. What was it like before the overwhelming disasters of these six months past? Was it only such a short time ago that she had dominated Middleton market and the Heywood Amateur Operatic and Dramatic Society? Once she had not existed. Would it be such a loss to go back? There was something she could not grasp, something about the asymmetry of the thought that struck her as odd.

Why, above all, could she not get rid of the anger, the resentment, the guilt that Bobby had left her with? She could have talked him down, if only she had arrived home earlier. Bobby appeared to her as a spectre-thin cheat of the natural span. What did she want to say to him? She had nothing. What was it that Georgie felt deprived of? Bobby's life, to be sure. But also more than this. Also an announcement, a portent of decline which would have allowed her to have become accustomed to the approaching end. We ask: was it expected? It is a good, sensitive and acute question. The inevitable needs to be prepared for and grief gradually stretches out to dilute the power of the shock. The longer this period of anguish before the fact, the more the end is a release, the less of a tragedy it becomes. The thought of Preston flashed through Georgie's head. When they had lived together he had often wondered, after a day in the company of the bereaved, why grief should be so unruly, so untidy, even when the death had been expected. Death, Preston used to say, should always be expected. But for Georgie night had fallen in a swoop and, for that reason, grief had not been able to hold her in its loving grip.

She had thoughts of Preston, of Bobby's state of mind on

the day of his death, of the metal that hurt her feet and of Mary upstairs. Here was the critical question: would Mary know what had happened if Georgie was not there in the morning? Who would have died? Isabel, the already gone? The young woman who changed her underclothes and smacked her across the face? The lunatic who shook her awake in the middle of the night? Across the road, the purplish-rose flower spikes of the loosestrife were swept back in the wind, enjoying the drizzle. Georgie picked up the Bible that Mary kept on the window sill. Mary read it most days. She was cramming for her finals. Georgie flicked through the chapters scornfully. Genesis, Exodus, Leviticus, Numbers, Deuteronomy flashed by, like a cartoon being made. Georgie still wanted the certainty written into its pages, but how? They promised her reassurance that life would go on. Death was just the start of the next adventure. Once these words had been a balm to her fear. But how? How?

Georgie settled on her plan. She wanted anonymity, to stop people talking about her. So, she would join those who made an appointment with death rather than those for whom it called at an inconvenient moment. She would allow the contents of the bottle five minutes to work through her and then she would call Preston to ask him to come round. He would get into the hearse at once and Georgie Lees (the body, distinct from the person) would be disposed of neatly before the sun came up. Either side of the darkest hour there would be light. Mary would rise with the hope of morning with no recollection that her daughter had ever come home and would see out the rest of her days blissfully ignorant of her own name.

Georgie read the label on the pills. There were lots of long words that she didn't understand but they sounded dangerous: cholinesterase inhibitors and so on. This paradise, this nearly was hers. Her chemical ignorance was the flaw in the plan. How long do sleeping pills take to work? And work to do what? To sleep was one thing. But to sleep not to wake, that was altogether different. They weren't designed for that purpose so how quickly did they manage it? She thought of calling Preston, to warn him, to give him a chance. Best to get on. If she waited too long for

146

sleep to approach Preston would come home and save her. He needed to arrive with a job to do. He would cope. Would he? If she had already taken the pills what could he do then? The thought of making herself vomit was far worse than the thought of taking the pills in the first place.

Georgie closed the curtains and took a sip of water. She gulped and steadied herself. She opened the curtains again to look at Nightingale Street. She turned her back on the outside and picked up the pills. They looked like microbes on her hand, germs that were always there, visible in some strange telescopic radar but out of sight until now. Georgie was trying to allow her mind to bring her arm up to her mouth. She took another mouthful of water, larger this time, and swilled it around the inside of her mouth, swelling out the cheeks. As her gaze dizzied on the pills on the hand, a key turned in the back door and Brian Wood came through into the kitchen. The first thing he said was, 'I bought you some bloody flowers and I forgot to give them to you,' which made Georgie smile. It also made her hurry to put the pills back in the bottle.

17

Dead Metaphors of Dark
and Night

Preston could not stop talking about work. During a marathon
five hours in the living room in Nightingale Street with Brian
and Georgie he mixed up his words into a paste and rotated
them in his head until they formed concrete phrases with hard
meaning. His monologue began with the realization that he had
buried Christine Wood, Brian's wife. Preston had pretended to
remember. The thing about Preston's job, though, was that the
people were all the same. Ashes were ashes, dust was dust. Really,
the living left behind wouldn't recognize their loved ones from
three burnt copies of the *Manchester Evening News*. But Preston
wasn't about to say anything like that. He didn't care for Brian
Wood but Christine was one of his own. The fact that he didn't
remember proved it.

Preston took the connection as permission to describe in
painstaking detail, punctuated by unfounded fears of invented
illness, the changes to his trade. The package deals of the mortuary trade now provided Preston Burns Undertakers with the
bulk of its income. While you were in the funeral parlour having
a relative dealt with, Preston would sell you an engraved coffin
and a twenty-four by twelve by four Barre granite headstone with
your name and a choice epitaph immortalized in a sand-blast. He
would arrange the regulation and administration for gaining a
slot in the graveyard or agree to conduct the tedious liaison
with the crematorium or negotiate with the landowners over
strange locations for the ashes to be sprinkled. He was trying
to go on-line. He was mulling over the British National Death

Centre's call for cardboard coffins but there were health and safety considerations. Brian wondered whether the important health and safety questions hadn't been settled by the time it came to argue over the material of the container.

Preston loved the salesmanship of being a mortician. He could not understand the strain in his profession that, following Jessica Mitford, disdained the florists and the clergy with their near-monopoly and disallowed the very prospect of death-related chain marketing of goods. He had pioneered beautiful women in coffins as a marketing technique. What better ploy than someone principally defined by the finish of her body? Pre-sale tender, he thought, had given new life to the trade, particularly for the dwindling band of independents now that consolidation had come to Heywood. Preston had knocked away three tempting offers from the Combined Funeral Experience, the huge multinational funeral company who take most people under these days. The independents, Preston had always argued, provided an intimacy of care that a multinational never could. You had to understand, said Preston, that death was not the same everywhere. The dead were the same everywhere but death wasn't. Funeral care should wear local dress and speak in a native tongue. The trade was split on the question of the correct approach, between antiseptic formality on the one hand and breezy friendliness on the other. Preston was an advocate of the latter, on which subject he had given a paper at the most recent symposium on the Mortuary Trade and Associated Matters, held at the Crown Plaza in Basingstoke. What was the collective noun, he had wondered, for a gathering of undertakers? A plot, a burn? A grief, a comfort? An order, a vigil? Or if you could have a murder of crows perhaps you could have a death of undertakers. Or a promise. A herald, a passage, a transfer.

And yet, for all his talk, Preston had decided to sell up. It was business, after all. The Combined Funeral Experience just had too much money. They had talked about the need to close down one or two businesses in the region – they were cannibalizing sales, they said, at which they all had a good sick, professional laugh – but they wanted to make Preston Burns Undertakers

149

the showcase for their business in North Manchester. Preston could be much bigger in the trade. He had potential. He knew the subject.

The loss of Bobby had turned Preston from an workaholic undertaker into a die-hard obsessive. He told Brian and Georgie at length about his themed funeral offer: Manchester City funerals, pitch and putt rites, ceremonies based on *Only Fools And Horses* and *Coronation Street*. Preston recommended the therapy of laughter to his clients who were, he stressed again, the living rather than the dead. He had a fund of jokes as a relief against mortality. We've all got one foot in the grate. For fifty quid more, he would say, you can take a friend free. I almost got killed twice today. Once would have been enough. I've been thinking about that and I'd like to be cremated. OK love get your coat on. Believe in reincarnation and leave everything to yourself. How much did he leave? Everything. Die? That's the last thing I'll do. What happened to Mr Young? He died Young. Used gravestone for sale, ideal for a family called Smith. And his professional chat-up line: Don't worry love, you don't need a nice personality, I only want you for your body. Preston was the living difference between telling gags and being funny. Responding to a quirk of demand, he provided novelty urns for those who wished to laugh in the face of the inevitable. Preston had seen people into the ground inside a pair of old socks, a tennis ball, a lap-top mouse, a portable CD player, a trophy for the winners of the Middleton Sunday under-15s league, a hollowed-out battery, a bottle of lemonade and an upturned shuttlecock.

By the time Preston had been persuaded to end his lengthy monologue, Brian had lost the will to live. Georgie got up to close the curtains as Preston reached his conclusion.

'All men, Georgie, are cremated equal. We are all socialists in the grave.' This was the closest Preston ever came to profundity. Georgie, who had heard him say it many times, had never quite made up her mind whether this remark was brilliant or stupid.

Brian was quite clear. It was stupid. Really stupid. 'You're a morbid bugger you are Trouser.'

Georgie sniggered disloyally at Preston's new nickname.

'Can we talk about something else now?'

'I wouldn't expect you to understand. I don't suppose you've got much understanding of more serious matters.'

'Don't insult me.'

Georgie intervened to prevent a resumption of the fight she had refereed through the night. When Preston had arrived at forty-four Nightingale Street to find Brian Wood already there, he had been apoplectic. Did Brian not know that Georgie was married? What was he doing bringing her flowers? Preston had plenty of flowers across the road. He didn't need a stranger delivering more. Georgie had told Brian that she was on the brink of a divorce, that the lawyers were looking at the papers. This had been an accurate portrait of her own view, but not of the facts, which were less advanced. For a full fifteen minutes Preston had not even cared to ask after Georgie, so intent had he been on excoriating Brian. While Georgie had put her bottle of pills back into the cupboard above the fridge, Brian and Preston had fought over flowers, Georgie, Mary, the Heywood Amateur Operatic and Dramatic Society, anything they could think of. It had been a long and dull dispute which had ended in a truce over two empty bottles of cheap whisky and had led seamlessly into a disquisition from Preston on the myth of still-growing hair and toenails and the business case for cross-selling flowers along with coffins and urns.

The night drifted away as the three of them sat up watching television. The two men began to enjoy chiding one another. Brian asked how often people died in Heywood and Middleton and, every five minutes, uttered, 'There goes another one, get your coat Trouser,' pointing Preston to the door. Preston responded by listing the stages of the area that the brilliant (but somehow unknown) comedian Brian 'Dead' Wood hadn't yet trodden. Preston had asked Brian who the bloody hell he was in any case and Brian had obliged with an autobiography.

He had had retired from the Co-operative Insurance Society, where he had been a health and safety officer, five years before. It was a silly job, he said. What's the worst that could happen

151

to anyone in an insurance office? Trip over a box of claims forms? A nasty paper cut on the end of a finger going gangrenous before Nurse could fix it with the Dettol? Brian's most important duty had been to make people sit properly with backs straight at their desks and to inform them of the dangers of chairs that spin around too quickly. He had yearned for a copy of the Association of British Insurers' book of regulations to fall from a cupboard and lay out an underwriter, just to give him something to do. Brian had always treated his job in the spirit it demanded, which is why he spent fifteen years in a small office, on the tenth floor, smoking a pipe, surrounded by posters small-printed with regulations, looking out on East Manchester's waste. Brian used this long period of paid inactivity to read. He absorbed the public crimes of the efficient state killers and marvelled at the twentieth century's ideological alibis for murder. He immersed himself in the avoidable slaughter of the Great War and shook his head sagely at the cavalier expenditure of life sanctioned by the officer gentry for whom he felt a class antipathy, inculcated by his lifelong activism in the Transport and General Workers' Union. During the time that Brian spent reading history books no mortal disasters, glad to say, befell the clerks of the Co-operative Insurance Society.

On his retirement, Brian had cashed in a life assurance policy. He resolved to spend the proceeds at once on the grounds that it was death, rather than life, which was assured. And there was no point to the policy then. He didn't believe in passing riches down. Then Brian's wife had died and he had, since Christine had gone and David and Lucy had left for college and then new towns of their own, filled his time with voluntary activity at the Blood Donors' Centre in Longsight, in singing tenor parts in the various Salford societies and visiting old ladies on the way round the twist under the auspices of the Florence Nightingale Hospital League of Friends. There was a lot of time in a retired day and Brian declared that he wished to close off every moment. That was why he was now turning his energy to the embroidery stall.

Georgie trooped in and out with cups of tea and echoed her

mother by herself doing the primitive dance of the gas fire: on–off, on–off. Georgie also felt a peculiar and lingering sense of disappointment. Her future had gone grey again. There had been something so decisive in her stipulation that she would take arms against herself. It had seemed so lucid a plan. It had a defined trigger and a ready execution. The only victim of the event would be Preston who, of all people, was schooled in coping. And yet now the moment had arrived and failed, Georgie felt foolishly melodramatic. Histrionics had a sort of desperate comfort. But she wasn't sure she had either the conviction or the courage. It wasn't clear to her whether she was inadequate to follow the histrionic option or whether it was an inadequate response to the world. In either case, the pills behind the frosted glass had lost some of their power. The simplicity and elegance of the solution dissolved into a white terror, a fear not just of the unknown destination but also of the sheer impossibility of dramatic action. Georgie realized how fossilized she had become, where even the escape chute was closed. Whether or not she had ever really gone to the brink that Bobby toppled over, the sense that the pills would never be used drained them of all power. Containing death, they had been a life-force.

When the insults had been exhausted and Preston had laid out his extensive business proposals, they discussed *Oklahoma!* which Olive Platt had chosen to be the next production of the Heywood Amateur Operatic and Dramatic Society. Brian tried to persuade Georgie that she should audition for the part of the state matriarch, Aunt Eller. Preston, naturally, disagreed and started an argument about whether the bereaved are better served by keeping busy or by keeping out of the way. After five minutes of his loquacious meandering, in which all sorts of verbal promises were laid down but not redeemed, Georgie objected to being talked about as if she weren't there.

Oklahoma! had been the first show that Georgie had ever seen at Heywood Civic Hall. Her mother had played Aunt Eller and it was that part that had lured her into amateur show business in the first place. Sitting in the stalls at *Oklahoma!* watching magic cowgirls swish their lassoos had captivated a young Georgie Lees and dropped her into love with musical theatre. So she was overwhelmingly well disposed to the idea to begin with. But there was, more even than this, an evangelical fervour about the way Brian discussed the show that attracted Georgie once again. When Brian sang, in a whisper, 'Oh What a Beautiful Morning', it seemed a lot more than a few hours before that Georgie had been contemplating her tinted bottle.

Summer was giving way to September and Preston was erecting his autumnal freshness. At three o'clock, for an hour and a half, Preston had gone over the road to his allotment. While he was out, Georgie and Brian had switched their drinking back from tea to spirits. Brian had this strange way about him that made Georgie feel he knew more than he should or could. She felt inclined to confess to him and was more indiscreet about the break-up of her marriage than was fair to Preston. Gardening in the dark, she said, was hardly the start of it. As Brian described his children – David, who was an accountant in Huddersfield, and Lucy, who was a nurse in Liverpool – the pair of them slumped on the sofa, inching closer with every glass. Brian extended his arm, in the pretence that he was stretching, and let it rest on top of the sofa, behind but not too close to touching the back of Georgie's head. She leant forward, just to make sure but, as the next glass of mouth-stripping gold liquid settled in, slouched back. Imperceptibly, nervously, their mouths moved closer together but did not touch. They fell asleep in this position, upright with the television on.

Preston woke them when he came back in. He was carrying a bunch of daffodils that he had picked for Mary. Brian had filled forty-four Nightingale Street with flowers and had, unwittingly, started a flower race with Preston. Hostilities had spilled over into the garden. Brian had arranged for the council to send someone to mow the lawn, at which Preston had objected. He had cancelled the municipal gardener but he hadn't got round to the lawn just yet. He kept promising to redo the garden as a memorial to Bobby but he was very busy at work. Georgie protested that no more people were dying in the Middleton area than usual – which was to say everyone

154

– but Preston wearily countered that she did not understand the demographics. Besides, people kept getting in his way just when he was planning to do it.

Georgie tried to be generous: 'Oh Press, they're nice. Are they for mum?'

Preston sniffed the flowers and murmured that they were.

'That's lovely of you. Thank you. She'll love those.'

The brain does not deteriorate at the same rate in all its sensory capacities and those parts responsive to perfume and music decay most reluctantly. Hence, since Brian had started visiting, Bach and Beethoven poured out of every room and flowers of every colour sprouted from vases on all available shelf-space. Preston pressed the daffodils in besides some sorry-looking fuchsias in a thin navy vase on the window sill. The weak light of the coming day was starting to drain the colour from the gauze-thin curtains. Outside, the plaintive aubade of the six-o'clock-in-the-morning birds could be heard. Georgie and Brian drifted away.

Her attention was suddenly taken by the blinking light of the television set which had begun to impart momentous news. She shook her head, to settle her confused senses, not knowing quite where she was at a moment when she would always know where she was. Georgie looked around the familiar room, winced at Brian snoring with his nose thrown back and Preston playing with the curtains, and heard a sliver of startling news. There are so many doors to let out life. Georgie listened for a moment until the news was repeated, until she could convince herself that this was not another dream.

'Press, listen.' She shook Brian. 'Brian, wake up.'

Georgie ran up the stairs to rouse her mother. The label on her bedroom door, 'Mary's room', reminded her of the plaque that she had bought for Bobby in Scarborough once upon a time. Brian had put reminders on every door, labels that said 'spoon' on the spoons and instructions on most of the furniture. It was as if their whole world were a stage on which Mary Lees read out the lines. Georgie shook her mother gently but Mary was dead to the world. She took a minute to come round and a

155

minute again to hear the sentence that Georgie repeated three times until it registered.

'Mum, Lady Di's dead.'

'What? Who?'

'Lady Di. She's been in a car crash. In France.'

Mary rolled out of bed and came downstairs. She concentrated on the news and ignored the presence of two men she did not know in this, a stranger's house.

The coverage unfolded across the news schedules in nothing-more-to-be-said extended editions. On-the-spot commentators struggled to find diction grave enough for their fortune in being there, then. They lapsed into cycles of dead metaphors of dark and night. The pictures were inarticulate too. Only the fact spoke. The fact of death.

Mary got her embroidery bag out of the sideboard and started to sew the nose on a wide-eyed cat. Brian encouraged Mary to sew more and more. As her cognition declined, Mary began to see the world in pictures rather than through language and her facility with a needle and a sewing machine was unimpaired, perhaps even enhanced. Brian's other artistic plans had been less successful. Mary was no oil painter. She wasn't a poet or a sculptor either and the experiment with her banging a drum had ended with Georgie's foot through it.

On screen, the condemned presenters filled out the contentless schedule and reporters on all channels talked to one another out of the cliché book of grandiloquence, adding to and supplementing the vague bulletin-bored obituary. Even Preston, the expert in death, was cowed into wordlessness. Somewhere out of shock, Georgie thought of Bobby. She also thought of the people who would be pained by this. Who among them would be truly pained by this death? Georgie didn't know but, whoever they were, she tried to think of them. She snappily demanded silence whenever Preston or Brian spoke.

Georgie searched for consoling parallels. But the new religion of celebrity, shorn of cosmic explanation, post-mortem destiny or any spiritual controlling hand, has none of the force of its predecessor churches. At crucial moments it is exposed as a shrunken fake. As one star is put out another lights in its place. Even the guiding star burns ephemerally. In the end it is a life which needs to find meaning either in its own terms or with reference to supernatural hopes. When the greater exposure is blackened out it leaves no traces and the martyrs of the new religion for that reason offer no comfort for the likes of Georgie Lees, watching spellbound on television. The only available lesson was to do with the human being on late display. Georgie thought once again that the fact of never being able to foresee the parting was part of the pain. Mary was at least having the good sense to decay in time, to grant her daughter, and all those who cared, the right to visualize the parting. This was the true shock of Diana's death. There had been no premonition, no preparation, no foretaste.

The circular rewording all left the fact essentially unembroidered. At the start of the fifth cycle of speculation, Georgie was shocked by a stranger clicking open the gate on to the allotments opposite. The stranger waved at the four faces who stared so oddly and directly at him. While a handful of private worlds were ending in public view with many million onlookers around the globe, this man, obliviously full of breakfast, began trimming a juniper bush. Mary got up to make tea, bored of the stories about this young woman she didn't know. After another hour of watching the same loop, Georgie went to bed, Brian and Preston began the drift back to their days and Mary got out her hat and coat in preparation for a long day at work.

18
The Last Drop

Brain had an idea for a last day out for Mary. The Last Drop Village. Saturday 6 September 1997. Princess Diana's funeral was being projected on to a big screen as if it were a football match. The Last Drop Village stands on a precipice overlooking Bolton. The car park creeps up one side of the ravine, climbing to the peak of an alarming fall on the other side. Parking in the dark was a perilous business for newcomers. The urban development on the valley's approach disappears out of sight and, behind the Inn itself, the bleakness of the moor is the more frightening for being so sudden. The Last Drop Inn was, Brian grimly joked, the ideal place to watch a funeral.

Brian helped Mary into the back seat and Georgie the front. Preston was working. Some poor nameless soul went on the same day and Preston's duty was to the local dead, not the dead on television. Mary was slipping in and out of being able to recognize Georgie but Brian Wood's almost perpetual presence in the house meant that there was no prospect of Georgie reviving her promise to herself.

On the way from Heywood to Bromley Cross, at the same hour that the funeral cortège was leaving Kensington Palace draped in the royal standard, Brian carefully enumerated Mary's likely regression: normal brain functioning had already given way to moderate cognitive problems and incipient dementia (forgetting to pay bills, domestic administration gone all wrong). Then, the passage that Mary was in: unable to decide what to wear, can't find a way home, cannot distinguish between the hot and cold

158

taps, not being reliable about who people were. But still, in this period, still the patient could have flashes of insight into the condition. The rest, he said, hardly bore thinking about. From then on in, it really was imperative, rather than just for the best, that professional help be on hand.

The course of dementia, Brian explained, is a strange and tragic return to the womb-state in which all the skills that the patient acquired as a baby are lost in exact reverse order to that in which they were acquired, to a timetable so similar that it invites us to imagine that fate is at hand. It is one of nature's cosmic black jokes. Control of the bladder and the bowels is lost, followed by a decline into nonsensical words and sounds presaging a loss of complex language and a final fall into monosyllabic noise until the very last word is lost. If nature really wants a cruel laugh, the first and the last words can be the same. Mobility goes next as the patient loses her facial expressions and the visage hardens into a corpse-like grin. Then the patient loses the ability to walk unsupported and takes to her bed. Special and constant attention is then required until the very final stage. At the very end, the patient assumes a foetal position, clamouring to die as once there was an irresistible pressure to be born. The final erasure could take years but Brian said that Mary was approaching the period in which she would finally fail to recognize anyone around her. Mary countered that Brian and Georgie would never be able to imprison her in their van when she had a pub and a shop to run.

Brian turned into the car park at the Last Drop and pulled up before the precipice. With an hour and ten minutes to go, the bar was nearly full but very quiet. The screen was already in place and a desultory commentary played over the loudspeakers as the first guests arrived at Westminster Abbey. In the Last Drop, people spoke only to order drinks, which were being provided free of charge as a goodwill gesture by the brewery. Towards whom and why was not obvious to Brian or Georgie, who had an incongruously republican discussion as the preamble rolled into the ceremony.

Mary ordered a roast dinner and abused the man behind the

bar when she was told that it was only ten to ten and food didn't start for two hours. Brian fetched two bottles of beer and a pernod and black for Mary. Switching moods as only a memory-trickster is able, Mary found it was very funny, all of a sudden, to say gottle of geer. Brian had reserved good seats, in the seventh row, with a clear view of the huge screen. The cameras were cutting between crowds in Kensington Gardens and reporters still talking, now in front of churches, in Parliament Square, the City and all around the country; trying to picture solidarity. The Last Drop was tense. The only break in the silence was provided by Mary Lees, who repeatedly tried to cajole Brian and Georgie into show songs as she drained her glass and licked the inside, giving her a purple-stained moustache and beard.

By ten-thirty, in anticipation of the arrival of the Spencer family, the journey to construct the community around the country had ended and the cameras had taken root outside Westminster Abbey. At the Last Drop, the chatter ended. So did the levity. As soon as the time was not filled with Brian's views, Georgie felt vulnerable once more. She stared hard at the screen, just as empty as she now ever felt. She knew she was being asked to conjure an emotional response and she knew she would fall short. The junior Windsors arrived at church. The Queen and Prince Philip set off from Buckingham Palace and the royal standard was lowered. Mary was already in tears muttering about the beautiful princess. Georgie had never really understood Mary's deep and uncritical monarchism. Not that she was a republican. She didn't care either way. She thought the Queen was a bit boring and not worth getting upset about. Diana was no different as far as Georgie could see. She had argued with her mother many times, going years back, that Lady Di was a spoilt young woman who hadn't married for the right reasons. Of course, she felt her death was awful, just as the loss of any life cut short is tragic. But she didn't really feel it was any more of a tragedy than that.

This led, of course, to thoughts of Bobby. The vision of her son on her mother's knee in Heywood Civic Hall flashed by.

She flicked her head, as if deterring a fly. Brian caught her eye and smiled solicitously. Gently, he ensured Mary could shuffle a row in front to get a better view. Georgie remained stoical as the newly minted service began. Like all such royal occasions trailing clouds of glory from time immemorial, it had been made up in the week before it happened. The novelty did not matter much to the people watching at the Last Drop. Everyone had come with something to give, something to leave behind. By the first hymn most of the confessors in the Last Drop were sobbing. Mary joined in because the mood was contagious. His wife Christine and his absent children got to Brian and he shed his first tears with the Prime Minister's reading of St Paul's letter to the Corinthians. Georgie offered a hand to Brian but, for her own part, she held on. She thought it was a lovely service. She was deeply affected by Earl Spencer's revenger's tragedy. God granted you half a life, he said. So what fraction was Bobby permitted? A quarter of a half. God granted you – vindictive deity, if at all.

'I would like to end by thanking God for the small mercies he has shown at this dreadful time.'

Small mercies? To think of thanking God for this. No, still the tears, stymied for so long, did not come. Through a glass, darkly.

Georgie was left alone with her own thoughts as, all around her, members of the congregation were alone with theirs. Georgie's dry face and miles-away stare was starting to attract attention when the big risk of the service whispered to her, one of those in pain. From the first plaintive minor key of 'Candle In The Wind' Georgie began to sob. The tawdry unpoetry of the words were given force by the mix with the music. Georgie forgot Diana Spencer. These words were nothing to do with her: empty days, this torch we'll always carry, nation's golden child, the truth brings us to tears, the joy you brought us. But encouraged by Brian and Mary, Georgie joined in the collective, public memorial for private grief. In the background, larger-than-life, Elton John and the body of Princess Diana provided the opportunity for this group of

161

strangers to commune with their own private sorrows and for Georgie Lees to join back in.

Georgie was at last released and she cried in a fury, rubbing her eyes to extract every last drop. When she at last lifted her head to look at Brian she saw that his eyes too were raw with red pain. His eyes had been remembering his wife and his two children who were too far away to be there serendipitously, when it really counted. Huddersfield, where his son lived, and Liverpool, where his daughter lived, both either part of the same speck on the global map or else far too far away, depending on your vantage point. Who knows what will happen and when we are needed? The trick is to be in the right place *all* the time so as to ensure that we are there at the right time. Brian's children came over once a month and this was not one of their scheduled times to visit. Their relations had become the typically silent transactions of welfare; a direct-debit parenting which would be completed with the final will in which Brian had arranged for his assets to be split equally between the two of them. So one of the moments that require us to pin our location for ever in our memories passed without them. Propinquity and losses of emotional memory are the price we pay for mobility. In this room, strangers were brought briefly together which only went further to expose their habitually silent relations. The service ended with a minute's silence. Brian held Georgie close as they moved a small step further on towards mastering their own lives. Many miles away, the coffin left on its journey to rest at Althorp.

19
The Pimpernel and Shepherd's Purse

There was no sign, no trace of Preston Burns. The aphides and tangled briars on the allotment, the sucking pests and wire-worms were allowed to flourish unfumigated or sterilized. The consumers of foliage ate happily without tasting poison. The pimpernel and shepherd's purse seeded in shallow ground, unhoed and unpulled by hand. Further down, deep bindweed took root, bracken crouched and twitched with ground elders and the family of dead nettles stretched into unattended space. At Preston Burns Undertakers, Gundappa and Lucy opened up, the postman called every day to drop more junk and bills through the mouth of the door and the phone rang and rang to announce another dust-biter. But there was no sign, no trace of Preston Burns.

Rumours were passed round the market about what had happened to Preston: he had run off to a woman, he had been abducted, he had become sick with death and left town, he had sold out to the multinational combine and gone on the trip he had always promised himself – to Vārānasi, the holy Indian city of the dead. He had been consumed with envy after a defeat in affection. But whatever the genuine cause of his flight, it was agreed that Preston had disappeared off the face of the earth and that his absence must have been the culmination of a plan. Preston liked to prepare his spontaneity in advance. It came without irony, with lots of exclamation marks. Let's have fun!!! Come on, join in, don't be a spoilsport.

But nobody actually knew where Preston had gone and,

163

whether or not he has any close friends, an undertaker is very soon missed. We hear tales of people whom the undertaker has failed to collect, lying among sewage and the carcases of rotten animals for weeks on end, but none of them is ever a funeral director. An undertaker has a renewable supply of acquaintances and the raw chimes of the telephone in the funeral parlour did not stop because Preston was not there to answer them. Gundappa and Lucy held up the service as best they could. But Preston had neglected to secure the succession. He had always assumed that Bobby would grow into the role. He had never offered anything beyond the most rudimentary instruction to his assistants. Gundappa and Lucy stalled and procrastinated but the dying can be made to hang on only for so long. The people of Heywood and Middleton carried on with their ordinary deaths even though Preston Burns had turned his back on them.

Three days earlier, Preston had risen for work as he did, a clock-stickler, at the same time every morning. From then on, his routine had varied. He had spoken to Georgie, for a start. He had gone into her room, woken her and shocked the life out of her with the announcement that he was going to file for divorce. Georgie was groggy from a brewing hangover and asked him to repeat what he had just said. He duly did, adding that he trusted his application would not be resisted, and then left for work. In the hour that he had before Gundappa and Lucy arrived, Preston neatly finished off the accounts that he had been preparing the previous night. He tidied up the back room of the parlour, which he had been allowing to clog up with baubles, and ran round with an air freshener, long overdue. He recorded a new message on his answerphone and wrote a note of apology to bereaved of Burnley whose mother he had promised to collect that morning. When Gundappa and Lucy arrived, Preston announced grandly that he was relieving them of all duties. He gave them an envelope each but refused all requests for more information and left before they could wheedle anything from him.

Preston sparked up the lead hearse and drove it very fast to the allotments in Nightingale Street. He parked, ran into his shed and came out with a rake. Preston dug its jagged edge into the regimental dahlias and rejoiced in the decapitation. When the peonies and delphiniums were littered with petals Preston extended the killing. He scythed without discrimination through hyacinths and narcissi, cutting off the hollyhocks, destroying with a passion the oriental poppies. In two minutes of wanton flagellation the exotic garden that had taken years of expertise and tending to produce had been obliterated. The *rosa rugosa*, the cultivars, the Chinese lanterns, he spared none of them. Preston replaced the rake and trampled the dead flowers underfoot, to hasten their return to the ground. Preston walked through the trees. He aimed a forlorn kick at a maple leaf and decided the trees would have to stand. He had a saw but it wasn't up to the job. The oak had an adamantine quality, a permanence about it that Preston was forced to respect. He took out this frustration on the ephemera: the sweet peas, the carrots and the spring onions which he kicked out of the ground and threw across the vacant dirt, some on to the perimeter fence, some beyond it on to somebody else's dandelions and some into the air where they were caught on the branches of the prunifolia and the Katsura.

Preston then calmly got back into the hearse and drove slowly round the streets of Middleton for an hour, at his professional, funereal, pace. And then he had driven off the slip road. On to the express way, over the hill and far away, picking up pace with every yard.

That same lunchtime, Georgie had lumbered out of bed with the intention of putting in an afternoon on the market. She had, as usual, missed the best of her trade. The stall was barely functioning. Deeply in the red, Georgie was now losing money as she lay on the sofa anaesthetizing her hangover with chicory. She got up and left the house at Mary's bidding. Georgie had the uncharitable thought that a place in Woodhall could not come up for grabs too soon. This was, in other words, a death-wish. Woodhall was full and so, like a car park, they had a one-out, one-in policy. Georgie opened the gate at the front of the house and looked up at the allotment. Out of habit, her eyes then wandered down to the ground in front of her. In a strange physical echo of her mood, Georgie had taken to walking with a stoop. She looked up again at once. The allotment! What on earth . . . ? What had happened there? From the other side of the road Georgie could get only a hint of the flattening and devastation that Preston had left behind. She ran across to check it up close. The vegetables had been bludgeoned. She found spring onions and carrot plants hanging like dead skin from the branches of a tree. Georgie ran on, through the border of the Japanese azaleas. The flowers had been bludgeoned too. Even standing over the dead blooms Georgie could not believe the philistinism of the act. Who would be so immune to beauty as to shatter all this joyful tending? She ran through the long grass, jumped over a barbed-wire fence on to another patch to find someone, anyone. There was nobody nearby. Three old gentlemen she recognized but did not know came back to Preston's allotment to look. They had seen nothing.

Georgie hurried back inside to call Preston. His mobile was switched off, which was unusual. Preston was always on call. She left a message. Georgie rang the office. Even more oddly, the call clicked straight through to the answering machine. Georgie heard Preston's voice and decided to leave another message. The litany of prices and services went on and on: 'Hello, this is Preston Burns Undertakers. We are a licensed member of the NAFD and subscribe to the NAFD/OFT Code. There is nobody available to take your call at the moment. We offer a full range of undertaking services. If you are a DSS applicant, and that refers to you rather than the deceased, press one.'

Georgie had been only half listening. She had been preparing what she would say, impatiently waiting for the beep. Preston had changed his message. He hadn't mentioned a new phone system.

'If you are a private client wishing for a tailored pre-care service press two. For a full funeral service including embalming and bereavement assistance press three. For our usual range of mortician services please hold for a funeral parlour service operative.'

Georgie held her phone to her ear. This was going on longer than usual.

'Our direct transfer service including mortuary provision, coffin supply and transfer to place of rest is available at £290 plus disimbursements. A basic funeral, in accordance with the NAFD Code of Practice including limited pre-care and provision of a hearse is available at £695 plus disimbursements.'

There was a pause.

'And if you wish to speak to a human voice you've called the wrong bloody place.'

Georgie looked at her telephone in amazement. She had to run through the whole message again to check that Preston had really put that on his answerphone.

Georgie went straight to the funeral parlour. She rapped hard on the door but the lights were off and there was no response. She called on the two shops on either side. Mr Greaves the newsagent had not seen Preston that morning, which, now he came to think of it, was a bit unusual. Mr Singh who ran the dry-cleaning business hadn't seen Preston that morning either. Georgie inquired in every unit in the parade: the baker, the shoe shop, the grubby café where Preston often had his lunch, the insurance broker and the solicitor, none of whom had seen Preston. Now they came to think of it.

Georgie went back home. Maybe he was out at a job. It was unusual that the shop should be shut. But perhaps all three of them had been required. Perhaps he was officiating at a ceremony. He hadn't said. He always said. Georgie rang the mobile and the landline again. Both clicked straight to the answerphone. She tried to find a number for Preston's assistants but failed. She left four more messages on each machine and then began seriously to suppose that something was wrong. Preston had, of course, come into her room that morning to declare that he wanted a divorce. Georgie hadn't forgotten but it had taken her a while to remember. It made sense to her. She called the crematorium, the other funeral directors in the area, the workshop that Preston ordered his coffins from, the whole-salers of urns and funeral paraphernalia, the officers in the

167

local authorities with whom Preston negotiated the registration of new deaths. Any or all of these people might have seen or heard from Preston this morning. None had. The registrar of deaths claimed not to know one funeral director from another, the wholesalers said they had received no contact from Preston for a day or two but that was not so unusual. He tended to buy in bulk on a monthly basis. The woman at the crematorium had not seen or heard from Preston for a week. So much for him attending a service. So where were Gundappa and the other one whose name she had forgotten, whose current sex she had forgotten? Two of the three funeral directors that Brian found in the Yellow Pages were closed. The third was out too but his boyfriend was able to confirm that something was definitely amiss. He had spoken to his partner the undertaker an hour before. He, the undertaker, was at a National Association of Funeral Directors' conference on *The Modern Pre-care Experience* in the Russell Hotel in Bloomsbury in London. Apparently, everyone who was everyone in undertaking was there. That explained the peculiar absence of funeral directors in the Heywood vicinity. Perhaps the collective pronoun was a dearth of undertakers. Preston, though, had not shown up to deliver his paper ('Corporate Social Responsibility and the Bereaved') in that morning's session. Preston had never mentioned any such conference.

Georgie walked back to the funeral parlour and did something she had never done before, which was to break a window. When the brick hit the glass it set off an alarm that brought the newsagent, the dry cleaner, the baker, the cobbler, the grubby café cook, the insurance broker and the solicitor out on to the parade. Georgie allowed the shards of glass to settle and pushed in the hanging edges. She threaded her arm carefully through the gap and opened the door. Mr Singh came in behind her and, to the great relief of the commercial gathering on the parade, worked out how to turn off the alarm.

Inside Preston Burns Undertakers, things were arranged much as they ever were. Georgie had not been back since . . . She ran round quickly, looking for any obvious clues. But there were no notes. That too was just too reminiscent . . . She thought of Bobby's grave at the crematorium. Perhaps he was there. She hadn't been yet. On the desk she found Preston's diary. He had begun his entries the day of Bobby's funeral. He hadn't mentioned it. Preston's entry for that day said that it had rained. Every day since he had recorded the weather, occasionally attaching a remark on the state of his allotment. Georgie suddenly felt overwhelmingly sad for Preston. Preston Burns had had a lot of trouble in his life, most of which had never happened. She was married to him. She must have seen the good in him once upon a time. It took another moment of pity like this for her to see it again. And, besides, she felt responsible. She added Preston's apparent disappearance to the list of things for which she felt responsible. Georgie left. There was neither sign nor trace of Preston here. She realized that if Preston had made any provision for the business the solicitors and accountants would know about it. She called them. Apparently not. And then, finally, when she got home, there was a call from Gundappa who had come back into the shop and picked up her seven messages. He told Georgie that Preston had dismissed his staff that morning, paid a month's notice and told them he was going on holiday, indefinitely. He had refused to say where.

20
The Brian Box

With a whimper, indeed, Mary Lees left forty-four Nightingale Street for a new home. She was so tenaciously attached to the idea that she lived in the White Horse Inn that a move from Nightingale Street to Woodhall sheltered accommodation swapped one irrelevant location for another. Brian had taken care of all the arrangements and a place was now free. On the morning of the departure, Georgie came downstairs at seven-thirty to find Mary sitting by the fire, as always. The skin on her shin was hot, raw, crackling and cracking.

At eight o'clock Brian arrived and wasted no time: 'Mary, come on love, we have to go.'

'Where to, love?'

'We're going up to Woodhall. In the van.'

'What van?' asked Georgie.

In the midst of Georgie's confusion about her business, Brian had taken a risk. When he had mentioned the idea of expanding the stall (a peculiar notion, thought Georgie, given that the one she had was going out of business), he had taken Georgie's expression of dreamlike interest as permission. He had arranged for the bond to be paid to the administrators in Bury, Oldham and Cheetham Hill. He had then bought an old van and had it engraved with the name of the newly christened embroidery business. Brian thought it was too early to put Bobby Dazzler's on the van. He wanted to keep that name for a shop, which was his next move. He hadn't told Georgie any of this but he had turned up to take

Mary to Woodhall in the new van. It was sitting outside, ready to go.

Brian collected Mary's bags and belongings and put them on the front of the seat. He came in and out of the house, carrying lampstands, chairs, crockery, cutlery, tables and cushions. They were going to furnish a flat that Georgie had rented in the centre of Rochdale. The house was stripped clean when Brian had finished. It was on the market, in the process of being sold. A newly wed couple were very interested. They were coming round that evening for a third viewing. Georgie had hoped to keep the house. It had never occurred to her that she would be made homeless by her mother going into care. But Brian had explained that the costs of Mary's care had to be met, down to a residue of £16,000, by the proceeds from the sale of her home. This was less of a wrench now that Mary had never heard of Nightingale Street. It was irretrievably hidden in the recesses of memory, the forty-four years of residence usurped by an earlier, more formative home at the White Horse Inn. The first sight of the 'For Sale' sign in the front garden touched Georgie as she looked out of the window at her old street. So much of her life had taken place in this little street yet she felt glad to be moving on and out. It had been her childhood bolt-hole and, then again, her refuge after Bobby. For that very reason, she did not feel any great sorrow. She was selling the family heritage but the family had all gone so it didn't matter. Georgie wondered to herself what she would miss about Nightingale Street and struggled to care too much about anything. It had all changed for her. The allotment, the view of the gardens, the vegetables and the flowers: she would take that as an abiding memory. Once Brian had finished his removals, Georgie closed the door gently behind them and Mary Lees left forty-four Nightingale Street for good.

When Georgie brought Mary out she was puzzled by Brian standing so erect and proud by the side of his van. Then she noticed that he had draped a white sheet over its back so that the ungrammatical engraving was invisible.

'Now then, I hope you won't take this the wrong way but

171

you said I could help on the stall and I said I might be able to get my hands on an old van from the Blood Donors' Centre. Well I've got one and I've had it engraved. It didn't cost much so it doesn't matter if you don't like it.'

Brian made Georgie stand back and then pulled the cloth away to declare their van open. Georgie stared at the inscription and, for a moment, Brian thought she was annoyed. Then she broke out into hysterical laughter.

'What? What's the matter? Why are you laughing?'

Brian had been trying to make Georgie laugh all the time he had known her. She had been like the princess who sits straight-faced while the succession of jesters try their damnedest. Now he had become Taper-Tom, the fool who succeeded in cracking her up, but he had no idea how or why.

'Look at that.' Georgie pointed to the inscription on the van.

Brian read it out loud: 'Mary Lees and Daughter. Fine Embroidery for All Occasions. Contact Brian Wood, oh seven oh six, eight oh nine four one four. There's nothing funny about that. It looks great.'

'No, it doesn't. Read it properly. Look at it closely. Go on, read it out loud, slowly.'

'Mary Lees and Daughter. Fine Embroidery for All Occasions. Contact Brian Wood . . .'

'No, stop, How do you spell Brian? B-r-i . . .'

'Oh bloody hell. Bloody hell. I can't believe that. Jesus bloody Christ.'

Brian looked at the inscription, which spelled out to the world that interested parties should contact some odd character called Brain Wood.

'Whoever did that must have been a right brianless idiot,' said Georgie, immensely pleased with herself for the joke.

'Bloody hell, look at that. What a bloody idiot. Sorry love, I'll have to take it back and get it re-done.'

'No, don't. Leave it. I like it. You're a right brian box, you are.'

Brian squeezed the end of Georgie's nose and mock-chased her into the passenger seat. She said skittishly that no self-respecting woman would want to be taken out in a badly spelled embroidery van.

'Right then Mary Lees, get in this van and we'll take you for the drive of your life.'

As he tried to start the unreliable engine, Brian declared that the van would now be known as the Brian Box. Georgie told him that he obviously needed brian surgery and, warming to the technique, asked him a series of brian teasers and declared that any time he lost his temper would henceforth be known as a Brian storm. She also searched through her head for famous Brians: Brain Blessed, Brain Clough, Brain Rix, Brain Cant. It was a real brian dump. Brian almost got annoyed. He very nearly had a brian storm.

Mary said nothing as they drove over Ashworth Moor, where the wind has space to run free, buttressed only by a pub, a restaurant and an outhouse on the edge of the reservoir. She still said nothing, and neither did Georgie who was wondering where Preston could be. It beat wondering where Bobby could be. Just. Brian began to whistle nervously as he dropped down the hill into Turn village.

Mary recognized the tune and shouted out that it was a beautiful morning, when everything was suddenly going her way.

'That's *Oklahoma*.'

'I know. We're doing it next at the Civic Hall.'

'I've done that one. I should come down and show you how it's done. I can still do it you know.'

'I'm sure you can. Why don't you do it for these old folks we're going to see. They put on shows.'

'I might do. I was Dolly in *Hello, Dolly!* you know at Heywood.'

'She never was,' interrupted Georgie.

'I bet you were like Betty Grable.'

Georgie thought sadly about Preston as Brian and Mary argued amicably over whether it was Betty Grable or Ethel Merman who once caused a stir as Dolly by flashing her legs in the dance routine.

Brian pulled into the long, immaculate gravel drive that led up to Woodhall residential home. The small white stones on the path were neatly combed into place. Through the long sitting room window, the residents could be seen, sitting in a single row, facing the window, as if two park benches had been knitted together.

Mary laughed as they pulled up. 'Look at them old buggers. Look half dead most of them.'

'They do a mean *Hello, Dolly!* though Mary,' grinned Brian. 'You should see the dancing.'

There was nobody to greet them. Brian led Georgie and Mary down the broad corridor, past square sitting rooms that smelt of old people and toilets that smelt of worse. The smell of over-boiled potatoes, cabbage, peas, carrots and green beans wafted on the air from the mass-producing kitchens opposite. The food in Woodhall had a smell all of its own, quite unlike any foodstuff in particular, the unappetizing smell of food in general. Brian whispered to Georgie that he would have to change some of this. He had been reading about a new technique called Snoezelen, derived from the Dutch for sniffing and dozing, which would improve the smell here, if nothing else. It involved different-coloured lightbulbs, vibrating cushions, armchairs in unconventional shapes, a soap bubble machine and pleasant smells. Georgie murmured in return, not very interested in Dutch sniffing and dozing techniques.

A tiny woman dressed head to foot in blue – cap to pumps – came out of the long sitting room to meet them. She introduced herself as Mrs Kavanagh. She said she was in charge.

'You must be Mary, is that right?'

'She's come to teach the old folk some singing,' said Brian.

'Sorry?'

'She's come to teach them how to sing. And to do some sewing. Mary's a brilliant embroiderer, aren't you Mary?'

'I can talk for myself you know.'

'Well, I'm glad to see you Mary. They could do with a good sing-song in there. There's some of them don't get too many visitors and they could do with cheering up.'

174

Mrs Kavanagh pointed to the women residents who were sitting in a line along the back wall of the narrow sitting room, staring at but not watching the ITV local news which shouted at life-threatening volume from the vast television. All of them, she went on to Brian and Georgie and, ostensibly, to Mary, were declining physically and plenty were on the way down mentally too. Most of those who did receive visitors didn't actually recognize them so tended to complain that nobody came to see them either.

'Is it all women here?' asked Georgie.

Mrs Kavanagh replied that there was a small group of male residents who, on the face of it, had nothing wrong with them at all and who claimed to like living there because it kept their wives out of their hair. In fact, none of them had wives. The men were all out with a volunteer, watching a football match at a park nearby.

'Do you always laugh at the patients you have?' asked Georgie.

'I do,' said Mrs Kavanagh unflinchingly. 'It keeps me sane.'

Mary wandered into the sitting room, where she was greeted by a tiny woman with a receding hairline and a fuzzy purple Afro.

'Hello love. I haven't seen you for ages. How nice to see you.'

In fact, they had never met. Mary did not respond.

'Would you like a drink love?'

Mrs Kavanagh explained that Doris, the purple woman, ran a pub.

Mary turned to Doris and smiled. 'Which pub is it love? I live in the White Horse.'

'The Rose and Crown. Up Milnrow way.'

'Oh lovely.'

Mary turned to Georgie and made the sign at her temples to indicate that Doris was evidently round the twist.

Doris noticed that Mary had company. 'Oh look love, we've got some customers. Can I get you two anything to drink? We've got all sorts.'

'A cup of tea'd be nice,' suggested Georgie, humouring her, as Brian had taught her to do.

'Oh we don't really do tea love. But seeing as it's you love . . .'

There was no telling who Doris thought Georgie was. Doris didn't know and so who did?

'I'll just go and have a look in the back.'

'I'll just go and help this young woman. I won't be long,' said Mary.

Mrs Kavanagh made Brian and Georgie a cup of tea and took them on a tour of the home, to show them Mary's room.

Mary decided that she would care for these poor abandoned old ladies in the sitting room. In the far corner she saw an old woman bent double over a piece of cloth. The lady took a needle from a leather sachet and started to slide it tentatively in and out of a tapestry of indistinct, poorly drawn white flowers. Mary strode over and took charge. By the time Brian and Georgie had returned from their tour with the blue lady, Mary was sitting on the floor of the sitting room, Buddha-legged and supple as a young woman, at the centre of an imperfect circle of sewers. The television had been turned off and all the women were gathered round on the floor watching eagerly as Mary was telling them how to make best use of the embroidery equipment that she had found in a box on the table in the corner. Every woman was holding a small piece of fabric, a needle and a thread. Mary began to berate them to sew faster as if they were all on exercise bikes rather than copying a pattern from *Silk Shading for Beginners* which she had found among the Catherine Cooksons and Barbara Cartlands and Mills and Boons on the bookshelf and recognized by its cover. Mrs Kavanagh's mother had been a supervisor in Heywood Mill and, when she had died, her library of volumes on practical ribboncraft had been her legacy to her daughter. Until Mary Lees joined the company the books had sat unopened on the shelves. Mary issued orders to ladies whose names she did not yet know and would soon forget, to fold open books of patterns. Mary conducted, arms in flight, as, all around her, the women of Woodhall wove colours into their fabric with new confidence.

Brian suddenly saw Mary's dream come true. Here was the road connecting 'Tommy's' and the itinerant 'Tommy's II' to Bobby Dazzler's and the shop in the parade.

He whispered to Georgie, 'That's it. Look at them. That's our Singapore.'

Here was the army of sewers he had talked about. Here were ten women with nothing to do, all day to do it in, and a collection of embroidery manuals to read. A free source of embroidery and the supply chain for the shop. Georgie looked at Brian as if he was as mad as they were. He called out Mary's name and waved to say goodbye.

Mary addressed her new team: 'Who's that young man? Is he your friend, Doris?'

'That's right. It's my daughter, Fred,' said Doris, with complete certainty. She went on: 'He's a brain surgeon is my Fred. Works for the army, mending broken heads. You'll meet his father, Eric. He lives in Stockport. If you go to Stockport you'll see him.'

'Just get on, Doris, will you love?' said Mary, who had got her new friend's number.

'I'll get everyone a drink,' returned Doris.

When Georgie got up to go Mary stopped her. 'You are coming back aren't you?

'Of course I am you silly.'

'When you come back will you bring your lad with you?'

Georgie did not know how to begin to explain. She could not face the prospect of reliving Bobby's death every time her mother asked. She chose to lie to be kinder to both of them. Mary told the story to her new friends, for her own benefit, of the time that Bobby, five years old at the time, sang 'Away in a Manger' on the settee in Nightingale Street after he had interrupted a party after the Christmas Eve mass. Georgie hugged her mother and agreed to pass on her love to young Bobby.

Mary had one final appeal before letting Georgie go: 'You won't leave me Georgie will you? Not before I've finished this dress for you.'

Mary looked into her embroidery box. She pulled out a

dress-in-progress that she was making for Georgie. It was for a small child. Georgie kissed Mary on the forehead and, with all her restraint, prevented herself from packing Mary's bag to go home. As Brian and Georgie jogged down the smelly corridor, Doris reappeared and called after them with two glasses of shampoo on the rocks.

Brian took Georgie back to Nightingale Street in the Brain Box to meet the couple who were to view it for the third time. He said goodbye on the doorstep and she let herself in. She had five minutes before the estate agent was due with the young couple. The nature of the area was changing. Young people were moving into Nightingale Street. It occurred to Georgie that this was what had happened in the mid-1950s when Mary and Jack had moved in here. She calculated that her dad must have been thirty-five when he had bought this house. In her lifetime, of course, it had always been home to people older than her, which is always the definition of old. But now Nightingale Street was growing afresh. Next door but one had sold up and moved in with their son and his children, at the bottom of their large garden on the Wirral, in a granny and granddad flat. Their place had been taken by a young family with two babies. Already, the trellis and the wooden window frames had been painted and the brickwork repaired. New flowers sprouted in the garden and crazy paving was laid leading round to the back.

Georgie walked through each room in turn, taking in the sounds and sights of the recent and diminishing past: in the kitchen the whistling kettle that Mary had refused to replace and which had outlasted either of them, in the back room the sense that the green shoots were climbing the walls outside through neglect. Now they peered, untended and unopposed, above the height of the window ledge. Jack's garden – it had always stayed Jack's garden – was a blaze of green shades, flowerless and a mess, a memorial to a lengthy abandonment. The back room had always been the living room and the view into the garden had luxuriated on the eye like paradise. Mary had stuttered into the front room where she had lived for her final months in the house because the angry gas fire was easier to manipulate than the coal fire in the back. Georgie turned the dial for old times' sake and the blast threatened to blow away the streets, as it always did. The survey on the house had identified the gas fire as a hazard to be removed at the first opportunity. It was a death-trap.

The doorbell rang and Georgie let the interested couple in through the front door that her parents had never used because it had stuck in the frame at some point in the late 1960s. Perhaps these new people would use the front door all the time. The estate agent, Tony, introduced the unfriendly new couple as Russell and Sandra. As they walked round the house Georgie shadowed them, eavesdropping on their conversation: 'That wallpaper will have to go. What were they thinking at with that stuff? Jesus, God.' That was Georgie's mum they were talking about. Russell and Sandra went into the bathroom. Georgie had emptied out all the cupboards, taken the toothbrush from the glass, taken away all the towels and plastic floor mats and removed the fluffy warmer that had cuddled the toilet for all her life. The only item that remained in the stripped bathroom was the picture of the harbour at Valletta that had always hung there even though nobody in the Lees family had ever been to Malta or even expressed a desire to go there. Russell picked it up off the wall. The white cord snagged on the nail, dislodging a sliver of plaster.

'I've been there. It looks nothing like that.'

Georgie pushed past and took the picture from this invader's hands. 'That's mine. Get your hands off.'

She pushed Russell back against the wall. She felt that people had invaded her house and were trying to steal her pictures.

Georgie followed them round, explaining why it was a lovely house. She felt very loyal to it though it looked very sorry and so much less deserving of her affection without Mary and her artefacts, her embroidery equipment and her colour-clashing furniture. There was one remaining item that caught Georgie's attention. Above the refrigerator, a small bottle of pills winked expectantly from behind the frosted glass cupboard. Georgie took the bottle out and popped it into her handbag.

She left the house clutching her sketch of Valletta and without saying goodbye to the new people whose offer of the asking price she had promptly accepted. Forty-four Nightingale Street was their house now and they could choose to embroider it as they wished. Georgie closed the back door quietly so as not to disturb them. She skipped across the road to the allotments which, Preston's wasteland apart, looked uncommonly adorable in the pale sunshine. The vegetable plots and unsightly functional goods, the produce that sustained life, had been pushed backwards. They were behind a wall comprised of the art of nature, the pointless, unnecessary, flowering beauty of inedible life. It looked as if it had been put there just for Georgie's delectation. The provenance of the art mattered so much less than the fact that it was there. It had been grown in serried layers and the natural heights of the flowers gave an effect as if the terrace had been purpose-built. At the bottom: low blue phacelias, violet larkspur and eschscholtzias aflame in yellow and tangerine. Behind them, lemon marigolds, candytuft and godetia and clarkia in pinks and mauves of medium height. In the top now, a deciduous tree stretched its branch arms in a motherly cuddle around the whole lot. From the side of the picture Georgie picked out a scarlet flax and a white love-in-the-mist. Meantime, the birds in the trees chatted in groups about the mess that Graham Collins, on behalf of Preston Burns, was making of his sweet peas. All the sounds of the earth were like music.

21
My Honey Lamb And I

It was dark by the time Brian and Georgie came out of their rehearsal for *Oklahoma!*. Brian offered to drive Georgie back to Rochdale but, when he should have turned down the dip in the hill past Nightingale Street and beyond, he carried on instead, along the bottom road towards Bury.

'It's down there Brian.'

'I know where it is. I'm not taking you home just yet. We're going for a drive. There's something I want to show you.'

'What is it?'

'And something I want to tell you.'

'What?'

Brian concentrated on the road. He headed through Heywood town centre and turned left on to the approach road to the Pilsworth industrial estate. He went past the factories and warehouses without telling Georgie where he was going. She assumed he was heading for the George, the one pub up here. But when he turned away from the George towards the multiplex cinema and fast-food joints, she thought again. Maybe they were going to the pictures. But no, they were not going to the pictures, which much was obvious as Brian drove by, out beyond the middle of the old industrial estate, towards the vacant lot where a pub once blew up on the Bury Road to Manchester. Or the Manchester road to Bury, as Brian described it. He had a very different view of the world sometimes.

That much was evident by the fact that Brian had turned down the lead role, Curly, in Olive Platt's *Oklahoma!* in favour of playing the violent, dispensed-with farmhand, Jud Fry. Jud Fry is horribly used by Laurey, the female lead (played with too much fake sex by Angie Rowles). Laurey has seen Curly (Colin Smethurst, back from his hit-and-run affair) talking to another woman and therefore agrees to go to the box social with Jud instead. She regrets her decision at once and Curly warns Jud to stay away, suggesting, into the bargain, that he might as well hang himself. Jud threatens Curly with violence in return. He purchases a telescope with a concealed knife which he all but persuades Curly to look into. At a shivaree for the inevitable marriage of Curly and Laurey, Jud turns up drunk and uninvited. In his struggle with Curly he falls on to his own knife. Aunt Eller, the matriarch of Oklahoma, insists, against the advice and authority of the sheriff, that a trial be held at once. The kangaroo court duly acquits Curly of murder and the death of Jud is promptly forgotten as the whole cast minus the farmhand sing and dance the finale. Brian and Georgie (Aunt Eller) had just played this scene at their rehearsal.

'He's a nasty piece of work is Jud. I don't know why you wanted to do it Brian; it's a rotten part.'

'It's not a rotten part. He's a misunderstood character.'

'Is he 'eck misunderstood. He tries to get the pretty girl, she doesn't want him so he comes looking for her fella with a knife.'

'No, that's not what happens. Curly stabs him and he gets off without a fair hearing.'

'It's an accident. Jud stabs himself while they're scrapping.'

'Does he? It's a bit convenient that isn't it?'

'He's only a farm labourer,' said Georgie.

'So what? So does that mean he's not worth as much as Curly?'

'Do you know that song that Curly sings about Jud? That's just plain nasty. Treating the rats like equals, which is right. That's what it says. You shouldn't treat anyone like they're a rat, no matter what they've done. The way they all get together at the end to have a big party just after someone's been killed. It's like you're nothing so why should anyone bother

182

if you're dead. I don't believe that. I think there's some good in everyone.'

Brian paused and prodded Georgie in the stomach.

'What was that for?'

'Because, Aunt Eller, it's you who organizes the whole bloody thing. That's your scene at the end when I get done. Thanks a bloody bundle.'

Brian steered the Brain Box round an acute curve in the valley which gave a view across three uninterrupted miles to Bury. Brian stopped the van and told Georgie they were getting out. She joined him at the side of the road. Down below, in the distance to their right, the cars on the M62 looked like two snakes, one white and one red, coiling in parallel in opposite directions.

Brian cleared his throat ostentatiously and began to sing, holding the first note for as long as he could manage. 'O----------klaheywood, where the wind comes sweeping down the plain and the waving wheat can sure smell sweet when the wind comes right behind the rain.'

'What you doing you, you loony?'

'Come on, join in. O----------klahoma, where the wind comes sweeping down the plain . . .'

'Hang on a minute, hang on a minute,' said Georgie, laughing. 'That's Heywood, not Oklahoma.'

'I can't sing Oklaheywood! It's not right.'

'Anyway, what's this waving wheat you're on about?'

'Look, there it is.'

'That's Asda. Do they have Asda in Oklahoma?'

'No, I meant that yellow stuff over there.'

'Grass, I think it's known as, Brian.'

'Grass is green.'

'Well it's not wheat is it?'

'You can't have everything. We've got plenty of wind sweeping down the plain.'

'That's not good enough. You need some waving wheat.'

'It won't rhyme if I say grass. Can't you just imagine it's waving wheat? You won't find any when we put it on in the Civic Hall either.'

'I'll try. I've never thought of Heywood like that though.'

'Good. Now will you let me finish the song please? I'm just coming to the best bit. O----------klahoma!, every night my honey lamb and I, sit alone and talk and watch a hawk making lazy circles in the sky.'

'Well a bat anyway.'

'Do you mind? I'm trying to build the atmosphere. A bat is our version of a lazy hawk. If Oscar had lived in Heywood he'd have written it different. But he didn't so as far as he's concerned it's a lazy hawk. Got it?'

Georgie nodded.

'Right then. Now altogether.'

Cars almost crashed and dogs ran away as two mad people danced on the spot singing Oklahoma! tranposing in their heads grass for wheat and bats for hawks.

The last notes rang out and Georgie laughed without restraint. Each laugh was precious, as if a magician had rematerialized an object that had vanished a moment before or the sawn-in-half lady had jumped out of the box with her bikini still thankfully in two pieces joined together by bare midriff. Brian and Georgie were briefly in love with their own music.

In the shadow of Georgie's laughter Brian sneaked in a plot point: 'Let's do this again.'

Before she had begun to consider properly, Georgie had agreed. Brian linked arms with her as he pointed out landmarks on the horizon. He had worked up here once, many years before. It had been a terrible job on a production line and he had had to get three buses from his mother's in Worsley. Georgie offered a standard elegy for the loss of the factories at Pilsworth. Brian turned it down at once. He didn't care what was up there, he said. He went there for the view. And the factories were awful anyway. Across the plain, towards Bury and beyond, the street lights blinked and the buildings looked like chessboards, some lights on, some lights off.

Brian started again on Oklahoma!, changing the words this time to try to include the retail park and view of Bury.

Brian improvised in the dark night and Georgie joined in the

184

lyric-writing. As Brian moved towards her, she was jumpy like a schoolgirl waiting for a dance. Brian jumped up and ran off. 'Chase me.'

Georgie gave chase and Brian ran, screaming, down the hill towards the Manchester road. Or the Bury road. He slowed down to let Georgie catch him and stopped suddenly so that she bumped up against his back. Brian seized the chance to take another big risk. He reached out his hand and took Georgie's fingers in his. She did not move either towards him or away. She was in a conventional dither with a conventional star in her eye. Brian swayed forward and swept Georgie up off her feet. His lips made contact with hers and Georgie recalled the long-lost sensation and taste of a man. Georgie felt the tough jaggedness of Brian's speckled skin and stubble. It seemed no more extraordinary a thing to happen than any of the events in this desperate year. But as Brian drew away and kissed Georgie softly on her cheek, it was, to be sure, the nicest physical sensation she had ever felt. Ideas went off in her head like a pub exploding. She pulled him back to her, their four arms rose as one and Brian Wood and Georgie Lees kissed each other greedily on the lips like love's dream. That was what he had wanted to tell her.

22
To Wuthering Heights

The summer smells of the thickets, the wild fruit trees and the white hawthorns fell into autumn. The violets faded and were covered over with leaves. And each Sunday morning Brian and Georgie lived on fast forward on their way to Nelson, to Colne, to Barnoldswick, to Helmshore, to Clitheroe, to Accrington. They went to the end of the land at Southport where they walked miles over sand so they could talk happy and count all the ripples on the sea. They went to another country, fabulously far, and instead of turning back at Todmorden had ventured on to Malham Cove, to Settle, to Rievaulx Abbey. And then to Haworth.

Brian parked the misspelled Brain Box at the foot of the perpendicular main street and pointed vertically upwards. Georgie and he slowly climbed the gradient, resting their hands on their thighs for help. They had a rest, halfway up the hill, in a deserted café. They ordered two plates of pastie and chips and a mug of tea each and, forty minutes later, still hadn't received anything. In due course the owners of the café finished growing the potatoes and served up two vast plates of tasteless, over-fried chips, plonked on top of a cold pastie each. Georgie ordered two more mugs of tea to wash away the taste. They filled in the waiting time by discussing Brian's desire to do a bungee jump. Georgie said she was worried that he might come off the elastic. Brian thought that was half the fun. A bungee jump was like going over to the other side without the horrible consequences.

When they came out of the café to finish the climb up Haworth's hill, the sun had honoured them with its presence. Brian consumed all the plaques and the information in the museum about the sisters whose books he had never read. He made a mental note to borrow *Wuthering Heights*. Reading a summary of the plot in the bookshop he declared that he was Heathcliff. Georgie, whose life had been devoid of romantic heroes except in the fantasies she borrowed in large piles from Heywood library and in the film of the book starring Laurence Olivier, laughed but did not demur. She thought that Brian could be who he wanted to be. Brian and Georgie carried on round the trail laid for tourists, not really knowing what they were looking at.

Georgie left the tourist track to go into the cemetery where Brian delighted her by discovering an Olive Platt on a headstone. Brian touched Georgie's shoulder, jumped up onto a grave and declared: 'Tig, you're on. You can't be caught if you're touching a gravestone. Graves are the den. Tig, you're it.'

Brian put his arms around Olive Platt. To give Georgie a chance he danced over the leaves and branches and the beechen green straw grass to a cluster of plots where he hugged Thomas Potts (1905–1984) for safety. Georgie waddled after him, running for the first time since she had tried to hit Preston with a pan fifteen years before. She chased Brian from Annie Smithills (1887–1973) over Raymond Lynch (1954–1963) to Harriet Jackson (1901–1988) but the gravestones were too crammed together to give her much chance in the game. Georgie was by now panting for breath so she sat down for rest at the feet of Eva Bunyon (1863–1939). Brian came up close, almost within reach. Georgie pretended not to notice him then snapped her arm out in a shot at a tig. But Brian was too quick and he leapt away on to the ornate raised stone under which lay Philip Crouch (1922–1985).

'You're hopeless at tig you are, Georgie Lees. Anyone'd think you've not played for years.'

'You're a bad lad you are, Brian Wood. It's disrespectful running on graves like this.'

'Don't be daft. I don't understand why dancing is such a big insult. I'll be chuffed if people dance on my grave. I'll join in. These people down below won't bother. Here, I'll ask.'

Brian kneeled down and lowered his mouth to the ground. 'Mr Crouch, you don't mind if I have a little bit of fun do you?'

Brian put his ear to the ground. 'Mr Crouch says he doesn't mind at all. It's nice to have company, he says. What was that Mr Crouch? . . . No, don't worry lad, we've not brought him. We don't know where he is if truth be told. We've lost him. You what? . . . no, I don't think so, I don't think he's come to join you just yet.'

'Brian, don't be horrible.'

Brian's routine had a momentum now. 'He bugs us every bit as much, you know. And we're not even dead yet. This poor bugger here's married to him. Imagine that. No sorry, Mr Crouch, that was cruel of me.'

Brian looked to Georgie. 'He's asking whether we've brought that bloody undertaker. He says he was glad to see the back of him. What was that Mr Crouch? . . . Oh, I bet it is. It's dark down there he says and he doesn't get out much these days.'

'Brian, stop it. You shouldn't speak ill of the dead like that.'

'I'm not. I'm treating them like I would if they were alive.'

Georgie relented and sat down on Philip Crouch herself. She looked down at his grave to ask him if he minded and then thought better of it.

'I wonder what he died of this, fella? When did he die?'

Georgie surprised Brian with her knowledge of the historical incidence of diseases. That was the kind of information you had at your fingertips if you married an undertaker with a scholarly interest in his craft. Brian strode away towards the cemetery gates. In front of the railings there was a thick oak.

'Here,' said Brian to Georgie, who had trailed after him, 'look what I've brought.'

He pulled out the many hidden functions and contraptions of his Swiss Army knife. The Swiss Army must have had to open a lot of bottles and carve their names in a lot of trees in the wars they fought. Brian began to carve delicately into the oak's age, ringed in bark. He traced the letters with loving attention, shielding them all the while from Georgie, like a primary pupil adding up sums. She was, in any case, lost in the familiar and yet unusual sounds of the wood. Georgie ran her hands through a flower patch of pansies, violas and saxifrages and walked into the blossom that was picked up by the wind. She squealed in delight at finding a family of snowdrops hiding behind Brian's oak.

After five minutes Brian unveiled his handiwork. 'There you are. Now that's immortality for you.'

He stepped back to reveal that into the tree's bark he had carved a message to all the walkers in the wood from that day on. It read: 'BW and GAL' and underneath the word 'ALWAYS'. The whole adolescent greeting was encased in a wobbly heart.

'What do you think of that then?'

Georgie kissed Brian chastely on the lips. He rudely broke off her embrace, tigged her and ran for dear life until he reached Jill Stone (1857–1900), to whom he clung as if the ground beneath his feet was tipping up. She followed him and, this time, when he jumped down off Jill Stone, Brian did not leap away, even though Nora Freeman (1932–1985) offered an easy safe haven.

'Tig.'

Brian raised an eyebrow and stood still.

'I said tig.'

'I know what you said. I'm not playing tig any more.'

'Oh that's right, change the rules . . .'

Brian took Georgie by the hand. He looked into her tawny eyes but then looked down at once. 'Georgie.'

'Yes?'

Even this moment's hesitation was enough to show that Brian was uncharacteristically reticent.

'What is it?'

'I have to tell you something. I should have told you before but there's never a moment that's right. If we're to, you know, step out together, you know.'

'What's the matter Brian?'

189

He fiddled with a twig that he found fascinating on the floor beneath his feet.

'You don't have to tell me if you don't want.'

'No, I do. I need to. At some point I would have to tell you so I might as well do it now.'

'Brian, what is it?'

Brian held Georgie with outstretched arms on both shoulders. 'There's something very important I have to tell you. I hope I'm not assuming anything and it might be that we stop going out together after the next time so maybe there's no need to say a word but . . .'

'Come on, you're sounding like Press now.'

'This is deadly serious Georgie. I've got to tell you Georgie that if we do start seeing more of each other like I hope we will, there's something you need to know.'

Brian's final six words were spoken in a softer voice than the rest of his spluttering speech.

'Nobody knows what I'm about to tell you except my two kids so please keep it to yourself. About three months ago I had a funny turn, nothing serious but I had to have the doctor out and he sent me along to the hospital to have it checked out properly. Well, to cut a long story short, they discovered that I had this condition. It's a blood disorder and I don't know much about it. I don't want to know about it but it means, when you boil it down, I don't know how much longer I've got.'

There was a silence like death itself.

'Brian . . . I don't know what to say.'

'There's not a lot you can say really. Look at this. This is what you can say.'

Brian led Georgie over to the view over the valley. 'Look at that view. It's spectacular. And it won't be there for long. It'll have gone soon so you have to enjoy it while you can.'

'Why have you not said anything about this before?'

'I don't like to.'

'Is that why you do so much?'

'Partly. But it's because I want to and I've got time to. Like most people, I got caught up in life, doing what you do on a daily basis, keeping insurance clerks safe and healthy and I never really had the time to stop and look at things. But I do now. And there's still things to do, you see. You know that road we've just come up? I remember when I was a lad I used to wonder where that road went. My granddad lived in Hebden Bridge then. I could see it disappearing out of the town up towards Haworth, well it looked like the moors to me, I didn't know what was there and I could never imagine going there. We didn't have a car and I wasn't up here very often anyway. And so when I got a car the first thing I did was to drive up through Hebden Bridge and out the other side to see where that bloody road went. And it came here and it's beautiful. But when I'd done it I was disappointed because I'd spoiled the excitement of not knowing where it went. I thought I'd never have the joy of finding out where the road went again. It is beautiful up here but I'll never not know the way again and it'll never be quite as enthralling as that first time. Do you know what I mean?'

Georgie didn't really but it sounded very exciting the way Brian talked about it. 'I can't believe this . . .'

'Look, don't get me wrong. I'm not about to pop it straight away. I could have ages left yet. And, anyway, a day's a long time if you use it right. And that's why I love the voluntary work and why I love being on the market. It's why I've been doing so much with you. Didn't you wonder what I was up to? Didn't it seem a bit funny? You never said anything but I thought you must have wondered.'

'To be honest Brian, nothing has happened this year that hasn't been funny.'

'I can feel the time disappearing, you know. It doesn't half concentrate the mind doesn't the thought of dying. It makes you cram in as much as you can. I'm even selling bloody cats knitted on to tea cosies these days.'

Georgie giggled and then stopped herself but Brian demanded the black comedy: to laugh at death, not with it. 'No go on, laugh. Laugh in the bugger's face. That's all you can do. I feel like those people on the guillotine and the last thing they do is comb their hair and smile. That'll show him. Anyway, the other thing about being on a death sentence is that life gets speeded up. That's why I was so determined to do *South Pacific*. Because you feel all of a sudden that being Emile de Becque is really important. That's why I wanted you to do it. It might not have worked out brilliantly but so what? Who cares? The important thing is that you've done it. You can't do it when you're gone. They don't put on pantos where I'm going.'

'They might do, you don't know.'

'Yes, they might do. But most of the religions have got it wrong if they do.'

Brian Wood lived with the ticking of the clock. He felt his time winding down, his own mortality intimating itself and pressing in upon him every day of his life. Brian lived as though he knew exactly the moment at which he would expire. It was as if he had it planned, as though *he* was one of those who had made an appointment with death. He was a Bobby dazzler, a man who knows he will be leaving soon and who treats that coming moment as an epiphany and a liberation because it allows him to notice living, to count and to make count.

'Can I ask you something Brian?'

'Course you can.'

'Are you not scared?'

'Funnily enough I'm not. I've never been scared of dying . . .'

Brian paused and settled himself before continuing: 'At least I've never been scared of me dying, and I'm not scared of it now. What's to be scared of? I won't be here to feel any pain.'

'Do you really believe that? You think you'll just disappear in a puff of smoke?'

'It won't be as dramatic as that. I'll just stop one day and that'll be that. I'll not be feeling anything for a while then.'

'There has to be more to it than that.'

Georgie suddenly realized that, throughout all her life, unformed but present all the same, she had been relying on an image of her mother, her father, her ancestors, herself, her Bobby in heaven. Bobby's death had thrown that unreflected notion back at her. Just when its consolation was most needed, the fold of certainty it promised had gone missing. The alternative response was fear but Georgie's control had stilled the terror. Now that her guard had fallen over Elton John and Brian Wood, she had a further glimpse of sheer fright.

Brian wasn't scared and he could read Georgie's face: 'Hey look, we're getting morbid here and I didn't mean that. I'm not a bloody funeral director you know. I know that sounds funny when I've just told you I've not got long to go but I don't feel morbid about it and that's why I told you. I told you because I want to see you again and I didn't want to do so under false pretences. So don't be upset, there's lots to be thankful for.'

'There doesn't seem like a right lot,' whispered Georgie.

'Yes there is. Yes there is. Yes there is. There's so much. Remember that.'

What is the collective noun for tomorrows? A promise. A promise of tomorrows. Brian swept a hand over the valley. He turned away because he was too proud to let Georgie see that he was crying.

23

Investing for the Future

The night frosts closed in, the plans speeded up and the leaves fell as 'Tommy's' grew afresh. Georgie posted herself on the market, now the other way round, and the stall began to turn over at a rate quicker than the hands of her mother's employees could sew. Mary had taken to her new role at once. She was a tyrannical supervisor of the ten sewers at her command. Spontaneity and creativity were sacrificed for a rigidly ordered roster. Mary drew up the plans and the patterns and allocated responsibilities for the production line. No single sewer even knew, at the early stages, what it was they were working on. The picture emerged at a late stage, like a drawing by Rolf Harris. Quickly she began to establish competence and specialization. Doris talked incessant gibberish but she had a skilled hand at the finer facial features. Mrs Kavanagh liked to join in too but she was the least adept of the company and Mary consigned her to basic background filling. And, of course, Mary Lees herself was the one with the gift. She worked harder than ever she had to meet her deadlines. No sooner could Mary finish off a portrait in wool of Bill the newsagent than Natalie from Poundstretchers wanted three jumpers with boats sewn on, one each for her triplet nephews. Then, as quickly as Mary could complete a tapestry of a bull chasing a cow in cross-stitch, Brian would persuade a Heywood housewife that she had always wanted it. Mary's fingers worked harder than ever, longer into each night. Output soared at no cost to revenue as Mrs Kavanagh would not take any payment, not even a gift to Woodhall. She said that the money would be no use to any of the residents as none of them was permitted out to the shops. Most of them, she said, were more liable to eat the money than spend it and the rest would have tried to smoke it.

Mary had settled into Woodhall easier than Georgie had ever anticipated. She had never once mentioned her old home. All that time Georgie had spent worrying that Mary would not be able to cope if she left Nightingale Street. Indeed, Nightingale Street had ceased to exist in Mary's memory. She lived in a pub where, each night, she pushed herself to sew faster. Brian encouraged Mary in this belief and had surrounded Mary with trinkets from her past to uphold her belief. It was important, he reasoned, that Mary enjoy this last stage of lucidity. Important too that Georgie not allow her memory of her mother to be dominated by a traumatic final phase. Hence he asked Georgie to bring all Mary's old photographs up to Woodhall and cover a notice-board with cuttings from once-upon-a-time newspapers and pictures of their ancestors. On their daily visit to see Mary, Brian listened patiently for hours as she told him stories that the mementoes brought spasmodically to her mind.

Brian was still working towards a shop. He had inhabited the dream, taken it up, like a baton carried from Mary to Georgie to Brian. He continued to insist a shop was possible, imminent in fact. He talked about it with an evangelical fervour out of keeping with the fact that it was someone else's dream. Brian hadn't ever given embroidery a first thought until he had walked into Mary Lees's house as a volunteer. Georgie had wondered why he was so keen. Perhaps, she had concluded, he was just lonely. Maybe he enjoyed the company that standing on the stall gave you. He was retired and needed something to do. So maybe it was just another form of voluntary work, like the time he spent helping out at the blood donors' place. But now she knew that it was to do with what Brian had told her in the cemetery. Life had to get speeded up.

On the first Monday after his extraordinary revelation in Haworth, Brian arrived at Middleton market bursting with

195

plans. The shop was all but ready for moving in, the way he talked.

'I've looked into the rent and it's not all that much. If we can get another stall turning over a decent profit then we can manage it in no time.'

'Brian, we can't afford it. A shop'll cost a fortune. We've never been able to afford it and no matter how many stalls we run we won't be able to.'

Brian was not interested in good economic sense like that. The jumped-up little monkey at the bank had given him a lot of that defeatist talk too that same morning. 'Look, we've taken loads this morning. I'm going to get a special bank account so we can save some.'

Brian began to expound a twelve-month plan towards a shop in the precinct. He produced from his pocket a huge folded piece of square-lined paper covered in arithmetic which proved, he reckoned, the feasibility of the business. He had been to see a supercilious graduate at the bank, at whose behest he had written a business plan. The plan was that they get lots of deranged old women in a care home to sew lovely clothes which they would then transport in a misspelled van to a shop where they would sell them for a considerable profit. This had been a bit too simple for the graduate in the bank who had wanted the same thing expressed in a more complicated way, preferably with rows of numbers and inarticulate diagrams. Brian had instructed him that if they sold a lot they would make some money and if they didn't, they wouldn't. If they sold a lot they would need more deranged old women or, if none such could be found, somebody else to help out with the production. That would be a nice problem to have but the shop could make money with the current suppliers. That seemed like business to him, wrapped up, as he said, in a pink bloody bow.

Georgie tried to be infected by Brian's drive but, ever present, there was the shadow of the truth. 'Brian, this is lovely you're doing all this but don't you think . . . I mean . . .'

Brian knew exactly what she meant. 'No, I'm making plans for the future, Georgie. End of story.'

196

The short future was Brian's driving force. He worked so hard because he had a deadline. Time was running out and a fate unavoidable was on its way and so urgency, like cost, increased with proximity to the end. Hurry up, get on with it, come on, get a move on, shift yourself, *dépêche-toi*, get a wriggle on, all these words are working to a deadline.

'I've got some spare money. I can pay someone to run another stall for a bit while it gets off the ground. That Asian chap who worked for Trouser's looking for a job. I had a word with him.'

'Has he heard from Press?'

He hadn't. Georgie, though, had. Through Preston's lawyers an application had been lodged for a quick divorce. Georgie had not contested it. The marriage was better off left where it was. Too much had happened. Georgie felt only flat sorrow when the letter came. *Decree nisi*. Brian talked on about his conversation with Preston's former assistant, Gundappa, while Georgie hoped that her ex-husband was fine. He had been in touch with his lawyer again to convey that he was well. He had refused to say where he was but he had made it clear that he would be coming back. Preston's lawyer didn't know when.

'Anyway, that lad, I forget his name, he said he might be interested. He said his dad works on Oldham market so he could do that one and I could open up in Rawtenstall.'

'Brian, you can't put your own money down.'

'Of course I can. I'm investing for the future.'

After a deliberate pause Brian said cheerfully: 'Just not necessarily mine.'

'But Brian . . .'

'What . . . ?'

'Well, you know.'

'Go on, say it. I haven't got any time.'

'Well . . . Brian, can I ask you something?'

Brian paused. The pace that Brian lived his life at, a moment without incident was a meaningful, deliberate interlude.

'How do you stay so calm?'

'How do you mean?'

'Facing what you are. You seem so calm. You'd never have guessed there was anything wrong. Maybe you're all of a tizzy inside but how do you stay so cheerful?'

'Because I'm not going to change anything being miserable. I won't get a second longer if I start whining so I may as well enjoy the time as best I can.'

'I know that makes sense. I'm not saying I'd have you any different. But *how* do you do it? Do you get sad at night? Do you get sad when you're on your own?'

'No I don't.'

'You must do.'

'Georgie, I don't. I've got it reckoned up. I know I'm going, like we all are. I just know my number's coming up a bit sooner than I'd like. There's nothing I can do about it and I've reconciled myself to that. So while I'm still here I'll do everything I can to enjoy myself.'

'But you could be near to dying. It could happen any time.'

Brian did not allow that there *was* anything near to death. He enumerated, only partly facetiously, some of the many ways in which the end may be passing by, closer than you know. For all the lightning that didn't strike, the cars that didn't crash, the hearts that didn't attack, the accidents still waiting to happen, Brian wanted to give thanks and think about something else. Georgie had no vocabulary for this discussion. Her only lexicon was the one she had inherited from Mary and which had now been emptied out, reduced to mere words.

'You'll be going to a better place any road.'

'I don't believe so.'

'Well you'll not be heading for damnation. You've not been such a bad fella from what I can tell.'

'No, I don't believe I'm going down there either.'

'Where you going then?'

'I'm not going anywhere apart from six feet under. I'm going down there to join Philip Crouch and Olive Platt and millions of others. I'll be worm food.'

'But your spirit goes out of you.'

'I don't believe that. I'm sorry but I just don't buy that. I

198

think that when you go, you go. Bang, that's it, that's your lot, thank you Brian Wood and goodnight.'

Brian could not see the case for divine presence or for an ultimate purpose, an evidenceless notion as far as he could see.

'I'd like to hear the good Lord explain the mystery of Olive Platt. How do you fit Olive Platt into a world created by the Lord? Bloody devil had a hand in it if you ask me. If he did have owt to do with it, he's made a rotten job of it. If he were on a contract fitting ducting he'd be sacked for that standard of work. I just don't buy it. It's worm food for me. It's you we should bother about, not me. You'll still be here when I'm gone.'

'But aren't you bothered that you won't be here?'

'No, why should I be? I won't be here to be bothered about it.'

'And you're not bothered by that?'

'What's to be bothered about? I'm no more bothered by that than who'll be Prime Minister in a hundred years' time. It's got nowt to do with me because I'll be long gone. Look at it like this. There was a time, millions of years in fact, when you and I weren't here, before we were born. Yet we don't get upset about that so why should we get upset now when we're going back to that?'

'Because we've been living in the meantime.'

'I know but the way I see it is that we have a span of time on earth and when your time's up you have to accept it and make the best of what you've got left. I'm lucky, I reckon.'

'How do you make that out?'

'Because I know when I'm going, more or less. So I can get on with things. The really poor beggars are them that gets killed just like that, without any prior warning. You know, like Diana. They've not had a chance to speed up their lives. There they are, living at normal pace, and then, snap, the lights go out.'

Georgie picked at the splinters on the stall. 'But what if you're wrong? What then?'

'Even if I am, are you telling me that the old fella up there's such a devil that he'll have his revenge? I doubt it, really. And if he does, he's not the fella you're expecting in any case.'

'I bet you'll change your mind.'

'I won't.'

'I bet you do.'

'I won't. I've thought about it a lot and I won't change my mind.'

'Lots of people think like you do but then they change their mind when it comes and then they want the parson to come.'

'You won't find me chickening out at the last minute.'

'I bet you do. I bet you that when it comes to the end you'll want to say a prayer.'

'You can say a prayer if you want, if that's what you believe.'

'I don't know what I believe any more. I used to but . . .' There were tears in Georgie's eyes.

'I know love. It's a good thing to have it if it works for you. My David'll say a prayer for me. He believes in it. Good for him, if it makes him feel better. That's the point isn't it? But I shan't be saying one. I've tried that and it doesn't work.'

The desolation that accompanied the death of his wife had been relieved by her parting words: have a good life Brian. You made me laugh. It had sounded like his own epitaph and one to be proud of, the best one. He had also learnt that prayer was a primitive technology. He had tried it on for comfort and found the emptiness just remained. There had been no answer there to his call and he had regretted what he had thereafter regarded as a lapse.

'Right, I'll bet you.'

'What good's winning the bet to me? I've no use of anything where I'm going.'

'I'll bet you a fiver and if you win I'll stick it in your coffin. And if you do wind up anywhere you'll have a bit of spending money. You can buy your way out of hellfire.'

'Right, you're on. It's a bet. Now then, that's enough getting morbid. You can't spend your life thinking like that, Georgie. What's the point getting depressed? Is that going to give me a second longer? Of course it isn't. You just have to get on with it as fast as possible. I've got plenty of time and that's

200

the end of that. Do you understand, Miss Lees?' Brian tweaked Georgie's nose.

'Yes Mr Wood.'

'So Olive can bugger off, do you hear?'

Olive was the name that Brian had given to his illness. He had considered calling it Stud but the illness was too precise and conclusive for that.

'You shouldn't joke about it Brian. It's serious.'

'That's why I joke about it.'

'You shouldn't joke Brian. It's, I don't know, it's awful.'

'It's not awful for me. I won't be here to be bothered by it. It's those who are left behind that it's awful for. They're the ones you want to bother about. It's my kids I'm bothered about and their kids. And you. I'm bothered about you.'

'You shouldn't bother about me.'

'Of course I should. We've just started getting into something and I know I'm going faster than you want but I have to. I appreciate it must seem a bit of a whirlwind but that's the only speed I do now. You'll have to get used to things coming on quicker than you'd expect.'

'I know that.'

'Do you?'

Brian reached inside his jacket pocket and took out a tiny box. He opened it to reveal a small diamond. The pace of relationships went haywire.

'Now I'll understand perfectly if you think this is a daft idea but I've had the notion that I might . . .'

'You might what?' asked Georgie, not really believing it.

Brian climbed up on to the stall and knelt. He squeezed out the last drop of romance and set love in a fight to the death.

'You might what?'

'I might ask you to marry me. Georgie Lees, will you do me the honour of marrying me?'

24
Brand New State

Georgie winced as Mary's hand slipped and painted a red gash on to her upper lip. She looked at herself in the bedroom mirror. She seemed to have lost weight. Maybe it was the flattering petticoat that she wore, maybe it was worry. Or maybe it was a trick of the glass. Different mirrors tell different tales and the plate in Mary's bedroom in Woodhall told comforting half-truths.

Georgie's face was powdered up to corpse-level. In the background, Mary's coiffure was competing for mirror space with Georgie's brittle confection. Both hair piles were held tentatively in place by an invisible bottle of lacquer. Georgie took the stick from her mother and painted herself a full pair of lips. Mary pulled their dresses down off the plastic coat hangers on which they slouched, poorly supported, the shoulders of the dress fitting poorly over the hanger. She held out the calf-length, off-white, thin-bodiced, flared-skirted dress that was her present to her daughter. Mary slid the dress with great care over Georgie's hair setting, taking care not to pull her pearl earrings, catch the matching necklace, brush against the slash of her lipstick or disturb her offsetting pastel eye shadow.

Georgie twirled around. 'How do I look?'

'You scrub up all right.'

'Oh thanks. I thought you might be a bit more pleased for me Mum, what with everything . . .'

Mary stepped into her own dress, which set blue and green flowers on a white backdrop.

'Isabel Jackson, stop this now. Come here.'

Mary held out her arms and Georgie bowed into her caress, pressing the top of her head into her mother's bony chest. Georgie held her mother close, feeling how thin and gaunt she was now, how very, very old, how close she seemed to needing the professional services of her ex-husband. Frail people always brought Preston to mind. The police were looking for him now, at last. Mary checked, professional as always, that none of her stitching, left deliberately loose to allow the dress some movement, had left any threads hanging.

'I love you little one, I really do. There, there. Good luck to you darling. You deserve some. Hey, stop it. There's no need for that. Come here. Look at you. Georgie with the dancing eyes your dad used to call you. He was a proper poet was your dad.'

Georgie sunk into her mother's chest and smelt the decay on underclothes from which no amount of washing could fully eradicate the odour of the body.

Mary began to sing the title song from *Hello, Dolly!* and forced Georgie into a waltz across the bedroom.

The Daimler arrived to take mother and daughter to the register office. Three times during the short journey from Woodhall, Mary took hold of Georgie's forearm as though she wanted to say something extremely portentous and then deviated once more. Every instance led Georgie to believe that Mary knew something ominous and life-changing, but every time it proved to be a trick. Georgie became more and more exasperated at her mother's peculiar conversational track, an odd circuit around which Preston, her father, her grandparents, Doris and the residents of Woodhall, and then Preston and her father again, ran in ever more complex variations.

Mary and Georgie arrived at Heywood register office at three-ten, ten after kick-off time, as Brian called it. Georgie ran in but she needn't have bothered. The registrar, who was an actor in his other life, hadn't arrived yet. The staff at the register office were frantically trying to find contact details for him and blaming each other, very loudly, in earshot of the small congregation, for not having his mobile or pager numbers. Eventually, a small bald man walked in as casually as if he had been half an hour early and announced himself as the registrar for the occasion. He pulled Brian to one side, to find out his name and other minor details like that. The room was so small that everyone heard the groom say twice that it was Brian as in Blessed rather than Ryan as in Giggs. When he was ready, the bald registrar nodded to the man who operates the tape recorder and three bars from 'The Bridal Chorus' from Wagner's *Lohengrin* were possible as Georgie walked round the corner from behind the door where she had been hiding.

She walked into a room that was spartan and bureaucratic. It looked like an office in a former colonial territory in which bored superior people pondered indolently on how little ruling required them to do on a daily basis. On the wall, the severe head-shots of three generations of council dignitaries looked out from within compressing black frames. The wedding was being observed by an army of men with anachronistic whiskers and black-rimmed glasses. There were three rows of wooden chairs, set up as if in anticipation of a miniature school assembly. Each row was half people half chair. Apart from a handful of people from Middleton market – Vinny Able in a velvet lilac suit and his hair like a bird's nest, Gareth Adams in a suit from which the smell of plaice and cod fillets had not been entirely eradicated – only Brian's friends seemed to have come. Georgie didn't really know any of them well. She noted in particular, with acute disappointment, that she couldn't see anyone from the Heywood Amateur Operatic and Dramatic Society at all. They had a show to perform that night – the last one of the run – and the cast party was going to be their wedding reception. Surely they had to be coming. Maybe they were all together and had got the time wrong. Maybe they were in the pub. Brian didn't seem worried, though. He said he was sure they'd be here soon enough. They were running out of time with the booking, though. There was another wedding coming in as soon as they were done.

The registrar-actor ushered Brian and Georgie on to two sub-thrones in front of his low wooden table on which the official papers had been lovelessly scattered. The betrothed couple were flanked by the groom's best man (his son, David), the matron of honour (Brian's daughter, Lucy) and the giver-away (Mary, standing in for Jack). The actor started his lines but it was a poor script. Georgie was used to the metre of the church service for which this prosaic businesslike menu-speak was a weak substitute. She talked through the responses in muted and disappointed fashion. The civil ceremony simply did not resonate for her. It was a strangely amputated wedding service. The image of a story that Preston had told her, about Idi Amin's wife who had all her limbs cut off and then sewn back on in the wrong places, came incongruously into her head. Then she realized that he had told it to her on their very first date and she began to wonder why things had gone wrong with Preston. She looked again to see who was behind her but there was only a small empty space, at the back of which was a scarlet curtain separating this room from the recess beyond.

And in there, Bobby . . .

This cold ceremony didn't seem like being married at all. It was all so very fast. This wasn't what Brian had meant, was it? That no care was taken, no pause permitted, no savouring. Even at the moment when the registrar announced that Brian and Georgie were married together, Georgie's heart stayed flat.

It was even worse when the bald registrar demonstrated why he was a registrar who did a bit of acting rather than an actor who did a bit of marrying. 'I'm a big *Star Trek* fan and as we Trekkies say, live long and prosper.'

He made a funny sign with his fingers which prompted Brian to do the same. Brian looked ready to throttle him. But then the curtain behind him was pulled with great force and Stanley Atkinson's voice declared its congratulations. Georgie turned and in astonishment saw the chorus of the Heywood Amateur Operatic and Dramatic Society. At the back of the further recess, Iris Chivers sat at a piano, grinning so hard her lips were splitting.

Brian counted them in: 'One, two, three, four . . .'

The company sang a fabulous, pitch-perfect first note. 'O----------!'

Olive Platt conducted with a manic semaphore of the arms.

'----------klahoma, when the wind comes sweeping down the plain and the waving wheat can sure smell sweet when the wind comes right behind the rain.'

Below the melody in a cheeky bass, Brian sang the words he had invented that night in Pilsworth when they had looked over at Bury and kissed. The song went on. Lazy circles in the sky. My honey lamb and I.

'Hey, them's not the right words!' said Mary, who was following Brian.

'They are now. They've changed them since your day,' said Georgie.

The Heywood Amateur Operatic and Dramatic Society did two rounds before they all came forward to give their best to Georgie Lees, their once and future dame, and to Brian Wood, whom they had very quickly come to regard and admire. The bald registrar trilled away in the background, telling anyone who would listen that he was the best Curly on this side of Rochdale and had anyone seen him play Billy Bigelow, the reprobate circus barker, in the Bacup production of *Carousel*? Billy Bigelow, Brian reminded him, kills himself in the first act.

The full cast bounced out of their cubby-hole, singing songs from the Rodgers and Hammerstein songbook. They all headed across the road to the Masons where Brian and Georgie had reserved the top floor and where a finger buffet – Georgie's doing – and a piano – Brian's – were waiting for them. Iris ham-fisted the keys and, like a man making his eyes accustomed to the dark, Brian groped around for a few bars before chancing on the place in the score of 'Surrey With The Fringe On Top' that Iris was aiming at.

'Don't you wish you could go on for ever, don't you wish you could go on for ever, don't you wish you could go on for ever and just never stop?'

Iris surprised them all by knowing the piano lines to a few

popular songs and the chorus of Heywood Amateur Operatic and Dramatic Society gave exemplary shouted performances of 'Hey Jude' (Hey Jud', Brian sang) and 'All You Need is Love'. For the rest of the afternoon, the chorus practised the songs from *Oklahoma!* to see if they sounded any better when they were all drunk. The consensus was that they did, definitely. What a lucky coincidence, said Stanley Atkinson, that they had a performance to do later that evening.

The cast arrived with twenty minutes to get made up. Lynn Riggs threw paint on them all at random and out they went. The first scenes of *Oklahoma!* passed quietly. Or rather, nobody would have guessed that the cast were drunk. It did not help that Stanley Atkinson, who was more drunk than anyone, had the big early number, 'Oh, What a Beautiful Mornin''. There was, indeed, a bright golden haze on the meadow. There always is after six pints of bitter. All the cattle were standing like statues, he sang in the second verse. They were too. They were painted on to the scenery. All the chorus were standing like statues too. They were frightened to move in case they fell over or took a bull down with them.

Oklahoma!'s chorus girls do not appear until the first act has run for almost three-quarters of an hour. This had the beneficial effect of keeping the ladies of the chorus, who were suffering most from the drinks after the wedding, away from the stage. But when they arrive there is supposed to be spectacular dancing. The can-can girls of Heywood filed on to the stage and wandered around aimlessly, arms and legs jutting out of their lines. They went from an oblong into a parallelogram into a figure-of-eight dance, all unplanned and free-form. Another innovation of the original Broadway production had been that a dancer falls on purpose and then gets up and carries on. Beryl Collins duly fell over but nobody believed it was part of the script. In fact, it wasn't. It was meant to be Lynn Riggs who fell over. She'd forgotten. It wouldn't have mattered so much if Beryl hadn't taken part of the Smoke House down with her.

Aunt Eller walked through the first half. She is scripted as the defiant matriarch, the strong point connecting the old ways with

Oklahoma's emergence as a fledgling state of the union. She is also the prime mover behind the romance of Curly McLain and Laurey Williams, to which the action proceeds, and which is a metaphor for the accreditation, in 1907, of the Indian territory of Oklahoma as a brand-new state. Word-perfect and in tune as she was, Georgie was shorn of all anger, her utopian passion fragile and spent. It was the beer, it was Preston. Her introspection led back to Bobby, as it always did, always would.

She stayed in the wings to watch the ballet sequence danced by Colin Smethurst, Brian and Susan Platt. From the beginning of the dance it was clear that Brian was catastrophically pissed. The dance scene is supposed to dramatize the struggle between Curly and Jud over Laurey. It ends with a victorious Jud carrying off the prize. This action, in which Jud spins Laurey around above his head, was way beyond Brian's capability. Unfortunately, it was not way beyond him trying. He lifted Susan Platt with a lurching strain on his back and staggered from side to side like a contestant settling himself in the clean and jerk. Then he completed the lift with a huge groan. Susan screamed and Brian tottered. As he began to topple over to his left he lost his grip on Susan's bottom and Colin, to a gasp and then a round of applause from the audience, caught her as she slid from Brian's hands. Quite apart from being hazardous for Susan Platt's good health, this symbolized just the opposite of what the story required, so Colin picked Brian up from the floor and handed Susan back to him. In the wings at stage-left Agnes Mills held her head in her hands. This was what happened when you strayed beyond the oblong comfort zone. The audience was killing itself, though.

Georgie spent most of the show where she was, in the wings. Farmers, cowmen, Graham Collins as an Egyptian peddling the elixir of life and Mid-Western ne'er-do-wells had to push their way past her as Aunt Eller refused to move. She returned to the wings after the interval for Curly and Jud Fry's big scene together. This was the one that Brian had told her about. It had been this scene that had made *Oklahoma!* such a sensation when it had first appeared in March 1943. *Oklahoma!* is innovative in a number of ways. It was the first musical to tell a serious story, the first to include ballet and the first to receive recognition as a literary drama. But it was the stage death and its questionable cause that inspired the critical accolades. Curly sings the mournful 'Poor Jud is Dead' which describes what people would say about him if he were lying in his coffin. Curly suggests in jest that Jud might hang himself and, in a macabre twist, persuades him to join in the song. As Colin Smethurst's reedy voice rang out across Heywood Civic Hall in praise of the rope in the smoke house, Georgie Lees stared at him from the wings. It seemed to tell her something about all the men in her life, from her father to her husband. Curly describes Jud as having a heart of gold. So he was her dad. So peaceful and serene, his hands across his chest, like her dad had been the last time she had visited his open coffin. It had made her feel better, that final visit. His fingernails had never been so clean; that wasn't her dad.

Bobby, little Bobby dazzler, with his clean fingernails . . .

Georgie had no tears, only a fixed glare into nowhere, a bad place, utopia lost. She missed none of her cues, flunked none of her lines, gave a steady and sober performance as the pivot holding the show together. She under-played every scene and her presence in the finale was particularly gentle. Ever since her conversation with Brian about treating Jud Fry as an end for their sport, Georgie could never play the kangaroo court with the scripted gusto. When the company was proclaiming *Oklahoma!* with an exclamation mark like a pole attached to the roof, Georgie was mouthing the words but giving out no sound. Brian tried to catch her eye to sing their own version but she sensed it and looked away.

Georgie stepped forward at the end of the evening to acknowledge the lukewarm, respectful applause of the audience at the curtain call. It was nothing like the exhilarating affirmation of life that Brian Wood had promised. After her final bow she quietly, without fanfare, left the stage. Brian lingered and took in as much applause as he could muster. He left the stage too, changed quickly and began to prepare their reception party that was to take place on the stage after the audience had departed.

The party was muted. The mystery of Brian and Georgie's bizarrely precipitous matrimony had hardly been approached. None of the cast knew about Brian's condition. As they resumed their consumption and topped up their inebriation, exaggeration started to stretch its legs from the truth towards nonsense. Veiled insinuations circulated about the peculiarly and conveniently coincident disappearance of Georgie's first husband a little matter of weeks before she broke the bottle on his replacement. Stanley Atkinson had seen things like this on the television. It was postulated that, in all likelihood, Preston was hidden away in one of his own boxes at this very moment. Georgie must, it was unanimously agreed, have been conducting an affair with Brian long before he had turned up to save *South Pacific*. People just don't get married so quickly. It was unseemly. Especially after, well, you know ... at this point, meeting the force of a serious object, the gossip abruptly stopped.

Georgie knew these yarns were being spun. She wanted to interrupt the cynical nastiness with the shocking truth. But Brian wished to choose his confidants for himself and Olive and Susan Platt, Stanley Atkinson, Graham and Beryl Collins and Colin Smethurst were not among them. Georgie's brave face was convincing enough that nobody noticed her lack of excitement. She did not feel trepidation or fear or regret but something flatter and less defined. And nobody had really noticed, she was sure. Until Brian asked fondly what was the matter. Georgie stalled and muttered something about Bobby being present in her mind and Preston ghosting in the aisles. Rather than insist on an answer, Brian called on Iris to take to the piano. He pressganged Georgie into leading the troupe into the famous Rodgers and Wood composition. Iris started the rhythmic introduction, before the song moves into the melody. Georgie exclaimed the status of the brand new state, flat and out of time. Georgie sang tomatoes where the book said termaters. It didn't matter. Brian and Georgie sang on, plenty of heart and plenty of hope, until they arrived at the great exclamation. Brian pointed his arm on the long first note like he had seen his children doing years before to 'Greased Lightning.'

'O----------' they screamed for four beats, '----klahoma!'

Next time round, the whole chorus joined in the finger pointing, led by Georgie Lees. For an encore, before they left for a night at the Last Drop Inn, Brian and Georgie performed a special version of the 'Twin Soliloquies'. Brian's careful enunciation brought some enchantment to the evening.

He took Georgie's arm and held her as he whispered the final words; promising, now he had found her, never to let her go.

He repeated the phrase and kissed Mrs Georgie Wood as their guests applauded hypocritically wildly.

Georgie did not find sleep easy at the Last Drop on her second wedding night. She jerked in and out of bleary consciousness and in and out of a dream-state. Brian started to breathe very hard to regain his composure. There was a large car. It hit him in the backside and he dropped straight, uncontrolled, until his fall was broken by his nose hitting the steel buckle of Georgie's suitcase. By the time Georgie got to Brian he was struggling mortally for breath. She gave out a terminal, piercing scream. She was dressed like a little girl again, clomping round in her mother's over-sized shoes, her lips smeared in her mother's lipstick. An ambulance arrived and took Brian to hospital. Georgie, too hysterical to know what was happening, was not permitted to travel with him. She was left behind on the station platform with a woman she did not recognize who claimed to be her mother. This woman assured her that Brian was not dead but Georgie was uneasy. She was not a reliable witness. She had an unreliable smile. He did not survive the journey. To the backbeat of early-morning traffic on the way into Rochdale, Georgie said a quiet prayer for Brian Wood. He moved for the last time, craned his neck slightly and shook his head as if to say, no prayers please. Georgie felt a great and everlasting terror. Even on the immediate threshold, Brian Wood resisted the fold of religious consolation. He passed away peacefully in an ambulance, stoical and unblinking to the end, a happy and philosophical death. Behind him he left terror on the faces of what suddenly became a host of companions: Georgie herself, Mary, Preston, Bobby, Jack, Jimmy Saville. Bobby's face stood out. It seemed to her to balloon up, to swell like a flaming

211

boil. On his face there was a peculiarly etched anguish as if he were in bodily pain. And then Georgie was in the ambulance after all. Somebody was banging hard on the flimsy ply-board door. She opened the door on this voice because she heard a man calling out her name, urgently, beseechingly. Georgie woke, screaming. Brian sat up and Mary leapt towards her as Georgie was attacked by an out-of-proportion, everything is in question terror of having lost her bet with Brian. She had a strong sense of loss, a feeling of early deprivation. Brian was already on his way to his appointment – she knew that – but serendipity did not feel any less malign for that. She wanted Brian's full, attenuated span, short as it was. The shortness made it all the more necessary that the term be completed. Brian kissed her cheek and told her that he had decided to do *Hellö, Dolly!*. It was the perfect thing to say and Georgie lay down her head on the pillow and went to sleep.

25

The Full Hand

The ten-rod allotment rose again. The deciduous plants detected the subtle shifts in light and temperature. The sap started to flow, the growth buds began to swell and burst and the routines of a new season – the growing season – were triggered into action. Eyes were cast forlornly up at the gifts from the weather: mildew on the roses, tomato blight, a plague of toadstools. The cool and the damp and dull days incubated blackspot on the roses and grey mould in the greenhouse. But then the cycle. It was not too long before the sun came again and the talk on the plots turned from rain and frosted evergreens to spring bulbs and fruit tree blossom. Men moved from weeding and mulching to their herbaceous perennials and growing again. Preston's plot was taken over by Graham Collins. Graham had long-term plans. He planted a line of conifers and cut out, from Preston's symmetrical groves, admixtures of vegetable, flower and fruit that showed no regard for the nourishment of the soil. Not sure if it was vegetable or fruit, Graham hacked up Preston's green tomato plant and let the land lie fallow. That was what Turnip Townsend had done in his schoolbooks and Carrot Collins wasn't about to defy the master. He had a plan to train sweet peas which he was scuppering with his lack of attention to the soil. But Graham didn't mind really. He enjoyed gardening because it got him away from Beryl without engendering suspicion. The allotment became his study and gardening was like writing in the ground.

Georgie was now settled into Brian's home in Swinton and

had started to forget about looking for Preston. Brian's deadline was pressing in on them and he was making arrangements for the opening day of his shop as if it were a real possibility. A lot more embroidery was needed for a full complement of stock before they could open. Brian had begun to doubt that the Woodhall sweater shop actually had the capacity or the expertise – Mary Lees obviously apart – to keep a serious business going. Though every garment he was expecting to have on sale on his opening day had been made in Woodhall – and he had no other plans for supply – it was taking a very long time to prepare. Brian was concerned that the replacement time of sold goods would be far too long and that the shop would crumble after a month. Georgie was sewing more herself than she had done since she had first started on the stall with her mother.

And, as if he hadn't filled up their lives with enough to do, Brian had committed himself to producing the next show at Heywood Civic Hall because Olive Platt had decided to retire. Brian's leading lady had been sentimentally pre-selected. Indeed, the leading lady had led the choice of the show. Brian craved for Georgie the judgment of the audience that he had inspired her with when he had persuaded her back into *South Pacific*. There would be no holding back, surely, for Dolly Gallagher Levi.

Georgie walked slowly down to the Civic Hall where Brian was already leading the cast in a rehearsal. He was keen to run through the final scenes which they had not yet tried. There were only six weeks until the opening night and they had still not joined up all the dots of the production. Brian rubbed the insides of his eyes and grimaced at Iris Chivers. When she asked if he was all right Brian barked at her and said he would be a whole lot better if people could start learning their parts. Brian was also getting more and more agitated at the noise of an electric saw in the background as the set builders constructed a replica of the inside of a New York milliner's.

The players went clunkily through some of the early scenes but Brian was keen to get to the point. Every scene in Jerry Herman's book points towards Dolly Gallagher Levi's big moment. She has been plotting to marry Horace Vandergelder, a wealthy Yonkers

214

merchant, while pretending to act as matchmaker for her friend Irene Molloy. Vandergelder (Colin Smethurst in a triumphant return to form) ends his interest in Irene Molloy (Susan Platt, released from the pressurizing direction of her mother), rather whimsically it has to be said, by the farcial interventions of his clerks, the comics Cornelius and Barnaby (played, despite the evidence to the contrary, by Graham Collins and a newcomer, Steven Green, replacing Preston Burns). Cornelius, with no apparent prior motivation, falls for Irene Molloy and, equally suddenly, decides to set up in business opposite Vandergelder. Brian encouraged Colin Smethurst to imagine how he'd feel if Graham Collins opened a butcher's shop across the road. Pretty bloody narked, Colin agreed. Dolly intervenes in the incipient rivalry to persuade Vandergelder and Cornelius into business matrimony. He then completes the set and concludes the plot by proposing to Dolly.

But this is all really so much comic foil for the single moment that the audience is waiting for. It is the to be or not to be moment of *Hello, Dolly!*, the bit where Del Boy falls through the gap in the bar. Dolly reappears, elaborately bridal, wearing a hat like a medium-sized water tower. Her spectacular entrance from back stage right, down two sides of a square, to front stage central, the last footsteps of which carry her on to an oval staircase in mahogany, is done against the backdrop of the 'Waiter's Gavotte'. The men of the cast run across the stage carrying trays loaded with drinks, duelling with enormous shish kebabs on skewers, bashing heads with plastic loaves of bread and deliberately tripping into custard pies in a nimble slapstick festival. All of this perfectly choreographed movement was supposed to leave no food on the floor and a clear way for one of the most sensational entrances in the history of musical theatre.

Agnes Mills gathered the men in a corner for a pep-talk. She walked them through the steps of the 'Gavotte', into which she had ingeniously inserted her trademark oblong.

Stanley Atkinson candidly assessed his own chances. 'I could probably just about manage that, Agnes, if you didn't expect me to carry a kebab while I'm doing it.'

The dancing in *Hello, Dolly!* is complex beyond the limbs of the men of Middleton. How to separate the dancer from the dance? Who knows, but it has never been more necessary. In 'It Takes a Woman', another routine they hadn't tried yet, the male dancers are scripted to leap from elevated platforms and to veer in and out of trapdoors, doing all manner of athletic tricks. When Brian had chosen *Hello, Dolly!* for the next show he hadn't given the dancing any mind. This was a show for Georgie which Stanley Atkinson's dodgy knees were threatening to steal.

Georgie limbered up her voice for her big number. The men walked through the 'Gavotte', groping for the right positions, trying to imagine themselves carrying kebabs. Brian stood at the back of the hall for a good view. He wished he hadn't.

'Come on, hurry up, will you? Give it a bit of bloody urgency will you? Do you think you've got all bleeding day? It's meant to be a gavotte, not a bloody stroll.'

He made the men go through the motions four times before he allowed Dolly her entrance. When, finally, he called on Georgie for her moment, she catwalk-shuffled down the stage to the front as the ensemble said hello in unison.

She was only two lines into her solo when Brian gave his verdict: 'No love, that's no good. Here, you need to give it some. This is the best bit of the lot, you can't treat it like it's singing at communion.'

Brian climbed up on to the stage and instructed Iris to start from the top. He swaggered downstage, hitching up an imaginary skirt like Betty Grable and throwing flirtatious glances at the kebab-imaginers. Brian exuded Dolly Gallagher Levi's sense of confidence. Brian was still certain, not at all prone to doubt, he knew what was what was what. That, he said, was what Dolly Gallagher Levi was like. She exuded certainty, sprinkled with a stoical disregard for the fortune that kept hinting it might cut her down. Brian took the song almost to the end. For most of the way through he was still going, he was still going strong. But then he fell, face-forward as in Georgie's dream.

Brian died later that evening, at home. The cast might have said of him that he would have wanted to die on stage but it wouldn't have been true. Brian didn't think enough of death to be sentimental about it. Georgie was by his side when he died. She did not cry, on his orders. On pain of death was the actual phrase he had used. She also promised to carry out a very simple funeral. Brian was adamant that there should be no fuss. He just wanted to bring down the curtain now that the comedy was over, the farce played out. Best to take a bow while the audience is still applauding. He left Georgie with the thought that Olive Platt was finally winning and with the conviction that somehow *Hello, Dolly!* contained the meaning of life.

As Brian lay, struggling for breath, his countenance was calm and Georgie could not resist asking: 'Would you like me to say a prayer for you love?'

Brian smiled for the last time and this time he knew it was the last time. The deadline. He shook his head slowly. If he was going he was going to be philosophical about it. For Brian, life was what he had and its loss was a terrible thing but only because it deprived him of so much, not because it was a terrible thing in itself. The final deprivation, indeed, was of the subject himself. And in that ultimate deprivation lay the fact that death was not terrible. The fact of death was that there was nobody left to experience it. The state of being dead was nothing, pure nothing, and the only rotten thing about dying was that it tended to end in death. A prayer was a form of therapy of which he no longer stood in need. Like so much of the ritual activity surrounding the death of a loved one, the prayer was for the one who prayed.

'No thank you. Goodbye Dolly.'

Georgie wrapped her arms around Brian, around this dying man who cared so passionately about the absurd trivia of pretending to be other people and breaking into song without provocation.

At the request of the deceased, Georgie gave Brian a quiet send-off. It was the simplest crematorium funeral Georgie could persuade the undertakers from Bury to arrange – they were suddenly overworked after a major change in the capacity of the local market. The cast of *Hello, Dolly!* came and a few friends of

Brian's from the Co-operative Insurance Society. But there were no theatrics or histrionics. Just a serious silence.

Georgie did not cry. She smiled, as she had been ordered to do. Brian's children kept up their fixed smiles too. It was, they all said to comfort each other, what their father, her husband would have wanted. Brian would have preferred a secular service but had left orders that Georgie should choose the form of his funeral. As far as he was concerned, which wasn't very far, the funeral was for her. As soon as she came to think about it, Georgie was thrown back to the church. Those words again. How different they sounded now, now that a full life had been lived. It did seem like a full life even though it had been cut off early. But what life isn't? Just as we're getting the hang of it off we go. As Georgie listened to the vicar saying the words she had recently heard she did so without the anger of the previous occasion. I am the resurrection and the life saith the Lord: he that believeth in me, though he were dead, yet shall he live: and whosoever liveth and believeth in me shall never die. And on: it is sown in corruption; it is raised in incorruption: it is sown in dishonour; it is raised in glory; it is sown in weakness; it is raised in power. Georgie did not laugh-scream this time.

Georgie said goodbye to Brian's children, their families and his friends at the door of the church. She promised she would come on for a drink, at the house which had, until yesterday, been her temporary home and which had now passed to the children. But first she wanted to go back into church, alone. Once she was certain that everyone had gone, that the vicar was in the vestry changing out of his magic costume, she took off her ornate hat (made in Woodhall for the opening-day sale in Bobby Dazzler's) and sat down on an uncomfortable wooden pew. She looked around, at the extraordinary beauty of the stained glass, the care that was lavished upon it, at the gargoyles on the front of the font and the restoration work going on in the roof.

She spoke out loud and sniggered at the echo that bounced back at her. 'Ta-ra Brian love. I bet you had a quiet prayer. I bet you owe me money. I'll be along to collect it before you know.'

She picked up her hat and walked down the aisle. Before

allowing the door to close behind her, Georgie took a final look at the altar. She had once believed in its power, uncritically, unthoughtfully. She had inherited it, along with the rest of her beliefs about the world, the bulk of which, referring to means of navigating quotidinal problems, had proved to be robust. But this big one was struggling these days. She had cast it aside, she supposed for good, in the unique event of her Bobby dazzler's funeral.

And yet she had a dim sense of some long-brewed transaction taking place as she stood in awed contemplation of the human care that had been collected in that musty house. She felt thankful that it was there even if she no longer counted herself one of the faith's uncomplicated adherents. She wanted to know that it would continue to be there, long after she had herself gone. It had become for her what it was now for most who bothered to acknowledge its presence at all: a place where they moved in and out of commitments, to life, to one another, to death. Even that much made it important. Life, one another, death. That's the full hand. She felt serious and, for the first time since the death of Bobby, settled, composed, consoled. It was a peculiar beliefless calm, not like her mother's positive conviction but distinct from Brian's atheistic certainty too. She knew she would be unable to put the thoughts into words but there was no question that she had grown, had grown wiser, surrounded by the people she loved: her father, her late husband, her boy. Somewhere in this air lay the key to joining up with them though the words and the claims of the people who come here are perhaps no better a rendering than these thoughts that Georgie settled herself with as she quietly closed the oak door behind her.

She went, as promised, to Brian's house to drink a toast to him. To wet the baby's head, as he had described it to her. David, Brian's son, was solicitous in his care for Georgie. He took her to one side and took Brian's Swiss Army knife from his pocket. His dad had always promised that he would leave it to him. David had wanted that knife so much when he had been a boy.

David held it out. 'He told me about the tree. I want you to have it.'

219

'No David I can't. He gave it to you. He thought about all his stuff. He gave it all out on purpose because he wanted to see your reaction when you got things. He said you'd always wanted that knife. It's yours.'

'Georgie, we don't know each other but I know how happy you made dad in his last days. He said he wasn't going to leave you anything because he'd given it all away, so I want you to have this. Please. Take it.'

Georgie took the knife and hugged Brian's son. The kindness of a stranger. It was an unsettling moment. She opened her handbag to place the knife inside

The next morning, Georgie was summoned to the office of Mr Keele, solicitors in Heywood, to attend the reading of Brian's will. She daze-walked to the Market Place. It was perplexing to be called in. As his assets had already been dispersed into his children's future, Brian's will had already been done. Mr Keele was very large, a very fat man who took twice as long to do anything, from opening the door to reading a will, as it really required. Georgie was beginning to suspect him of a theatrical relish in cranking up the suspense, when he finally began reading Brian's will. As Georgie had helped Brian prepare its contents, none of it came as a surprise. The house went to his children, as he had promised them. The residual bank deposits went to the Blood Donors' Centre and the Florence Nightingale Hospital League of Friends. Georgie got the ungrammatical van. The Brain Box. It was the only thing she had wanted even though she couldn't drive. She'd decided to learn.

But there was something else. Two more things in fact, said Mr Keele, stringing it out. Mr Keele opened a sky-blue envelope. He took a document out and began to speak, very slowly: 'You may not be aware but Mr Wood had accumulated a number of savings plans not currently dispersed in the arrangements settled so far. Taken together they amount to a total of £42,000. Arrangements have been left for them all to be liquidated on this day and for a cheque for that amount to presented to Mrs Georgie Lees.'

Georgie gasped.

Mr Keele handed her the envelope. 'The money will account

for the other documents included in these papers which are the deeds relating to ownership of the business premises of 42 Market Place, Middleton, currently owned by the Combined Funeral Experience Company and lately occupied by Preston Burns Undertakers but henceforth to be occupied by Georgie Lees's wool shop, pending agreement by the production line manager, Mary Lees and her executor, the proprietor, Georgie Wood Lees.'

Georgie was incredulous. She just shook her head, completely unable to think of anything to say.

Eventually, she found a word. 'Really?'

'Yes, really.'

'Really?'

'Yes, Mrs Wood, really.'

Georgie hugged Mr Keele because he was the closest she could get to Brian.

She got up to leave but Mr Keele called her back. 'We've not quite finished. There is just one more thing.'

Mr Keele reached into his desk, with elaborate pauses punctuating every movement. He produced another envelope, plain white with her name written unfussily in black ink. To intensify his drama, Mr Keele decided not to read it. Instead, he handed the envelope to Georgie.

She opened it and read: 'Georgie Lees. My dearest darling. I have always maintained that I would go with a smile on my face. You may remember that I put my money where my mouth is. Or was, by the time you read this. In the unlikely event that I did fall on my death bed into religious prayer I bequeath to you the princely sum of £5.'

Georgie shook the envelope and a dirty fiver fell out on to the floor.

'If, as I imagine, I did not fall into any kind of superstition at the last moment, then you owe me money darling. I'll not be needing it though. Frame it and remember me. This is how we live on. Yours for ever, Brian Wood.'

He would have the epitaph he had wanted: beneath this sod lies another. The daisies in the dell will give out a different smell because poor Jud is underneath the ground.

26
Forget-me-nots

It was now a year ago. And still Georgie had not been to Bobby's graveside. Bobby, his soul and or his ashes, depending on whether one took Georgie's or Brian's view, lay in the soggy ground, flanked by lupins which flowered in the half-light's shade at the graveside. Georgie fielded her mother's insistent questions as they walked across the squelching plots of grass. Mary was clearly finding the recollection of Bobby impossible. Georgie gave a painstaking reply to her mother's demands for a biography of this old man they were going to visit. For the first time, Georgie was able to describe the facts of the matter clearly. She described Bobby's life, never bloodlessly but calmly. She told the tale of his death steadily and truthfully and declared that he was not to be blamed for what he had done and that God would look after him if God was at all true to His own promises.

Georgie looked at Mary after she had delivered this consummately difficult speech. Her mother's struggle to connect with the person described was visible and unavailing. Surrounded by so many stone reminders of mortality and framed by cold white flowers, Mary had never looked so frail, so in need of protection, futile as protection was. The fragility was seen in the brain, not in the body. Though Mary was smaller and much thinner than before, her tyres of fat having dropped out of middle into old age, she still had a flinty durability. She walked quickly and without hindrance; her facial features were more sharply defined than before as the amorphous puffs of skin had stretched away and she bent down to pick a dahlia with a suppleness and dexterity that Georgie herself would have taken pride in. No, the loss was not bodily and there was a lot be to thankful for in that.

And, as Georgie stood by Bobby's grave, she was thinking not of her son, who had chosen his own fate, but of her mother who would be angry and tenacious to the end and yet who was dying into another internally created world. The loss was not bodily but still Georgie witnessed a loss. Mary Lees was not a bag of bits, bones skeletally and recognizably arranged, covered over and skin-held in place. Mary was Widow Twankey and Aunt Eller and Dolly Gallagher Levi and Bloody Mary and the moment she could no longer remember the words was the moment that Mary Lees was dying. And suddenly, there was the thought of Jack, her father. If this was true of Mary, that death is as much a question of character as it is a question of cell reproduction and the cessation of consciousness, then so must it have been for her father. She thought that the closure of oxygen may just conceivably have been the physical confirmation of the death, rather than the death itself. No murder takes place, only the holding up of hands before the obvious and the inevitable.

Georgie stepped away from the small grave. On the stone the marks read simply: 'Bobby Graham, died 1996, nine years of age.' Dusk now hung round the graveyard. As she sat down by the graveside Georgie spoke, unfalteringly and out loud, without shame. Mary said nothing.

'Hello love. Hello love.'

Georgie left a pause for Bobby to reply, which he did.

'Sorry I've not been before. It's not been easy though, love.'

Pause.

'I've got some bad news for you love. I'm afraid your dad's disappeared.'

Pause.

'Had he been to see you much?'

A pause for Bobby to reply.

'He never was one for being organized wasn't your dad. I know he came a few times though because he was always badgering me to come. He's a funny fella sometimes is your dad. He sort of got side-tracked with his job. I often wonder what he would have turned out like if he'd been a plumber. He wanted to write about cricket when he was a youngster. He was obsessed with cricket. But then he found something else to get into and it turned him morbid.'

Georgie paused again. Bobby insisted she go on. Georgie shouldn't have raised it if she didn't want to talk. It sounded interesting and Bobby didn't get much conversation these days. He had always thought his dad was a bit odd, in the way that children sniff out a weak spot, for purposes of bullying disabled people and satirizing weirdos.

Georgie tried to explain why Preston had gone. 'He got into a bit of a tizzy. It was when I was marrying Brian really, that was what did it. Your dad wanted me and him to get back together but I just didn't think it was right . . .'

Georgie paused, a little shocked by Bobby's reaction. 'Oh Lord, I haven't told you have I? There's so much been going on lately. Sorry love. I know it must have come out of the blue a bit. It did for me to be honest. I thought I was past all that. Anyway, me and your dad got divorced. We weren't getting on. Well, you knew that didn't you? And that after . . . well, you know . . . I got married again anyway. It came on really soon. I hope you don't mind love. He was called Brian and he was a lovely man. He used to come to look after grandma. Grandma's here. I know she's been to see you before. I'm sorry I've not been. It's not been easy love . . .'

Pause and a change of subject.

'Yes, he was a lovely fella was Brian. But he died. It was OK though because I knew he was dying. I mean, well I knew he was going to go quite soon. I don't feel sad about it because he had his time. He enjoyed his life.'

Georgie took Mary's hand. 'He was a kind man, Brian. You'd have liked him, you would honest. He would have been your new dad.'

In the following pause Georgie looked up. Three solitary figures were hunched by the sides of their own dead, talking silently. Georgie turned away so that Mary would not see her distress.

'Have a word with your grandma, love. She's not so good at remembering these days. She talks to you though, I know that.'

Mary spoke. 'I'll be a while before I join you yet.'

Pause.

'No, he was an absolutely lovely fella was Brian. I wonder where he is now . . .'

Pause.

'He was ill but he was always making a joke of it. He used to call it Olive Platt. His illness, that is. Do you remember Olive? She was that funny woman in the hat at the show. You did meet her but you probably don't remember.'

Pause.

'But you can't make a joke of it all the time. It's not that funny really.'

Pause.

'You never talked about it Bobby. You never said.'

Pause.

'I had to leave the house afterwards. It was too empty without you rattling about inside.'

Pause.

'You should have said Bobby. You could have talked to me, you know. You didn't have . . .'

Pause. Georgie knelt in front of Bobby's simple, unadorned stone. She picked a lily from the graveside and dropped it gently.

Mary spoke and pointed towards the plot where her husband had settled down for a long night. 'I'd better go and say hello to Granddad Jack love,' said Georgie.

Mary interrupted her attempt to move. Mary began to speak to Bobby: 'I've got something else to tell you love. It's about your dad.'

Mary started out on a motiveless anecdote. She had no purpose but her unreliable lucidity penetrated into the details. 'Your dad did something wrong when Granddad Jack died. Well, I don't know if it's wrong, you see. I want to know what you think. You see Granddad Jack wasn't very well by the end. Do you remember, you were a little 'un at the time and your dad thought it was best to try and ... well I don't know how to put it really.'

Talking to Bobby forced her to attempt to elucidate the meaning of the act. That forced her to interrogate the source of the act, its motivation.

'Mum, don't. Bobby doesn't want to hear about that.'

· Mary went on, trancelike. 'Well your granddad was very poorly. We all knew he was dying. Do you remember me telling you that we had to get ourselves ready? Granddad Jack was hurting a lot. Do you remember when you went to see him and he couldn't answer your questions because he was so out of breath? Your dad used to work with Granddad Jack, did you know that?'

Mary paused again for the words.

'He thought he was doing it for the best. He saw your granddad was suffering and I think he thought that he'd be better off not suffering any more.'

Bobby could understand that sentiment.

'And I'm sure that your dad meant it for the best but I didn't like it, I must admit, and I've never really taken to your dad after that.'

'You wanted to go as well Bobby love, didn't you? You decided not to carry on, didn't you love? I don't know why. I really don't know why. Maybe you were suffering too love.'

Georgie listened for a few minutes.

'I can't understand what you did love. I've tried but that's why I've not been to see you because I've not been able to work out what's going on.'

Pause.

'Anyway love, as I was saying, I'd better go and have a word with Granddad Jack. And then I'd better be going. Before Fungus the bogeyman gets me.'

Georgie and Mary circled the plot where Jack lay. As she approached, Georgie was sure she noticed a furtive, fugitive figure moving in the dark, close to Jack's grave, in vandal-attendance to it.

Georgie called out, frightened: 'Who's that?'

The voice that called back came from the figure in the dark. Of all people. 'Bloody hell Georgie it's you. You frightened me then.'

Georgie was incredulous. The invisible mourner was Preston Burns. She passed over the obvious questions, the where-have-you-beens and the when-did-you-get-backs?

She surprised him with wistfulness. 'Oh Press, I'm glad you're back. We've missed you.'

'You haven't. I know what happened Georgie. I know all about it.'

Preston wandered off. From fifteen yards away and barely visible in the dark that had fallen quickly, he said: 'I'm giving up the business . . . I've had enough of dead folk.'

Preston gesticulated towards the mares' tails and pimpernels that were controlling and patrolling the ground round about Jack's grave. He pulled out a flower of bracken by the top of the stem, leaving its root in the soil to recover for another day.

'Where have you been Press?'

'India.'

'India?'

'I've always wanted to go there. I travelled all over. It was fabulous.'

'What did you go there for?'

'I don't know. I just had to run away and I've read about the City of the Dead on the Ganges so I went to have a look for myself. I sat on the steps next to the river and had a think about everything. And then when I'd finished and I'd sorted it all out I came back.'

'When did you get back?'

'Two weeks ago.'

'Where have you been since then? No one's seen you.'

'All over the place. I've been travelling. Just getting on buses and trains and staying in a B&B. I couldn't cope with it, you know. With what happened to our Bobby. Everyone thought that because I was an undertaker I was used to it. Nobody thought to think that I might not be able to cope. I couldn't make head nor tail of the whole thing. And then I thought that you and me

227

might be all right after all and I'm not sure it would have been the right thing to do anyway but then it sort of fizzled out and I just couldn't stand the whole thing any more.'

'So what you going to do now? Are you going to keep running all your life or are you back now?'

'I'm giving up undertaking. I've spent all my adult life worrying myself about dead folk and about people who are worrying about their relatives. It gets to you in the end. I want to do something that's not so morbid before I snuff it myself. I'm going to set up as a gardener. I'm going to put some adverts up. There's plenty of work doing people's gardens. I was always talking about gardening with relatives while they were waiting to have their dead buried. I don't know why but people liked to talk about the flowers when everything else is so miserable. And then they used to talk about their own gardens and how they were getting more and more messy because they never had time to look after them properly. People don't know what they're doing in the garden any longer. My grandad was a genius in his garden and he taught me when I was a kid. Parents don't do that any more. Nobody knows how to stop a garden from weeding.'

'So have you started?' said Georgie, purely to forestall Preston's lecture on gardening.

Preston did not answer. In the silence Preston didn't realize that he hadn't answered. He was away with the ideal site for a garden. It was not too overlooked by neighbouring plots, it sloped away from the house, preferably to the south. It had a deep soil and a sub-soil that retained its moisture. The soil would be about eight inches to a foot in depth with a sub-soil of marl or clay. The flower garden and the lawn should be placed nearest to the house, the less pleasing vegetable and fruit gardens relegated to less conspicuous parts of the plot. At the front section of the garden, all manner of ornamental jiggery-pokery was required. But the garden had to be usable. There was no point with a keep-off-the-grass garden where children were around. They had to learn to love the sight and the smell of the garden and that delight could never be developed if the lawn was out of bounds.

228

Georgie gazed and gazed at Jack's grave. She moved softly over broken branches to where Preston was standing.

She held out her hand in the dark.

'Come here Press. Come here.'

They shook hands, stiffly and formally in the dark. Preston whispered that he had a wart forming on his palm. He thought. Preston put his hands on Georgie's shoulders. He moved them round her neck and kissed her on her lips. She did not resist. Far below the surface of the earth, the release from dead tissue of enzymes was pushing the process of autolysis. The pancreas had digested itself and putrefaction had spread to show sagging, slipping skin wearing blisters. To the scenting of worms and bugs, hydrogen sulphide and methane soaked into the earth. Eyes bulged, tongues protruded, blood-stained fluids burst from the opening orifices. The colour of the skin was changing from olive to purple to black. It began to recede on the hands, teeth and nails began to loosen, tissues liquefied and main body cavities burst open.

Far below the surface of the earth the roots of the clematis vitalba stirred, stooping for spring in its climb. Georgie and Preston stared at the ground as, in the dark, the flowers opened and sang. The loosestrifes and blazing stars drank contentedly in the valley on the moisture that they required to thrive. They were a natural disguise covering the earth, painted over to kid us into forgetting the endless purposes underneath the ground in which they are rooted. The flowers hold a truth they do not disclose. The veronicas stretched out to cover a pauper's grave to their left. Arid patches of ground were suddenly covered over with mauve, shaggy blossoms of erigerons and late-summer anemones. Out of the ridges formed by the cold, like the steps left on the sand by the sea, ice plants, frightened of frost, opened their childlike eyes and rings of purple black and orange yellow pointed their way to the stately tulips which were formally massed by the specially marked graves in the enclosures of the graveyard, flanked by forget-me-nots. Around Georgie and Preston, invisible life stirred and moved.

27

A Change, How Strange

The queen of embroidery had also brought her musical heritage with her into Woodhall. The residents, under the direction of Doris's son Terry, put on regular shows for their relatives. Of course Mary Lees had decided to take control. Terry's name appeared on the single xeroxed programme sheet but it was Mary Lees's variety bill. Georgie was shaking in the front row as Mary Lees strode out on to the shallow low stage in the converted main room at Woodhall and sat on one of the two stools. Mary looked up at the audience, smiled and then looked aside, as if she were seeking the help of a prompt. In fact, there was no script. None of the players could reliably remember who he or she was. A script was no use, except for lyrics which, tied to music, miraculously escaped the chute of memory. Mary slapped her forehead and left the stage to bring on her prop. The residents of Woodhall and their relations chuckled as Mary led Doris, dressed as a boy scout, on to the stage. Doris's shiny pumps slid across the vinyl and Mary deposited her on the smaller of the two stools. The audience tittered at Doris's purple candy-floss hair crammed down under a scout cap which, throughout the act, threatened to spring off.

Doris began to speak before Mary was ready with her lip synching. 'Hello everybody.'

'Sit down you devil,' said Mary, breaking out of character before it had even been established.

Mary wrenched Doris by the spine. The joke of their act was that Doris the dummy couldn't remember the words. As there was no script, there weren't any words to forget.

230

But Doris forgot that she was meant to forget the words that weren't there and said the first thing that came into her head. 'What are all these people looking at us for? They're all sitting very still. Are they dead?'

'Shut up Doris.'

'I don't like the look of them. They're not doing anything.'

'Doris, be quiet.'

'It's not very good this show is it? When are they going to start?'

'Be quiet Doris. You're not to say anything.'

'Oh look, he's funny. He's got a nose like the dry ski-slope at Rossendale.'

The audience laughed at Terry, Doris's son, who covered his vast protuberance with his hand and blushed. He had been the victim of comedians ever since the playground and now his own mother unerringly picked out the vulnerable warthog in the audience for her comic prey. Doris's gaze settled on a man with abnormally elephantine ears and set for a vulture swoop when Mary gave her a Mr Punch slap to the side of her head.

Mary addressed the audience: 'Hello everyone.'

There was silence.

'I said hello everyone.'

The audience murmured hello. From her stage suitcase Mary took out a bubble perm wig and a fluffy green scarf which she draped around Doris's neck. This next section of the act had been Brian's doing.

'Now who do you think I am?'

Doris replied: 'I don't know. You look funny though.'

'But who am I?'

Doris had no idea. Alarmingly, neither did Mary.

From the audience Preston shouted: 'Keith Harris and Orville.'

That sounded familiar and Mary offered a prize to the gentleman who had called out the right answer.

'You're a duck Doris. Go quack, quack,' shouted Preston.

'You're a duck yourself darling,' said Mary.

'I'm a dead duck I am,' offered Doris.

231

'Now then children, say hello to Doris.'

The audience, not a child among them, said hello to Doris.

'Now Doris here has not been so well, have you Doris?'

'I'm all right.'

'No Doris, you've not been so well.'

'I'm not so bad. Our Terry's got a rotten head cold though. It must be that new beer. I don't think much of it, do you? There must be something wrong with it. Our Terry was as sick as a dog when he came in last night.'

Mary was miming frantically, trying to keep up with Doris's impromptu rambling. They had agreed that the climax of the act would be that Doris the dummy dies on stage, or at least appears to. Mary would make frantic attempts to revive her, including sitting her up and ventriloquizing on as though nothing had happened. But every time Mary tried to set up the gag Doris misread the lead-in. Doris would not play dead and, after five minutes of trying to kill off her dummy, Mary lost her temper.

'Bloody hell Doris, will you start bloody dying? You're meant to fall over. Can't you just die when you're told to?'

'I don't want to die. I'm not ready to die. What you talking about dying for?'

'We've all got to go to Doris. And now your number's up.'

'It's not yet. I've got years left. Who's going to look after the pub? Oh no, I can't go anywhere just yet.'

Mary pressed the tip of her finger into Doris's exposed spine. She gave out a yelp of pain like a hyena on the prowl. Mary announced that the finale of their act was a rendition of the well-known show tune 'Hello, Doris'. At Mary's insistence, the audience joined in a hall-filling reading. Doris stared out into the space like a dummy with a beatific smile fixed on its face, as the whole audience sang her song. It never once occurred to her that this was anything other than entirely normal behaviour.

Mary and Doris left the stage to prolonged applause. The other stars of the show, and there were plenty, came on to take over. As she always did in the theatre, Georgie had drifted off into a collage. An image of her father had dissolved into a blurred picture of Preston which had become in its turn a polaroid of Olive Platt, Brian, Bobby Dazzler's, the dream shop-to-be that Brian insisted he would live to see (against any evidence, the stall's growth having reached, it had seemed to Georgie, a natural plateau formed by the fact that there were only two of them. Now she knew why he was so sure.) And on to Mary, Doris, the dummy and the ventriloquist, Bobby, the iron curls, the plastic hangers, the pills behind the frosted glass. But then Brian again, overriding the default pictures. Brian in Pilsworth, Oklaheywood, where the waving grass for wheat can pass. And then Preston, the man by her side, who was unquestionably changed. How strange.

Suddenly Georgie was shaken out of her reverie. A parade of comic grotesques had taken the stage while she had been sorting out her life. She drifted back in as four old women ambled on stage, walking with gentle steps to a crackly recording of 'Down at the Old Bull and Bush'. If and when Agnes Mills moves into Woodhall she will be gratified to discover that the residents already know her dance steps. And next, the audience was treated to a man called Bert spinning plates, mostly on to the floor, a mock-magician and saw-the-lady-in-half merchant and a man whose party trick was to pop his false teeth into a pint of ale while singing 'She' in a fragile impersonation of Charles Aznavour. Charles Aznovoice, said at least ten members of the audience. It was like the very worst of won't-be New Faces, reconvened thirty years after they had failed the audition, for one final folly.

After three-quarters of an hour of life-enhancing comic defiance, Mary Lees came on again and shattered the prior quality with a tender reading of 'Ev'ry Time We Say Goodbye' that belonged in a different show. A change, how strange. Every time she said goodbye, Mary lived a little. Her voice commanded a silence which was broken by heavy applause and, as the rest of the cast joined Mary to take their bow together, tears streamed down Georgie's face. This was the end she craved – the laurels that Brian had promised when he had persuaded her to go through with Bloody Mary in *South Pacific*.

But nothing in this show was as it might have been expected to be. This was not, after all, quite the end. The cast left the shallow stage but, without leaving the line of sight of the audience, came straight back into place. All except Doris and their leader, Mary Lees, who went backstage to change. This had been a show led by its star, the costumes. Mary shouted at Doris to help her into a luxuriant dress in green taffeta. While Mary struggled into the huge swishing confection, Doris noticed the word 'hat' pinned on to a flat cap hidden in ostrich feathers. Mary pressed the hat to her head without taking the label off. On stage the music had started. It was Mary's favourite moment in all musical theatre. Guided by an innate musical discipline that survived her illness, Mary swaggered across the back of her colleagues and down to the front of the temporary stage, word-perfect through the title song from *Hello, Dolly!*.

28

Bobby Dazzler's

The coffins and caskets floated silently six feet above the ground, out of the parlour into a removal van. They were followed by a procession of flimsy black drapery, rotted not-quite-white lilies, plain brass plaques awaiting engraving, a trinket-shop volume of thick candles and clean stone under which one-as-yet-not-visible was in hiding, ready for the mason to find the name that was on it. Two tables, still dressed in unadorned white lace, came out in a diagonal walk, a leg at a time. They were followed by their companion chairs. An argument between red seats erupted on to the pavement. The creaking legs cracked as they fell, defeated, into the deadly pile of rubbish with which Preston was blocking the pavement outside the Market Place. After an hour of white sheets and drab brown boxes, the funeral procession was over. When the shop was empty Georgie asked for a five-minute delay, as if to allow death one final look around the premises before it vacated them for good. Preston observed that it would be back soon enough even if it went visiting elsewhere. Death, said Preston, back in the old way, comes to all shops. The only difference at his place was that he used to stand on the threshold, inviting it in. Georgie wanted to chase the ghosts out, to fumigate the insides, spiritually. The driver of the removal van started up the noisy engine and the reaper's bag of tricks drew away.

Georgie and Preston stepped outside and sat on the sloping bench inside the bus shelter.

'I don't believe this, Preston. It's just unreal.'

After the five-minute hiatus for respect, perched on the badly designed bench in the bus shelter, Preston went back inside where he started to fill the empty space with their goods. The brown and the black and the white lace of the parlour were splashed with all the colours of the embroiderer. Red appliqué, rayon threads in rouged scarlet, a hand couched navy and a petit point, afresh like the greenness of the new trees, danced from the Brain Box (which Preston had driven down to Heywood) to make a new home in the former funeral parlour. Their variegated patterns clashed with the garish formica of Preston's cheap customer service tables. Time was served on all memory of the previous use. Ten minutes later the tables had been cleared of formaldehyde, glycerine, borax and phenol. The shelves that had once groaned to hold books filled with the price of dignified human disposal were soft with balls of wool. The wood itself seemed to buckle into a smile. The bare window was dressed with crewelling in the space that Preston had allowed for dust. Preston had been circumspect about advertising his wares. Detailed as he was in death he had always thought it better not to rub people's noses in it. But embroidery? That was the very life-blood itself and Preston picked all the most bounteous, most joyous sweaters and bobble hats and mittens and scarves and tea towels and tea cosies from the tables and threw them into a heap of light and gold in the bay of the shop's window. When his design display was complete Preston brought in a new cash register to replace his old machine which he had, indecorously, placed at the front of the shop.

Georgie bustled in and out from the van with soft-covered books of knitting patterns. Preston followed with a box of needles that swayed as he walked, like reeds on a pond. He carried them with great caution, fearful of one breaking his skin. A cut could so easily get infected and, before you know it, gangrene has set in. Georgie came back with her wedding present from her mother, an electric sewing machine which she took into the back room, the one where Preston had prepared so many bodies, Bobby among them. Preston staggered back in under the weight of two tubes of thick, woollen Middleton-Moroccan rugs. He dropped them just before they took him down. Georgie shuffled into the main room and stopped in the bay window that Preston had left bare and which he had now begun to fill with sewed cats and dogs and farmyard animals.

Preston had placed free-standing shop-rails along the back wall, cupboards down the sides and shelves in the alcoves. The stench of the previous owner had miraculously gone. In its place was the odour of new fittings. Georgie gradually filled the rails with her colourful merchandise and the shop came into being. When the rails were full with the items she wanted on display, she opened the cupboards where she found a row of empty metal coat hangers. Georgie pressed them all together so she could carry the bundle by wrapping her index finger around the iron curl. She told Preston that she was just going out. He looked at her in amazement as she left the shop carrying all their coat hangers. Georgie walked to Ethel Austin's clothes store where she waited her turn in the queue to be served.

'Excuse me love, I'm just opening up across the way and we've got a lot of wool garments that don't really hang well on these metal ones. They cut into the fabric, you see. I was wondering if I could swap these for some of your plastic ones.'

'We don't really do swaps, love.'

'Oh, I see.'

'We've got some plastic ones you can have if you like. How many do you want?'

'As many as you've got.'

The shop assistant brought out a large bag of plastic coat hangers. Georgie couldn't carry it so left it behind the counter, to collect later.

She walked, with her metal coat hangers, towards the market. She attracted a few odd looks but she didn't care. She saw Geoff Webb haranguing the man, whose name she had never known, who sold very poor ornaments and painted gold jewellery. Gareth Adams saluted like a soldier. Vinny Able shouted a warm hello. Georgie approached her old stall. It was still empty. Geoff hadn't found a new tenant yet, but he would. The market was thriving. Once it had seemed that it was going under but that judgment had been premature. Georgie arrived at the bare stall. Without the adornment of Mary's embroidery it was only a wooden table. It was a sorry sight without any goods on it. Droplets of rain dripped down between the panels. Georgie stopped, looked around and then thought better of it. She had a deadline, things to do. Life goes on, all that stuff, better hurry up, so little time, so many sweaters to sell, so many songs to sing. She laid the metal coat hangers carefully on the stall and walked back to the old funeral parlour, picking up her new coat hangers on the way.

Preston kept repeating the same words. It didn't seem real. None of this seemed real, all of this odd tale; where on earth was it all heading, throwing up all things into the morning air? He didn't blanch when Georgie opened the cupboard and filled it up with new coat hangers. He knew nothing about embroidery. Metal hangers were probably all wrong. Georgie walked round the near-empty shop that was set to open three days later as Bobby Dazzler's Embroidery Emporium. Bobby Dazzler's, that little Bobby Dazzler. She bounced off every wall to check that it was all real. She opened the door and reached her hand up into its frame, so as to touch the very bricks and mortar of it. Georgie tried again to reach the moment but just shook her head instead. It just didn't seem real. Preston whispered a comforting line in her ear and she smiled at him.

Preston left Georgie to complete the moving in. He went out, ostensibly, to bring in some lunch. Preston checked that Georgie wasn't watching him through the window, got into the Brain Box and drove away. Georgie was beginning to wonder what had happened to him by the time, an hour later, he returned.

Preston came back in and called Georgie through from the sewing office. 'Look love. Look who's come to visit.'

Georgie ran out to the front. 'Who?'

Mary Lees walked very slowly in through the door. She had come to look at her concrete dream. She looked up at the ceiling, gazed at the shelves heavy with wool and the garments that she dimly recognized. She had made or supervised everything in there. The shop was a riot of colour. It looked quite beautiful

238

to her but the pained look on Mary's face made Georgie think that her mother was struggling to grasp its significance.

'Mum, this is our shop. Your shop. We've done it. We've got a shop. Look, this is going to be it. This is where we're going to sell all the work you do.'

Mary clearly had no idea who Georgie was. She walked right past her daughter, not even acknowledging her. Mary took hold of a red rose-patterned sweater and ran her fingers over the bump of the skilled embroidery. Georgie began to harangue her mother, imploring Mary to recognize her. This is our shop, Mum. It's here. We've done it. Look Mum, a shop, a shop, a shop. Can you believe it? Haven't we always said we'd get there? Didn't you always say that? You said we'd do it, you always said we would. It didn't seem real, no matter how many times Georgie repeated it. Mary walked around. Out of irrationality come occasional moments of lucidity. Mary nodded. It seemed that the dream, the promise that she harboured all her life, was still present in her head. She seemed to know what the moment meant. Or so it appeared to Georgie from her reaction.

'I know this place. I've been here before.'

'It was the funeral parlour till yesterday Mum. Dad used to work here. We're making it into a wool shop. This is where all your sewing will be sold.'

Mary stopped in the middle of the room. Her eyes moved around the room as if her head was on a pivot. She nodded, to herself, and whispered, so low that she was inaudible, 'Yes. It's grand is that.'

Preston brought out a bottle of champagne which he had hidden under some dog-tooth quilting in the Brain Box. He shook it up and aimed the cork at Mary. It flew across the room and landed, with a pleasing cushion, in an elaborately embroidered pinny, while the spray drenched Mary's just-set grey hair. Preston gave each one of them a ball of wool which they raised in a toast to Bobby Dazzler's as they took it in turns to drink from the bottle. Against the rules of the Woodhall care home regime, Mary got extremely drunk. So did Preston and Georgie, so much so that when Preston moved from a congratulatory embrace into a passionate kiss, he thought nothing of it and she did not resist. They drank two bottles of champagne between the three of them and fell asleep on the floor of Bobby Dazzler's soon-to-be-opened Embroidery Emporium.

29
Hello Dolly, Well Hello Dolly

Georgie woke up with a hangover that split her head in two. She lay on Preston's sofa all day watching the hopeless television, trying to recover in time to play Dolly's opening night. In the event, she fell asleep as the six o'clock news was starting and did not wake until seven, by which time the players at Heywood Civic Hall were in chaos. They had less than half an hour before the show began and Dolly Gallagher Levi had not arrived. Colin Smethurst, who had taken over as producer when Brian had passed away, decreed that if Georgie did not show up within the next fifteen minutes then the show would have to be cancelled. Yet another one. Colin was running through the car park in a panic (on an orthopaedic foot Colin always ran in a panic) when Georgie stepped out of a taxi in front of him. She ran into the dressing room, where she received a huge round of applause born of relief.

Georgie cleared her throat, sang her scales tunelessly and sat down for Lyn Riggs to apply her make-up. Georgie was uncommunicative but she was not nervous. She was looking forward to this moment. It seemed to her like a continuation of her solitary communion in St Stephen's church. That might have seemed a blasphemous thought but, not requiring any belief, her religion did not contain the idea of blaspheming deviation. There were five minutes to go before the curtain went up and Colin Smethurst was conducting his pre-show pep-talk. It was an uninspiring rhetorical anti-flourish and the principals were not listening properly, preferring to concentrate on repeating to themselves the first words they were expected to say when they appeared on stage.

Colin's ramble was interrupted by visitors. Preston Burns opened the door so hard that everybody turned to look at him. He rubbed his shoulder, which he'd stretched a little. In his left hand Preston had such a vast bouquet of white roses that his face was invisible behind it. His voice was instantly recognizable in any case: 'Hello everyone. You can stop worrying now. I'm back.'

As all the cast had seen Preston wandering the streets of Heywood and Middleton and some had even had a drink with him since he had returned, this was a less dramatic moment than the oratory Preston was lavishing on it.

He bounded like a puppy over to Georgie and planted the flowers in her hand. With them he said he was worthy of her. 'Good luck love. You slay 'em out there.'

Georgie hugged him. Preston was different now, she thought. He was throwing off people's expectations of him. Gardening suited him; he had begun to suit it. He stopped Georgie as she was about to go into the wings for the show to start. She liked to prepare herself psychologically by watching.

'Hang on a second. There's someone else I want you to say hello to.'

Preston went back out of the dressing room and, hand in hand, brought Mary Lees in.

She spoke directly to Georgie. 'I've played this part. And I'll tell you what, I could still play it. I'd be better than you, there's no doubt about that. Why don't you get out of that dress and let me on. I was like Betty Grable I was. That's what the *Manchester Evening News* said.'

'Oh Mum, come here . . .'

Mary and Georgie hung on for dear life.

Mary whispered in her daughter's ear, recognizing her, burning, raging just as she was required: 'Give us a belter love. Go on, you deserve it. I'll be looking out for you.'

Preston saw Mary out to their seats in the front row. Georgie

242

went to the toilet. She had one more thing she had to do before she was ready to go on.

Georgie sat down on the plastic seat, fully attired. She reached into her handbag and took the tinted bottle full of pills. She pulled off the white top and emptied the little white keepsakes into her flat palm, taking great pains not to spill any. She needed every last pill to do what she had to do. She belatedly locked the bathroom door with her free hand. Georgie then pulled down her dress and panties and used the toilet, her hand held tight. She got up and made herself decent with her spare hand. Then Georgie opened her hand and stared at the little white entry tickets which seemed to glisten on her flat palm as she held them upright to catch the light. The now familiar collage of the recent past again reeled through her head. The shows, life counted out in shows, *Carousel*, *South Pacific*, *Oklahoma!*, the pantomime. Archie Gregson, the ventriloquist-dummy, Bobby, the coat hangers bouncing in their pleasing symmetry, snagging into the soles of her feet, Preston, Brian, Mary, walked on and off stage, all there together, all explaining one another. The story had a new ending this time. The serious air, the saddening and consoling silence of the doors that let life out. Georgie turned her palm over with a violent twist and the pills clattered noisily against the white enamel of the bowl before settling with the gentle clamour of raindrops into the deep yellow pool of urine. Georgie clapped her hands together hard and repeatedly, as if brushing away memories, rubbing out the events that had been collected in a glass bottle, like the malignant genie of the lamp. She thrust the handle and flushed the toilet, turning pills into sewage.

Georgie went back into the dressing room. She began to be very nervous all of a sudden. Colin Smethurst assured her that she would be fine once the show started, but actually her anxiety was amplified as the show began. Suddenly there was so much riding on it, as if it could propel her back into the black if it went awry. The early scenes were not vivid. As Cornelius (Graham Collins) and Horace (Stanley Atkinson, a barely credible casting) went through the comic scenes Georgie realized that Dolly really had

243

to hold this show together. Graham and Stanley were so bad that Georgie began to crave Preston.

But the comedians can be rubbish and it can not matter. This is really Dolly's show, all the way through to the spectacular resolution in the defining moment at the end. In fact, all the conflicts are mere ornaments to that moment. It is a set-up designed to provide a single moment of hair-standing sentimental joy for the title girl herself. Any great moment requires intricate prior tedium, without which it will not work. The great art of drama is the difference between writing and stand-up: the dull bits. *Hello, Dolly!* was like a compendium of dull bits, stripped out of other shows and assembled in order to provide a wondrous pay-off at the end. The rest of the show is perfunctory by comparison and Michael Stewart's music also refuses to upstage the show-stopper and show-ender it has stored up for the conclusion. The Heywood players went through the stage directions competently and without incident. Georgie carried the plot along through the melodrama of overreaction, the randomness of breaking into song and the hyperbole of jealousies and petty envies. It was all there to set up her glorious return. As Georgie went out to begin the second half Colin Smethurst asked her if she was enjoying the show. She was amazed to find herself saying that she was. She was looking forward to the end more than the audience were. She even risked a little wave to her mother and ex-husband in the front row.

The second half led on, up to the point. It seemed to take for ever. The audience was all waiting for it as much as Georgie was herself. And then the end came.

The whole cast gathered on stage for the story to be settled. Ronny Rose's set was simple and appropriately spartan. The point was that the eye should be trained on Dolly. A single raised walkway came out of stage left and ran across the back of the stage before swinging, perpendicular to itself, down to face the audience. It was a catwalk. The backcloth was a painted ballroom. A crystal chandelier hung on a wire above and spiral staircases were painted on swaying cloths on either flank, and centre-stage, leading off the suspended catwalk, an elaborately constructed staircase spiralled down to the footlights at the front. The action took place either side of and behind it. The dancers walked around pretending to talk to one another as the orchestra played its last overture. Colin's quietly effective directorial touches were evident. He had stretched this moment out to make the audience wait. This put a premium on the skill of his actors in wasting time productively on stage while not betraying that they were simply waiting for the main event. The largest strain of all was on the leading lady herself, who wanted, so wanted, the moment to come.

Finally, the ritual preliminaries were over and Stanley Atkinson announced that Dolly Gallagher Levi had arrived at the Harmonia Gardens. The spotlight focused on the entrance at the top of the central stairway with the waiters lined up on both sides. There was another almost-too-long pause. And then Georgie Lees appeared, resplendent in a full-length red gown made by the hand of Mary and her deranged team, set with onyx and emerald and all but hidden under a headpiece of feathers. At the turn of the set, as she changed direction and faced the audience, Dolly Georgie Levi wiggled her hips, shuffled a two-step and winked at the crowd on and off stage.

She was sure she heard a cheer but she was too far gone really to separate the hubbub in the audience from the chatter that Colin Smethurst demanded on stage. As Dolly walked down the catwalk, the conversations on stage dissipated and there was only Georgie Lees. And the music and the words which, coupled with the tune, lost all the triteness that they exhibit on the page: 'Hello Dolly, well hello Dolly, it's so nice to have you back where you belong. You're looking swell Dolly, who can tell Dolly, you're still going, you're still going, you're still going strong.'

The cast of the Heywood Amateur Operatic and Dramatic Society sang as if their lives depended on it. By the third round of the chorus the audience was joining in. The glorious song ended too soon – it always ends too soon – and the Civic Hall pealed with applause. Before the hands had stopped slapping the orchestra reprised the song and the cast moved into their comedy couplings. Georgie ran off the stage like a prima donna offended at having to share the limelight with these mere mortals. When the lady dancers and the waiters and the other principals had taken their call, they all turned to look at the back of the stage.

The theatre was filled with the music. Georgie Lees stepped forward to take her moment of judgment which was, for this moment, the only judgment which mattered, the judgment of the audience. Georgie with the smiling eyes dissolved into her pain as the audience, every man jack of them, stood to acclaim her.

Georgie Lees went to bed that night and slept soundly. The following morning Bobby Dazzler's, emporium of embroidery genius, shop window for the art of Mary Lees, Bobby Dazzler's would open for business.

www.ingramcontent.com/pod-product-compliance
Ingram Content Group UK Ltd.
Pitfield, Milton Keynes, MK11 3LW, UK
UKHW022246180325
456436UK00001B/33